She needed to have a handle on Adam.

Yolanda liked thinking about him being this happy-go-lucky, free-spirited boy who always landed on his feet. Lately, though, she was seeing him as an amazingly talented adult man who pitched in when his family needed him.

Conflicted. That was what she was.

She should avoid him at all costs. And not because she didn't respect him. After everything he'd done for her this past week, helping her with the mystery, he'd gained her respect and maybe a little more than that.

Subtle attraction.

But she knew him too well. Right now he was shouldering his responsibilities in Scorpion Ridge, but what if an offer he couldn't refuse came along? Or, an even better thought, what if his father got better and Adam wasn't needed?

He would leave, and this time he might not come back.

Dear Reader,

My love of books started in second grade. I remember the author who lit my fire for reading. She was Carolyn Haywood and she wrote the Betsy books. They were like chocolate. I couldn't get enough. Neither of my parents were readers. My mother got her first library card when I was in second grade so that I could check out enough books to keep me occupied until the next library visit.

My father was in his sixties when he got his first card. I was home from college for a few weeks and there was a book I wanted to read. The library wouldn't give me a card because I didn't have a local address, and I guess I'd lost the old one. Dad came and applied. Of course, I had him check out a romance.

In *Small-Town Secrets*, Yolanda is the book connoisseur. You don't see it on the pages, she's too busy uncovering town secrets and getting closer to the hero, but she's definitely harboring a Harlequin Heartwarming book in her bedroom, a mystery in her purse and a paranormal beside the cash register.

My hero, Adam, also likes to read. Not everyone sees past his easygoing manner to his steadfast heart. Yolanda didn't at first. He's the kind of man who would say to his love, "I'll clean the house—you sit back and read." He's also the kind of man who isn't afraid to fend off any attack. Yup, don't be fooled by his soulful brown eyes. He's a black belt. Which might come in handy as he and Yolanda discover more about the history of Scorpion Ridge, Arizona, and the secrets of their own families...

So settle back, enjoy the story and ask yourself about the secrets your family holds.

If you'd like to know more about the Heartwarming authors, please visit heartwarmingauthors.blogspot.com. If you'd like to know more about me, please visit pamelatracy.com. I love to hear from readers.

Pamela

HEARTWARMING

Small-Town Secrets

—

USA TODAY Bestselling Author

Pamela Tracy

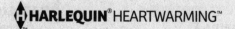

HARLEQUIN® HEARTWARMING™

Recycling programs
for this product may
not exist in your area.

ISBN-13: 978-0-373-36727-6

Small-Town Secrets

Copyright © 2015 by Pamela Tracy Osback

This edition published by arrangement with Harlequin Books S.A.

For questions and comments about the quality of this book, please contact us at CustomerService@Harlequin.com.

Printed in U.S.A.

Pamela Tracy is a *USA TODAY* bestselling author who lives with her husband (...the inspiration for most of her heroes) and son (...the interference for most of her writing time). Since 1999, she has published more than twenty-five books and sold more than a million copies. She's a past RITA® Award finalist and past winner of the Christian Fiction Writers' book of the year award.

Visit the Author Profile page at Harlequin.com for more titles.

To my brother Danny Crawford, who has the soul of an artist (music instead of murals) and the kind of steadfast heart that his sisters need.

We love you, Danny.

CHAPTER ONE

THERE WERE TWO things Yolanda Sanchez didn't want to see in her somewhat restored Queen Anne Victorian, whose ground floor now housed the Twice Told Tales used bookstore.

One, a leaky roof. Leaks were bad, very bad, for books. But as she was a worrier, she'd already thought about the roof and installed a new one. Now a roof leak shouldn't be a problem, especially since her bookstore took up the first floor.

The second threat was fire. Fire was bad, very bad, for books. That's why the puffs of smoke floating and fading in the air near the history room couldn't possibly be good news.

Yolanda quickly set the three books she'd been carrying to the children's section on the nearest empty shelf. In her haste, she misjudged how much room she had and two of the books tumbled to the floor. She ignored them and hurried through the rows of popular fiction, self-help and romance.

She'd been in the history and nonfiction room

just this morning doing inventory. Some of the books there were so old she'd put them in Ziplock bags and was considering putting them on display next to the cashier instead of keeping them in their genre area. They were rare and a book lover's dream, with brittle covers, ragged corners and yellowing pages. They were the most precious of firewood.

No! Not on her watch!

She rounded a corner and stopped so abruptly that her shoes made a squeaky sound. The noise didn't seem to disturb the room's occupant. Amidst the books was a tiny lady wearing a light brown sweater and dark brown skirt. Her clothes—right down to her brown, flat shoes—looked dull and faded next to the bright purple walls of the history room. The expression on the woman's pale face was serious. Without blinking, her bright blue eyes perused the shelves, peering closely to read the titles that even Yolanda couldn't make out on a good day without the use of her glasses.

"We're not open yet," Yolanda sputtered.

What she'd wanted to say but couldn't seem to form the words was, "Who do you think you are, smoking a cigarette in the middle of my used bookstore?"

The woman reached up to finger a strand of

pearls around her neck. "I realized that when I arrived and there was no one to help me."

The judgmental tone didn't inspire Yolanda to feel generous. "The sign on the door clearly states that we're not open yet."

Obviously, Yolanda needed to work on her assertive nature because the woman merely shrugged and said, "I'm looking for a book about the history of this town."

Oh, yes, this was a seasoned smoker, with the telltale throaty voice. Yolanda gritted her teeth—customer relations and all that—shook her head and gently suggested, "If you want something immediately, you'll need to go to the town museum or one of the gift shops on Main Street. We don't open until Friday."

The woman's expression remained disapproving. She didn't seem bothered one bit by the fact that the used bookstore wasn't open and that she didn't belong there. Instead of looking chastened, like Yolanda expected, she looked determined. She inquired, "Do you have other books about Scorpion Ridge? Besides what is in this room. Old books, I mean, perhaps written by someone long ago who lived in this town but who only published for themselves or their family. I'm not finding the book I want. I've been to the little museum. They don't have it. It's a particular one, probably written a little more than a hundred years ago. I'm looking for proof."

"Proof of what?" Yolanda asked.

"Just you never mind."

What a curmudgeon. Unhappiness and anger oozed from her.

But there was something else in her eyes, too, an emotion so fleeting that Yolanda almost didn't see it. This woman had suffered loss and never recovered. Yolanda gentled her response. "I'm still working on this room. You need to come back some other time. I've not quite un-packed…"

Just like that, Yolanda's eyes teared. And not from the smoke. She love, love, loved that she was living her dream, but she was struggling with all the changes, not only to her way of life but also to her way of thinking. She was living in her grandmother's house. The history sec-tion of Twice Told Tales was located in what used to be her grandmother's bedroom. Now Rosi Acura, who told everyone she was a little over seventy but who really was quite a bit over eighty, lived in a retirement group home close to downtown.

The home's director had a bit of a crush on Rosi. Yolanda figured he believed the woman really was in her seventies.

"I love being at the home," Gramma Rosi

kept telling Yolanda. And Yolanda didn't doubt that she did. Rosi's best friend lived in the room next to hers. The group home's caretaker—who had been Yolanda's history teacher way back when—enjoyed squiring her grandmother around on any errand she wanted. Plus, a van took her shopping, to bingo and once a month on some sort of touristy excursion. That, combined with helping Yolanda's new venture, did a lot to distract Rosi from the grief of losing her oldest child.

A year ago, Yolanda's mother died, quietly, without pain.

Yolanda's mom, Trina Sanchez, had invested wisely and had lived frugally. She'd left six figures, all to Yolanda. Yolanda would rather her mother have taken her to Disneyland when she was ten, to the beach once or twice, or even a few excursions to the big city of Phoenix and a movie night or something. Instead, Yolanda had spent many hours alone in the house while her mother worked. Mom had been adamant about the security of savings and worried about every penny spent.

Maybe at the end, though, her mother had reconsidered her practical philosophy. Because a stipulation in her will emphasized that the inheritance could only be used to build a dream.

Possibly because Trina had not fulfilled her own dreams?

"This room looks quite full." The raspy voice snapped Yolanda out of her reverie. The woman's eyes swept the room. Her lips pursed, as if she didn't like what she saw. "Do you have anything in storage? I'd be glad to help you unpack. Or perhaps you've a special place for your really old books?"

Yolanda straightened to her full height, which put her eye to eye with the petite woman's just over five-foot frame—and that counted the curly top of the woman's gray hair. In her most commanding small-business-owner voice, Yolanda said, "Ma'am, we're not open, and even if we were, smoking is not allowed on the premises."

Finally, the woman's expression changed but only marginally. Her red lips pursed when she glanced at her cigarette as if just noticing it. She then looked around for a place to put it out. As the ash was almost at the length where it would soon drop to the floor, Yolanda reached for the bright yellow coffee cup she'd left on the windowsill this morning. It was from a set of four that her grandmother had given her. Butter yellow with an orange daisy painted on it, three cups had survived a household of kids.

"I can search through the trunks in the attic,"

the woman volunteered, giving the cup a disdainful look before dropping her lipstick-tipped cigarette into the coffee cup as if it were a gold-plated ashtray meant just for her. "It would have to be now, though."

"That won't be necessary," Yolanda said. Only one trunk of books remained to be unpacked from her Gramma Rosi's attic, where the remnants of Yolanda's ancestors were stored, gathered by her family for the last hundred years and maybe even earlier. Yolanda wasn't sure. The books in the final trunk appeared to be as old as the house and just as precious.

Used books were the lifeblood of Yolanda's new business. That the first ones shelved had been from her attic made the venture all the more special. Besides yard sales, friends simply giving her their already read offerings, and buying the surplus from a used bookstore in Phoenix, Yolanda had also snagged more than five hundred books from the town of Gesippi, just an hour to the north. Its library had closed just two weeks ago, and Yolanda had purchased a good deal of their inventory, but she hadn't had time to go through all her purchases. They were in the carriage house.

For a moment she thought the woman would argue, so Yolanda continued. "We're right on schedule for the opening, and I have plenty of volunteers. Come back on Friday."

The woman gave the shelves one last perusal. "Did you put any books on reserve?"

"We're a used bookstore, not a library." Yolanda'd been patient long enough. "Who are you?"

"I'm staying with relatives right now," the woman said. "Maybe you've heard of Chester Ventimiglia."

Yolanda didn't know a Chester, but she did recognize the Ventimiglia name. Richard Ventimiglia and another man named John Moore had been the town's founding fathers. There were still a few Moores in Scorpion Ridge, but the Ventimiglias had long since left or died out.

"I do know the name, but…" Yolanda's words tapered off as somewhere in the old Victorian something clattered to the floor, the sound as effective as a fire alarm. Yolanda stepped from the room, listening. Maybe the old woman wasn't the only one snooping in the used bookstore before the grand opening. In the silence she moved closer to one of the vents where now she could clearly hear talking—singing?—and relaxed when she recognized Adam's voice. He'd said he'd be by later, something about replacing the hinge on one of the saloon doors he was hanging for her.

"This isn't really yours," came a throaty whisper.

When Yolanda turned back, the woman was gone.

FOR SUCH A little thing, Yolanda Sanchez sure made a lot of noise. So much so that Adam Snapp stopped his singing. Last time he'd honored the Beatles with his limited musical talent, she had poked fun of his voice. Poking fun at him was something she'd done since fifth grade, when she'd noted that he'd worn two different colored socks to school by accident. Used to be, he'd tease her back, saying something like, "Across America, socks are standing up and shouting, 'We don't have to all be the same.'" He'd said it loudly and made sure there was an audience. Yolanda hadn't seemed fazed.

Today he wanted to quip, "Better to sing off-key than not to sing at all."

For the last few months, though, his ability to joke his way through life had taken a severe hit. Which was why when his father got sick and the family business went from profitable to precarious, it had been a simple decision to come home and help. He'd not told anyone the mess he'd made of his once-in-a-lifetime opportunities.

Straightening the toolbox he'd accidentally stumbled over, Adam listened to Yolanda's stomping and huffing. Occasionally, she'd call out, "Ma'am?" Something or someone had her riled; he was glad it wasn't him.

Picking up a Phillips screwdriver, he held the door level while screwing the pivot hinge into the doorjamb. The blank surface beckoned him but only for a moment. Personally, he didn't think saloon doors belonged in this late-nineteenth-century Queen Anne. And they were a ridiculous choice to separate a private office from a place of business. She'd get no privacy.

She, however, thought they were pretty.

He reminded himself that he'd signed on to help her complete general handyman duties and to follow her directions about decorative shingles and dormers and enclosed breezeways. His job was *not* to tell her how she could make the two-story Victorian even more authentic and artistically pleasing.

The house was her canvas, not his.

She came up with ideas; he obliged to the best of his ability. Like these pressboard saloon doors that she wanted him to paint brilliant orange.

The old Adam Snapp would have painted

books on one side; after all, this was to be a used bookstore. Then he would have added real covers and used shellacked fanned-out pages for a 3D effect. He'd also have painted a caricature of Yolanda, her nose in a book, as it always was, on the other panel. He'd have glued a pair of glasses above that perfect little nose. She, all female with slim lines and slight curves, was a painter's dream. She often displayed a Mona Lisa smile. Her hair, black and straight, would look simple on anyone else: normal, everyday. On her it accentuated big, smiling black eyes filled with determination.

Her lips had always been a challenge for him to capture. For some reason, whenever he'd painted her—and he had many times back when they'd both been teenagers working for the local animal habitat, BAA—her lips had come out bigger than they really were and always seemed pursed. She'd gotten mad at him on a few occasions, accusing him of making it look as if she'd just swallowed a pickle.

Yes, he could picture exactly how he wanted the saloon door to look. He clenched his fingers. Desire rose, fell, disappeared. It didn't matter what his heart told him to do. Right now, when his fingers grasped the pencil so he could start to seriously sketch, nothing happened.

Nothing.

So it was best to just tighten the screws, adjust the hinges, check to make sure the doors were level, paint the stupid panels Kool-Aid orange and be done with it.

"Ahem."

Adam looked down. She hadn't used to be able to sneak up on him. He was really off his game. But then, in the weeks he'd been working for her, she'd been too involved with the plumbers and electricians to pay much attention to him. Almost gave him a complex.

"What was that noise? And did anyone come past you?" Yolanda demanded, all righteous indignation. When he didn't answer fast enough, she added, "There was an elderly woman over in history and nonfiction. I turned around, and she was gone. I've searched the nooks and crannies of the first floor book areas. I even went upstairs to my private suite."

Adam hadn't been up there yet. Yolanda's priority was the bookstore. As a result, he had a to-do list in his back pocket that would keep him busy for a year. He'd make, he figured, not even half of what he'd made the last five years painting murals, and he'd work harder. It would take longer to get it done.

Up until a couple of months ago, his life had been about creating art, murals specifically. Most of his creations had been done outdoors.

Now he was indoors, hemmed in, without space to call his own. To Yolanda, creativity, when it came to her old house, was categorized as either "That's not practical" or "Not in the budget."

Not that Adam had much creativity himself these days. He wasn't sure where his muse had gone off to and doubted it would come back. And right now he was too worried about his dad and his family to go after it. "Adam," Yolanda said impatiently. "Did someone go by you?"

"No, I haven't seen anyone." He watched as she peered past him, as if someone really could have sidled by and taken up residence in her tiny office. "The front door was open when I got here. What about the back?"

"I thought they were both locked," Yolanda stated.

"You should start checking." The last five years Adam had lived in a few off-the-beaten-path neighborhoods. He'd learned to value a good door lock. When she finally focused on him again, he said, "I'm glad you're here. Check this out."

He opened and closed the doors a few times. "Hear anything?"

"No, but I heard something earlier. What did you drop?"

Okay, so she didn't appreciate his handyman skills. "I tripped over the toolbox."

She looked down. "I can tell by the assortment of tools spread out on the floor that today is 'Get rid of loose hinges' day."

"Hey, I can't believe Hallmark hasn't thought of creating such a holiday!"

Yolanda didn't laugh. In all the years he'd known her, she'd never responded to his humor. She'd been the straight A student who kept trying to tell him, "You should try harder," while he'd been the class clown responding with a "Maybe later..."

And she'd been right. When *later* came, he'd been ill prepared. He'd had the opportunity of a lifetime the last few years and because he'd not had good business sense, he'd made one mistake after another.

Yolanda continued, "I think I'll use that shade of orange on the upstairs baseboards. It will add a little character to the place."

Adam shook his head. He might make poor business decisions and have no clue when it came to women, but he knew that would be wrong. This house was almost three thousand square feet of historical space and sculpture. The shade of orange she wanted hadn't been invented when this house was built.

"Of course," she continued, "I shouldn't even be thinking of the upstairs until after the bookstore is a success."

It would be a success, Adam thought, because she'd poured her heart into it. Per Yolanda's orders, he'd painted every room—the foyer, study, parlor, dining room, bedroom, bathroom, enclosed breezeway and kitchen—a different vibrant color. The grand lady, a Queen Anne who probably missed her flowered wallpaper, had never shined so bright. Next he'd be working on the second-floor bedrooms. When he finished that she wanted him to turn the upstairs of the house's two-story garage, which used to be a carriage house, into an apartment she could rent out.

He might not agree with her color choices, but he appreciated the work to take his mind off his mistakes and his family's problems.

"This old dame doesn't need any help with character. She's loaded with it."

"You did a great job," she admitted. "But I'm more concerned about the woman I just spoke to. Are you sure no one went past you?"

"I didn't see anyone."

"She was old, really old, and tiny. She had gray hair with a hint of blond left. The cut was straight and close to the scalp. Her eyes were blue. She wore tiny pearl earrings and a matching necklace. Her face was as wrinkled as any I've seen, and she was smoking a cigarette."

"I don't smell anything."

Yolanda frowned. "I don't smell it anymore, either. That's so odd. Come, help me look. Maybe you can figure out how she just vanished."

Adam followed her into what used to be the living room. Now it housed popular fiction. From there he passed her, meandering through horror, true crime and mystery before finally stopping in the history section.

"No. No lingering smell of cigarette smoke. Are you sure she had a cigarette?"

"I caught her right here, in this area. I didn't recognize her, and when you made such a noise—" Yolanda glared at his tool belt as if it were somehow to blame "—she somehow got past me. I've never seen her before, and I didn't get her name. I was hoping she came by you so you could fill me in."

"What did she want?"

"She wanted to know if I had any old books about Scorpion Ridge."

"Sounds harmless enough," Adam said, "except for the cigarette."

"I used to catch people trying to sneak cigarettes at BAA, but they always did it in some out-of-the-way corner. This woman didn't care that she was breaking the law," Yolanda said.

Adam had also been vigilant about smokers during his tenure at Bridget's Animal Adventure. He'd taken the infraction a bit personally, as his autistic brother was bothered by smoke, so much so that he often demanded to be taken home if he smelled it, no matter how important the event the family was attending.

"And," Yolanda continued, "the expression on her face wasn't harmless. She stood in the middle of the room as if she had a right to be here."

"At BAA we called that attitude entitlement."

"Yes," Yolanda agreed. "That's exactly the attitude she personified."

Adam glanced around the room loaded with history books. It even smelled old. This was not a place he would normally spend much time. His taste bent more toward true crime and horror.

"You really think people will buy old school history books?" he asked.

"I used to."

"Well, you've always been a bit strange."

Her color deepened, exactly the response he'd hoped for. He bent down, picking up a book that had fallen to the ground. "*Soiled Doves of the Desert,*" he read. "I'm thinking these aren't the kind of doves that squawked."

Yolanda took the book from his hand and placed it on the shelf. "I'm being serious. Something about her wasn't right."

"Well, she didn't come past me. I'd have seen her."

Annoyed, Yolanda said, "Which means she went out the back door, which is definitely not a public exit. And just how did she know where it was?"

"Are you talking to me or just muttering to yourself?"

"Both," Yolanda retorted. She patted a bookshelf, moved a book then looked at the shelves below and above. "Oh, I almost forgot. She flicked the ashes…"

"What?"

Yolanda had gone pale. Not a color he liked seeing on her. She whispered a response, "She used my favorite yellow coffee cup as an ashtray. But the cup is gone."

She kept searching the shelves and then went to the end table and chair in the corner of the room.

"You think she swiped your cup?" Adam asked.

"I can't imagine why. This makes no sense."

"You're probably overreacting."

"I don't overreact, ever."

That was true. She was always in control, always did what she was supposed to do. Yolanda had once been in a school play, and the stage had collapsed under her feet. She'd kept saying her lines even as the actor playing the cowardly lion helped her out of the hole.

"You had to have seen her."

You have to pay more attention...

He'd heard that a million times growing up, mostly from his father. They'd never seen eye to eye on anything, particularly after he'd dropped out of high school, and Adam had been desperate to leave Scorpion Ridge as soon as possible. Now he was back.

"No one walked past me. She must have gone out the back."

"But—"

He ruffled her hair, knowing it would distract her. "It doesn't look like anything's missing. It was probably some tourist who wandered in, realized she'd made a mistake and then wandered out."

Yolanda nodded, though she didn't appear convinced.

Adam checked his cell phone and turned to leave. "I've got to be at the Tae Kwon Do studio in thirty minutes, and I still need to finish the door."

"Tell your brother I said hi."

"I will."

Snapp's Studio, his family's business, had employed the whole Snapp family for years— except for Adam. He was there now, though, once again working for his father. Only this time if his father made a request, Adam jumped to it, trying to make his dad's life easier.

Tonight Adam was scheduled to give a lesson to a beginner class. His twin brother, Andy, would be there stacking mats, folding towels, offering advice from the side of the room. If the noise and chaos got overwhelming for Andy, he'd go into the back office away from everyone. But usually it was where Andy felt most comfortable.

Right after his brother was diagnosed with autism, a well-meaning counselor had handed Adam's mother a pamphlet and recommended a group home for him.

Both parents decided that was not in Andy's future.

Adam respected all they'd done to keep that from happening. Snapp's Studio was the result of taking what Andy loved most and making it his life's work.

Yolanda followed Adam. "You know, the old woman didn't give me her name but she did say something about a relative. Have you heard of Chester Ventimiglia?"

"His name is on the courthouse wall. On a plaque."

"Trust you to remember that. If an historic politician is commemorated anywhere in an artful way, you'll know. Are you sure you don't mean Richard? Wasn't he a judge?"

Adam bent down, opened his toolbox and soon cleared the floor.

He was sure. *Both* Chester and Richard's names were written on the courthouse, but they were two different engravings.

All his life his father had been telling Adam to pay attention to what went on around him, not to lose himself in whatever project he was engaged in.

And he'd been right.

Adam Snapp had become a successful artist, but he hadn't been able to balance art and life. His art had become his sole focus.

All the while, the rest of his life had fallen apart.

CHAPTER TWO

IF ANYONE HAD told Yolanda that Adam would become Mr. Fix-it, she'd have laughed. He was a dreamer, an artist and a wanderer. His family and friends had always worried about him, sometimes even more than they had about his brother. But Yolanda had to admit, Adam always seemed to land on his feet, albeit wobbly.

After dropping out of high school, he'd managed to become a pseudo artist-in-residence, surviving by doing caricatures during the weekend and then masterminding most of the artwork—mostly murals—at Bridget's Animal Adventure. Back then, a whole five years ago, he'd painted during the day and during the night, acted as a security guard in exchange for room and board.

Yolanda's mom had called him a loser. But Trina Sanchez had thought only a man wearing a suit and tie and bringing home a four-digit-a-week paycheck was to be admired.

Yolanda had never met that man. Her memories of her own father were shadowy. She remembered that he was tall and that his chin and cheeks had always felt rough to her touch. He'd smelled of ink, as he'd worked in Phoenix at some type of print shop. He'd died when Yolanda was four. Her mother hadn't talked about him much, simply saying he should have had more drive.

Yolanda had long suspected that no one possessed enough drive to please her mother. Yolanda certainly hadn't.

When it came to Adam Snapp, Yolanda couldn't get a handle on whether he had *drive* or not. He was passionate about his art, and never seemed to worry about anything else, like rent or food. In his teens and early twenties, he'd been content to live in an old house, more a caretaker's cabin, on BAA's property. Existing day to day, almost like a hippie. Yolanda had almost envied him this worry-free existence.

Unfortunately, there'd been only so many walls to paint in Scorpion Ridge, which was just a tiny spot on the Arizona map. Fortunately, his talent had gotten noticed, big-time, and he'd left Scorpion Ridge with a suitcase of clothes and four suitcases of art supplies. At least that's what Yolanda's grandmother had heard from Mr. Teasdale, who'd heard it from… Well, the small-town grapevine had many roots.

What Yolanda remembered most was that

when Adam left Scorpion Ridge, her mom had shaken her head and given him six months before he came back, head hanging, to move in with his parents.

Yolanda had refrained from mentioning that *she* still lived with her parent. And, although Yolanda nodded in agreement with her mother's prediction, secretly she believed Adam would do something great with his talent. She respected that he had the motivation to follow his muse to other places. She'd been so busy making sure she got straight A's that she'd not had time to develop a muse. Wasn't sure she knew how.

And, though she'd never admit it, especially to him, she thought Adam was quite good.

To everyone's surprise, two years after Adam left, an article in the *Scorpion Ridge Gazette* reported that he'd won a national competition and was becoming fairly well-known, with patrons willing to pay in the five digits for his art.

Even in black-and-white, the winning mural featured in the newspaper was riveting. It was as if Adam had only been practicing when he'd painted all the murals at BAA. His real talent lay elsewhere.

And now he worked for her, removing hinges.

"Yolanda."

Startled, Yolanda blinked, realizing that she'd

followed Adam to the front porch and had just stopped, afraid to go back in the house but unsure what to do next.

"I'm fine."

He shook his head. "No, you're not."

Yolanda started to protest, but stopped. Adam, of all people, could read people's moods. He'd been doing it his whole life, watching out for his disabled brother by diffusing emotional situations before they got out of hand.

"You're right," she admitted, "for some reason, I'm overreacting."

"Not like you," he admitted. "How can I help?"

It felt strange to accept help from him. She and Adam were usually adversaries—she promoting the side of logic; he on the side of risk.

She glanced back at the house, almost asking him to walk around with her again. Help her figure out where the woman had gone, how she'd disappeared. He'd do it, she knew. He would never walk away from someone who needed him.

"Nothing right now," she finally said. "I'll figure it out."

He nodded, not looking convinced, and he took a couple of steps down the front stairs.

She didn't want him to go.

"Adam, why'd you come home?"

He raised an eyebrow, clearly surprised by the question. "Haven't you heard? I came back to help my parents."

Yolanda knew that his dad had hurt his back while teaching a Tae Kwon Do class, and that the doctor had found something suspicious in the X-ray. But Adam's parents were young. Probably in their fifties.

Her mother had been young, too, even though Yolanda had been a change-of-life baby, a complete surprise, born when her mother was forty-six. She'd passed away at seventy-one, too young. Yolanda still wanted her mother. And Gramma Rosi was eighty-six. Maybe eighty-seven. No one was quite sure.

"I heard that but didn't realize your father was so sick that you had to give up your career."

"Sometimes family comes first."

No, Yolanda thought. Family *always* comes first.

But she didn't buy that his father's illness was the only thing that had brought Adam home. Something had to have happened, something that had stymied his paintbrush, filled his eyes with sadness and erased the smile from his face.

Yolanda didn't know what, but right now she was glad he was here because his over-six-foot frame made her feel protected. She rather liked the sensation. The old woman must have really spooked her, enough so that she walked to the edge of the steps, closer to him. Funny, she'd never realized just how tall he was.

"I've got a class to teach," he reminded her, but he didn't leave. The street in front of her wasn't busy. It was a small-town kind of Monday, paced for the beginning of the week. Tuesday and Wednesday would see more people out and about. By Thursday the out-of-towners would arrive not only to enjoy the wildlife habitat but also to stay at the many ranches that catered to weekend cowboys.

It was Yolanda's town. The Acuras had arrived here just after the Moores and Ventimiglias. She liked the close-knit Scorpion Ridge community, quaint downtown and the feeling of a rich history that came with it. Adam had always been meant for bigger and better things, however.

He stood for a moment, watching her. "If you're really afraid, you can always come to the studio with me. I doubt your ghost will be signed up for a beginner's class."

"She wasn't a ghost. Ghosts don't smoke." Yolanda stepped around him and settled in one of the two rocking chairs on the front porch and studied her surroundings. Across the street, a young woman pushed a stroller. The woman's husband worked at a nearby mine. Maybe someday she'd come in for a romance novel for her and a picture book for the baby. Another neighbor raked his yard. A car—Yolanda recognized it as belonging to the minister—traveled down the street and turned right.

Nothing was out of place or suspicious.

"She's gone," Yolanda muttered.

"Who's gone?"

Yolanda started at the new voice. "Gramma Rosi, where'd you come from?"

"I was sitting in the backyard on the swing, enjoying the garden. I thought it was time to come in."

Rosi Acura still owned the house, still had a key. She could visit whenever she wanted... and apparently leave doors unlocked so people could wander in off the street.

Right now she called a lot of shots in Yolanda's life. Her biggest stipulation: "Even though I'm giving you the house, I still want things in my name. I'll pay the gas and water and such. All the taxes."

When Yolanda protested, Gramma Rosi merely scoffed and added her two cents to Yolanda's mom's wish that her daughter live her dream. "In the world today there are people who love what they do and people who don't know how to love. You are a lot like your mother, but you don't have to live like she did. All my life I worried about that girl."

"Hello, Mrs. Acura," Adam said. He took two steps down the front stairs, apparently feeling it was okay to leave now that Yolanda wasn't alone.

"Adam, I love what you've done to the floorboards. They look like they did when my family first moved in."

"When was that, Mrs. Acura?"

"Nineteen hundred and forty-six... maybe earlier, or later. I had just turned sixteen. Until now, it's always been a private residence." Gramma Rosi gazed up at the house, all smiles, something in her eyes that Yolanda didn't understand.

"It's still somewhat a private residence," Yolanda reminded her. "I'm living upstairs, remember."

Maybe Scorpion Ridge was too small a town for a used bookstore... That had been her aunt Freda's comment. Rosi's second daughter. Yolanda had always thought it magical that her grandmother had had two families. First, she'd had Trina. Then, when Trina was grown and gone, she'd had two more children.

"They kept me young," Gramma Rosi claimed. "Also, it made it so much easier to lie about my age." Freda had moved to California the day after her college graduation. They saw her maybe once every three years.

You'll have to take care of your own insurance, both life and medical… That had been her uncle Juan's contribution. He was Gramma's youngest child.

He lived life to the fullest, always had, yet seemed to land on his feet and make good decisions. Yolanda, on the other hand, needed prodding to take risks and sometimes took so long deciding which course to take that she missed out on opportunities.

But Rosi had made the decision to open the bookstore easy by giving Yolanda her house. "You, more than Freda or Juan, deserve the house. Take it now while I can enjoy watching what you do with it."

True, Freda was in California. She didn't want it. Juan lived in Phoenix in a gated community, complete with wife and children and all their activities, although he did love to come visit.

Grandma had another stipulation. "And I'll work for you. You don't even have to pay me."

Just what Yolanda needed. Gramma Rosi would give away books if the customer didn't have enough money, or worse, she would lend him the money. And if a book that had questionable content—maybe it was a bit too sensual—

wound up on her counter, she'd accidentally misplace it. Even if a buyer was right in front of her.

But her immediate concern was the mysterious older woman. "Gramma, did anyone leave out the back door while you were sitting in the backyard swing?"

"No, why?"

"I found an elderly woman in the history section. She said she was searching for a book. I turned away for a moment and when I looked back, she was gone."

"It was someone you didn't know?"

"She said she was related to the Ventimiglia family."

Gramma Rosi's smile disappeared. "You must be mistaken," she said. "That family died out. They'll do no more harm."

"Harm?" Yolanda said.

"What did she look like? What did she want?"

Quickly, Yolanda described the woman and mentioned the book she'd asked after.

"Phhh," said Rosi, still frowning. "Probably some reporter thinking there was a story. The Ventimiglias used to own just about everything in these parts. If she appears again, you find me."

"But—"

"Just do it," Gramma Rosi said.

With that, she went inside. Yolanda watched her climb the wide stairs, slowly and stiffly.

"I've never seen her like that," Yolanda remarked.

"I'm curious, too, now. Let me call GG," Adam offered, setting his tool chest on the porch. "If there's a Ventimiglia relative still living and hiding somewhere, she'd know."

For a moment Yolanda thought about saying no. Her grandmother had been so upset. But why?

"I guess it wouldn't hurt."

"They're about the same age, your grandmother and mine."

Which meant that Adam's great-grandmother Loretta, who wouldn't let him add great to her title and so was called GG, was nearing ninety.

"She was a Realtor for all those years," Adam said. "What she doesn't know about Scorpion Ridge isn't worth knowing." He fetched his cell phone from one of his many pockets and soon was busy trying to get the lowdown on the Ventimiglias.

Yolanda sat down on the top step, wrapping her arms around her knees and listening.

"GG says she thinks the family has died out, too," he reported. "And she's never heard of a Chester. GG wants to know if you're sure the name was Chester and not Richard."

"I'm sure."

"Guess neither of you noticed the plaque on the courthouse in the middle of town," Adam teased before returning to the call. He paid rapt attention to Loretta, nodding exaggeratedly before sharing, "The last Ventimiglia, not named Chester, left decades ago, more than six." He listened some more, finally saying to Yolanda, "GG says they were not a nice family, and everyone was glad to see them go."

"Well, your great-grandma and my gramma agree. Hmmm, why'd they leave?" Yolanda wondered.

But Adam was still intently listening to Loretta. "GG says she's not heard the name Ventimiglia in a long time. She's sure you're mistaken about the name."

"No, I'm not. And the name sure got a rise out of my gramma."

Adam shrugged and handed Yolanda the phone.

"The Ventimiglias are long gone," Loretta Snapp said, her voice guarded. "Died out, and I don't recall there being a Chester. But my grandson says his name is on the courthouse wall. Adam's always had a good memory. It's been years since I've even thought about the family."

"Did you know any of the Ventimiglias?" Yolanda asked.

"The person Adam described sounds like Ivy, but she died a long time ago. Why, she'd be almost ninety if she were alive."

"Sorry," Yolanda said, thinking that Loretta hadn't really answered the question. "And she didn't have any children?"

"Oh, she lived the life she deserved, went off to college, but never married or had any children."

"Are there any distant cousins or such?"

"Not that I'm aware of. The family left town when I was still a teenager. It caused a bit of a scandal."

"Any idea what the scandal was?"

"No."

"So my elderly visitor was probably somebody doing a bit of research on town history," Yolanda decided.

"If you want to know about old families, ask me about mine. I was born a Munro. I married a Snapp, who've lived in Scorpion Ridge for over a hundred years. I can also tell you about the Moores and the Sheldons and—"

"That's all right," Yolanda said.

Adam held out his hand, and after thanking Loretta, Yolanda returned his phone. He said goodbye and hurried down the steps to his ancient minivan. He was the only guy she knew who willingly drove one. It had always been full of paints, brushes and old towels.

It perfectly represented his vagabond life and reminded Yolanda that she'd only be able to rely on him temporarily.

Heading back toward the house, Yolanda couldn't help but feel that Adam's grandmother, who apparently was well versed in the whole history of Scorpion Ridge and its oldest families, knew more than she was telling.

SNAPP'S TAE KWON DO studio was in a strip mall nestled between a nail salon and a doughnut shop. It would celebrate fifteen years of service in a few months. In some ways the studio was a blessing. It gave Adam's autistic brother, Andy, a productive way to earn a living. But it had also been a huge change for the Snapps. When Adam was eleven, his father had walked away from a six-figure white-collar job and purchased the studio. The Snapps had gone from buying whatever they wanted, whenever they wanted, to spending on a budget.

And Adam had been angry. He'd liked having a television in his room, being able to get any video game he wanted and the best art supplies.

It had been the beginning of his strained relationship with his father. Adam had just wanted a voice, to be heard, but his dad had never seemed to want to listen.

This afternoon the parking area in front of their studio was fairly empty, as the Scorpion Ridge schools didn't get out for another hour, and the two morning Tae Kwon Do classes, one for tots and the other for seniors, had ended before Adam rolled out of bed.

"Hey," his mother greeted him as he stepped into the foyer. She was at the front desk taking advantage of the lull by counting out fliers to be delivered to the local schools and anywhere kids or any potential client might be found.

"Andy feeling better?" Adam asked.

"No, he's been in his room all day. Doesn't want to come out."

"Still don't know what triggered the mood swing?"

"Not a clue."

Andy was a creature of habit, a connoisseur of routine. If his day got out of whack, he closed down.

"Want some help?" Adam offered.

"No, go on back and see your father. He tried calling you earlier." Marianne smiled at him, as she had his entire life. She'd been his champion, but she hadn't really understood him, either.

Adam figured his dad was checking up on him, calling to make sure he would fill in for

Andy and the three-thirty class. Adam didn't need reminders. He was here to help out, and that's what he'd do.

Well, that was the price for arriving early: too much time to talk. His dad might have traded a suit and tie for a white sparring uniform called a dobok, but he still harbored the soul of an accountant. He liked every task to be itemized, completed and checked off.

Maybe that was where Andy got his extreme need for routine.

Robert Snapp was hunched over his desk, muttering about paperwork and frowning. He still believed, even after almost a decade, that somehow Snapp's Studio would turn a decent profit. Maybe in the big city, but here in Scorpion Ridge?

Getting sick had only made him want to succeed more.

"You wanted to talk to me?" Adam had ignored his dad's phone call, but it was harder to ignore the man.

"Sit down."

Adam reminded himself that he was a foot taller than his dad and that he'd been living on his own a long time: two years working at BAA and five years in three different states as a well-paid muralist.

But all he could remember was that every

time he was called into his dad's office, whether it was here at Snapp's Studio or at home, he would hear how displeased his father was with him. Adam had sat through hundreds of lectures grilling him on grades that were never the best, goals that were not met and how in the Snapp household everyone had a job.

Problem was, the job his dad wanted him to do and the job Adam had been born to do were two different things. Choosing a paintbrush over a "reliable" career had put the two men on opposite sides, and neither was willing to swim to the other.

Until Dad got sick.

"It's good to have you home," Dad said, his smile not quite reaching his eyes.

Adam started to remind his dad that this was temporary, but stopped himself. Adam had had five years to miss his family and to consider the real meaning of home.

"It's good to be home."

One thing his ex-girlfriend Stacey had taught him was that home was temporary and love wasn't always unconditional. To some it was the means to an end.

Now, though, his dad needed him. Dad had injured his back three months ago at the studio. He still moved slowly, and a wrong move would put him in bed. But then a blood test had turned up something more serious: pancreatic cancer. His parents had been very optimistic about treatment and recovery, but Adam hadn't thought twice about coming home. He wanted to see the world and work a career he loved, but he could put his family first for a while.

Taking a deep breath, Adam reminded himself to keep thinking as positively as his parents, because thinking any other way made the truth all too clear.

His father could die.

So until his dad's health returned, Adam would teach the classes that his brother and the other instructor, Mr. Chee, couldn't.

"Glad you're here early," his father said. It was his idea of a compliment.

"I was working over at Yolanda's. She'll be opening on time." Adam waited for the chitchat to end. His father wanted to talk about something more important than what he'd done that day.

"She's a hard worker. So was her mother." Adam's dad approved of hard workers, whether they be a waitress at the local restaurant, or a grocery store clerk, or a housekeeper.

Roving mural painter didn't make his list, though. It didn't make Yolanda's list, either. She'd stopped speaking to him when he dropped out of school, muttering something about people not knowing when they had it good. Back then, he'd thought she was talking about his dropping out, home life and art. Now, after working with her these past few months, he realized she'd just meant his home life.

She was right. He'd taken his family, especially Andy, for granted. His talent, too. Now that both were in jeopardy, he realized just how much he could lose.

Adam smiled, thinking about Yolanda. At first glance she was quiet, deceivingly hesitant, but underneath she was all fire and opinions. But she never got flustered. Not even when they'd worked together at Bridget's Animal Adventure. If they'd had a problem, she'd just calmly tug on his sleeve and say, "The anaconda is loose" with no more concern than if she were asking for a tissue.

But she'd made it clear that she felt he should charge for his murals. She was a bit more impressed that he did caricatures for pay on the weekend, but only a bit.

She was too much of a Type A. Always with her calendar filled with tasks and no time to watch the sunset. Let alone enjoy it.

Just like his father.

"You had something you wanted to say to me?" Adam chose not to sit but remained standing. He didn't want his father looking down on him.

His dad closed the folder he'd been fingering. The pause was typical, but had a different feel. Adam started to worry. Finally, his dad said, "Shut the door."

Adam did as requested.

"Your mom and I are going to get a place in Phoenix for a while, close to the Mayo Clinic. The doctors want to do exploratory surgery to see what can be done—either good news or bad."

"Will this improve your chances?"

"I'm not going to sugarcoat this for you anymore. It might give me five more years."

Adam's breath left his chest like a vacuum taking air from the room. The lights seemed to dim. And Adam, who didn't cry, felt his throat close and his eyes water. He couldn't talk.

His father continued. "We'll be relying on you a bit more."

Adam nodded. His parents couldn't stay in Phoenix if no one was around to take care of Andy, not just at home but here, at Snapp's Studio. "Sure, I'll do it." Unbidden came the thought: this might be the last thing my father asks of me.

His dad blinked, clearly surprised. "You will? It means working more hours at the studio and some real time with your brother."

"Of course. When will you be going?"

"We're working on—" his dad hesitated "—on getting the money together."

Adam swallowed. He'd have money to give his parents if he'd been a little wiser. If he hadn't trusted in Stacey's supposed love.

Stacey Baer had wanted to be an artist, so she claimed. He'd met her when he'd been commissioned to do a mural for the town of Wildrose, Illinois, and she'd insinuated herself into his work and his life almost immediately. She'd climbed right up on the catwalk beside Adam as he started sketching the train and all the history of Wildrose, population two thousand and three—counting him.

He'd loved the old building the town was turning into a museum. It had character. No one was threatening to paint it Kool-Aid orange! Having someone next to him who appreciated art had made the job all the better.

He'd shared his craft, his apartment and his money.

Growing up in Scorpion Ridge, he'd been insulated. No one had taken advantage of him, ever. And he'd made sure no one took advantage of Andy. They were the Snapp brothers. People admired his family, especially his dad, who'd sacrificed so much. They were pillars of the town. They paid their bills, attended parades, went to church… It had ill prepared Adam for the realities of life.

Six months later, as soon as he finished the mural, Stacey had cleaned out his bank account and broken his heart. Last he'd heard, she was in Boston. That is if she hadn't run out of his cash. He hadn't been able to paint since.

"You need money, Dad?"

"I'll get it."

Which probably meant Adam's grandmother was already involved. She'd been careful with every cent, but still couldn't have that much to spare. More than ever, Adam wished he had the money he'd earned and the muse that Stacey had taken when she left. He'd been foolish. And now he realized the cost.

"How much will the surgery cost?"

"Between medical bills and living expenses… at least twenty thousand dollars. But I don't want you to worry about that. The operation's been scheduled for a few weeks from now."

"You gonna be able to get around okay until then?" Already Dad was missing work, sitting down a lot when he used to always be on the move. He wasn't eating much, either.

"I plan on giving it my all."

"Andy know?"

"Not yet."

Adam wasn't sure he wanted to be in the

room when Mom told his big brother about the change in his routine. Older by just two minutes, Andy was brilliant, which sometimes made living with his disorder harder. People started to expect him to be brilliant in everything, which was impossible.

Looking around his father's office, Adam took in the pictures. They were mostly of Dad and Andy. Andy was shorter than Adam, coming up to Adam's chest. He was thicker, too, but not by much. Tae Kwon Do was to thank for his fairly slender build because Andy loved to eat. They both had the same brown, unruly hair, the same nose, same smile. Adam was a bit more prone to whiskers, though. Adam was in a few of the photos. He and his brother both were featured in the one where his dad had been painting the words Snapp's Studio onto the building. Each brother held a paintbrush and was looking at the camera, both innocent still, not realizing how much time and energy this new endeavor would take.

Adam had gone the whole route, all the way to black belt. He'd competed and done well. But in about eighth grade, he'd backed off, realizing that Tae Kwon Do was something his brother needed more.

And really, Adam had his art. Snapp's Studio was awash in murals. It had been Adam's first blank wall and the one time when his father hadn't shook his head at the waste of time.

"Are you going to ask—" Adam began.

"GG already said she'd move in, too, while we're gone."

"Did you talk her into teaching the senior session?"

His dad laughed. For all their angst, Dad's disappointment and Adam's disregard for "going into a profession where you can make a living," they shared one trait. Both fiercely loved and protected their family, especially Andy.

Adam wondered if the bond between him and his brother would have been as strong if Andy hadn't had autism. He doubted it.

When Adam was in fifth grade, his mother had told him that having an autistic brother made the family more of a unit, working together for the good of the whole. Andy didn't get other people's jokes, often said the wrong thing and liked routine. He was perfect at Snapp's Studio, though. He'd laugh at the little kids' jokes no matter if they were funny or not. In turn, the kids didn't notice or care when he said the wrong thing. And, as long as the kids tried to follow him, that was routine enough. Best of all for them, he clapped no matter how the students performed.

"You'd need to move back home," his dad said.

Adam nodded. He really liked living in the groundskeeper's cabin over at Bridget's Animal Adventure. It was off the beaten path and felt right. His best memories were there: learning how to make it on his own, realizing that he could make a living off his art. Best of all, he could paint there and leave his supplies where they lay. The house he'd grown up in hadn't offered that option. It was a "clean up when you're done" kind of atmosphere where get-er-done meant get-er-done in one setting. Most of Adam's projects took a week if not more.

"I wouldn't ask if it weren't important."

"I might be able to handle things without GG needing to move in," Adam offered.

Loretta was in her late eighties and still sold realty. Granted, those transactions were few and far between and mostly just for dedicated clients—most as old as she was. But she had her own routine, and it wouldn't jibe with Andy's.

"We appreciate it, Adam. You can make the guest room your own," his father offered.

But it had been a long time since Adam had felt anything was his own.

CHECKING HER WATCH, Yolanda decided to finish stocking the last few rows of the children's room. The decor there was the opposite of the history and nonfiction room. The room had not a shred of seriousness in its atmosphere; instead, it was bright, colorful and inviting.

She'd already spent way too much time investigating what was probably a harmless old woman who simply wanted to read about the history of a town her forefathers helped create. With that in mind, Yolanda went looking for the books she'd left waiting on a shelf in the middle of the second floor.

Two Ramona books were on the floor. Yolanda picked them up. Their author, Beverly Cleary, had started life as a librarian before writing some of the best children's books. Five-year-old Yolanda had begged for a chapter of *Henry and Beezus* each night.

Two books remained on the shelf where Yolanda had placed them earlier.

Two?

Yolanda frowned. She only remembered carrying three books in the series. Two were on the floor; only one was supposed to be on the shelf.

"How funny," she whispered as she picked up the top book, which was clearly not intended for the children's area. It was dark blue, dusty and had faded embossed gold lettering proclaiming the title *Stories of Scorpion Ridge, Arizona*.

Unease followed Yolanda as she walked toward the history and nonfiction room. She really wished that Adam hadn't left. She was sure this book hadn't been in her hands this morning when she'd been interrupted by the old woman. The book certainly hadn't made its way to the shelf by itself.

Someone else had been in her used bookstore.

Or perhaps the old woman had found the book—without Yolanda noticing?—and then realized it was the wrong one.

Yolanda might have chosen to forget the whole incident if she hadn't been a stickler for details. Inside the cover page a name was written. Black ink, perfectly formed letters, all caps, looking almost like one word.

CHESTER VENTIMIGLIA

CHAPTER THREE

TUESDAY MORNING ADAM'S phone sounded way too early. He'd always preferred to wake up when his body wanted to wake up rather than when the alarm said it was time.

Nowadays he woke up a lot earlier. Mostly because he wasn't painting way into the night.

"I'm awake," he muttered into the phone.

"I'm trying to find Adam Snapp," a voice said.

"You found him."

"I'm William Woodhull Huckabee. I'm just outside of town. I own—"

"You own all the ostriches."

Huckabee chuckled. "That would be me. Huckabee's Harem is about to expand. We're trying to bring more visitors to our door. I've seen your work around BAA, and I wondered if you'd be willing to do a mural for us?"

"No," Adam said, swallowing hard. "No, I'm not doing murals anymore. But I can make a referral."

Huckabee paused before saying, "No, I don't

want a referral. I was hoping to do a bit of tie-in with BAA. After all, they don't have ostriches, and when we get visitors to town, having two places to visit is a plus. If both attractions have a similar look, we can maybe combine our advertising. I can make it worth your while. What do you usually charge?"

He'd been paid twenty-five thousand, plus room and board, for the Wildrose job. From start to finish, it had taken six months. Since then, he'd had three more offers, all in the same price range. He'd turned the jobs down and come home with an almost empty checking account.

Huckabee's Harem, however, was not a twenty-five thousand dollar kind of establishment. And Adam, still licking wounds that weren't healing, couldn't take the job. Didn't matter the payoff.

But the money could go right to his father. He paused for a moment, running the idea through his mind, trying to picture himself with a clean slate.

No picture came; only a clean slate remained.

He'd make the money some other way. He could do it. Would do it.

"Sorry, I've gotten out of the business. I'm doing something else now." It wasn't a lie. He was teaching Tae Kwon Do classes, taking over the care of his brother and remodeling Yolanda's Victorian.

None of which would bring him the money he needed to help his father. Maybe he should take a lesson from Yolanda. At least once a day she sat down with her spreadsheet and made sure that she was sticking to her budget, following the business plan she'd created. If Adam were lucky, he'd break even this month and manage to put gas in his van and food in his belly.

He was right back where he started: just getting by. Proving his father right. But his lack of career had also made him available when his father needed him.

Getting back that career would help his father even more.

"Tell you what," Huckabee said, "I'm not in a hurry. I'll give you a few weeks. You change your mind, give me a call. Better yet, come on out. We're fairly new, and the locals haven't really taken to stopping by. I'll show you around. Bring the family."

Definitely not an outing that would fit into his brother Andy's routine. Adam had taken him to BAA, but he hadn't been able to handle all the noise and chaos.

"Okay, I appreciate that." After a quick goodbye, not giving Huckabee a chance to say any more, Adam rolled out of bed.

Good thing Huckabee had called. Adam had to teach a class this morning. After a decent breakfast, doughnuts and milk from the grocery store in town, Adam made it to Snapp's Studio where his first step was to head down to the dressing room and change into his uniform. He had a ten-thirty class with ten students, all at various levels. One was actually better than he was. Two were beginning their second week. There was even a mom.

An hour later Adam applauded his class for being the best they could be and went through his list of reminders: their next lesson was on Thursday, there was a competition in Mesa this coming Saturday and they still had time to sign up and that a School Special started in just over a week. For the month of September, anyone who brought in a spelling test with a perfect grade got a ten dollar coupon for a Snapp's Studio T-shirt.

His dad believed that Tae Kwon Do had to include the whole student, not just the student who showed up for lessons a few hours a week. Adam's dad monitored the school kids' homework and attitude.

Nobody dared mention Adam's own past grades or bad attitude.

Changing back into his regular clothes, Adam tossed his uniform into the laundry bag and headed for the front lobby. There would be another lesson at four, but it would be taught by Mr. Chee.

Adam's dad and brother were in Phoenix volunteering at a food donation center. They'd been going every Tuesday morning for a decade. Andy was a natural at sorting, and sorting was just what the donation center needed.

Adam had gone with them a time or two. But the repetition, standing still, had made him want to scream. His dad, however, never even blinked at the challenge.

Adam's mother was up front. The beginning of the school year meant his parents put out a rash of advertising. She had stacks of brochures ready to go, all crisscrossed with sticky notes marking their destination.

"Want me to deliver these, Mom?"

She looked up at him, a half smile on her face, but tears were shimmering in her eyes.

"Mom, you all right?"

"No. Yes. There's just such a lot going on. And I appreciate you staying with Andy while…" She didn't finish. Instead, she came around the desk and reached up to hug him. He realized just how small she was, and yet she always carried so much: his dad, his brother, him.

He was more like her than he was his father. She was the decorator, and he'd gotten his love of color from her. When he was six, he'd helped her paint the living room as well as put tile down.

After a while she let go and stepped away.

"I'll do whatever you need me to do, Mom."

"Your delivering these fliers would really help."

Ten minutes later, he stood in front of Snapp's Studio, staring at the sign, at the advertisements posted on the windows and at his mom still working at her desk inside.

It was in little more than a strip mall.

His dad had traded the highlife for such a venture. His dad had had a good reason, though. He'd not given up on his old life; he had instead given his all to what mattered.

Adam wasn't sure he could say the same. But he was determined to change that.

YOLANDA HADN'T SLEPT all night. Every noise she'd heard had had her grabbing a flashlight and heading downstairs. Plus, when she'd showed the book to Rosi, her grandmother hadn't remembered owning such a book and refused to even look at it, muttering that she didn't want to remember the Ventimiglias.

Odd.

Yolanda had then spent an hour going through the books she still had to shelve. None were on

the history of Scorpion Ridge. Later that evening Gramma Rosi begged off Yolanda's offer
to take her out to dinner because her favorite
television show was on. Gramma Rosi never
put television before family.

So she'd taken the mysterious book to bed.
Now on Yolanda's nightstand was a book that
didn't belong to her, but possibly did belong to
a woman who'd not only disturbed Yolanda but
had also disturbed her grandmother.

Adding to Yolanda's anxiety, the book's letters were small and handwritten, the words running close together—forget paragraphs. There
were no indentations. Her head started hurting
after reading two pages. So at midnight, when
she realized sleep was a goal not to be realized, she settled on reading the pages devoted
to a Ventimiglia: Richard. Chester wasn't mentioned at all.

What she did like about the book were the
drawings. Hundreds of thumbnails all about
Scorpion Ridge. Some were faded and impossible to make out. Others, though, were still
crisp and clear, almost jumping off the page in
bold strokes.

Bold strokes? Now that was an Adam Snapp
term.

The pictures were of homes and people—
mostly faces. Most of the places were long gone;

most of the people had passed away. She recognized her own house, looking much the same only with a stable. The other house she recognized was downtown and housed the Scorpion Ridge Historical Society Museum. The drawing showed the building with a door in the middle and two windows flanking it on each side. It looked the same today, except the front door had been moved, and there was now a swamp cooler on top. Yolanda had been there many times and remembered that the hardwood floor creaked and the ceilings were low. The back porch was big enough to sleep on. It was an old adobe dwelling with a plaster coating, same as in the picture.

Next came a drawing of an old mission that looked a lot like San Xavier Mission in Tucson. Under the drawing was a name, but Yolanda couldn't make it out. The last structure she recognized was the old Scorpion Ridge courthouse. She remembered hearing about it in school. The old building had burned down in nineteen hundred and forty-six and had been replaced with an ugly cement structure.

But Adam had mentioned there was a plaque on the wall that mentioned Chester Ventimiglia. Here was something Yolanda could actually investigate! She finally fell asleep knowing how she'd spend her morning.

Her alarm sounded and she rolled out of bed at the first ring. Today she'd strive for good mood and peace of mind.

Not always easy. Yolanda had always been a worrier. Gramma Rosi blamed Yolanda's mother for passing on such an unnecessary pastime. Yolanda knew that worry was a choice, and one she needed to make differently. She got up, got dressed and made an easy breakfast: cereal. Then she checked her to-do list before spending the next few hours stocking the last empty shelves in the children's area.

Tired of bending, dusty from the books and needing to get outside, Yolanda locked the front door behind her and walked downtown. It took her three blocks and ten minutes. It would have only taken her eight minutes, but there were plenty of people to say good morning to. All asked about her grandmother. Two asked about the opening of her bookstore and promised to bring her some gently used books. And one offered a marriage proposal.

"No, thanks, Otis. I'm too busy to get married."

Otis Wilson gazed past Yolanda at her Victorian. "I used to love a girl who lived there, you know."

Yolanda wasn't surprised. According to legend, her Gramma Rosi had been quite a looker.

Of course, Gramma Rosi liked to weave her own legends. Whether they were true or not…

Yolanda arrived at Scorpion Ridge's courthouse at the same time as the mayor, who'd been her third grade teacher. Janice Kolby had handed Yolanda her first Ramona book. "I hear the bookstore's coming along," Mayor Kolby said.

"Every room is stocked."

"Make sure you take advantage of all the tax breaks given to female business owners." With that, Mayor Kolby hurried through the front door. According to Gramma, the mayor was just as good at fiscal responsibility as she was averaging classroom grades. Which meant Gramma was pleased because Scorpion Ridge was debt-free.

Yolanda hoped her bookstore was a success and she could continue to be debt-free. If the business failed and she lost all her mother's money…? Maybe she should have taken a "real" job. One that had benefits and where she didn't need to prove herself.

Or maybe she should have bought the Corner Diner. She'd been offered that business, one already established and making a profit. Lucille Salazar, the owner, had been wooing Yolanda for years.

"You're the best cook in town" had been her first compliment. "Come work for me."

That had been a mere five years ago, and Yolanda had been attending college and working as a housekeeper for Ruth Dunbar, who used to be a Moore, owner of one of the other still-standing houses in Yolanda's book.

Not *Yolanda's* book—it was Chester's.

Then Lucille had tried, "A little restaurant is easier to manage than a mansion. Come work for me."

Yolanda's hours had been flexible when she'd worked for Ruth. The pay had been good. And Ruth had treated Yolanda like a daughter who happened to help around the house.

Ruth had paid for most of Yolanda's schooling because no one—not Yolanda, Gramma or Ruth—had known that Trina was a miser.

Eventually, Lucille said, "I'm wanting to retire. I'll give you a good price." But Yolanda didn't want to own a restaurant. She loved books. They opened windows to adventure and took readers to new worlds. So if she was going to take a risk, she wanted it to be for something she loved.

Today, however, Yolanda's adventure was the Scorpion Ridge courthouse, and it was nothing to get excited about. When the original building depicted in the book had burned down, only the iron doors had been salvaged. Adam was right, though. A bronze plaque was on the front wall, down a bit from the doors, and now partially hidden by a giant bougainvillea bush. Yolanda had to step off the walkway in order to read the words. They were weathered, time-faded and neglected. She brushed away a bit of mud that obscured the first word. She traced the engraving, so worn away by time that it could barely be read.

Erected in nineteen hundred and fifty because of Richard Ventimiglia and by Chester Ventimiglia, by his hard work and money.

She'd once known a poet who'd said, "I'd rather write a book than a poem. Much easier to get everything said."

This plaque boasted sixteen words, and Yolanda immediately realized their depth. *His* hands not *their* hands. *His* money not *their* money.

"So you never noticed this before?"

Yolanda jumped.

Adam grinned, only one side of his mouth going up in a lazy, devil-may-care expression. "Didn't mean to scare you. I was delivering a stack of advertisements—" he held up a flier with Snapp's Studio pictured across the top and a twenty percent discount coupon on the bottom "—to the woman in charge of parks and recreation."

Must be an easy job, Yolanda thought. Scorpion Ridge had one park and very little recreation. Maybe that was why it was debt-free.

"I didn't hear you come up, and no, I've never noticed this before."

"One of my art teachers brought us here when I was in fourth grade," Adam said. "We used butcher paper and charcoal to make a rubbing. I still remember how what we re-created was clearer than what we could actually see." He reached out a finger and traced what looked like bumps and grooves. "These are actually two angels holding a banner."

"What does the banner say?"

"Impossible to tell. The teacher guessed that it was something about God. I never thought that, though. None of the letters resembled a G to me. And what we decipher of the letters didn't form any biblical saying I could think of."

"Oh," she joked, "and in fourth grade you knew quite a few biblical sayings."

"You'd be surprised."

"I'm surprised that I've never heard of Chester, only Richard. And I can't find any information about Chester. I searched last night, both online and among some of my grandmother's books." Yolanda peered at the plaque, now noticing the top. "You know, this could easily be restored."

"At a cost, and no one really cares," Adam pointed out.

"It's part of our history."

"Forgotten history. Maybe if there were some Ventimiglias still around…"

"That woman yesterday said she was visiting relatives of the Ventimiglias." Yolanda truly wished Adam had spoken to the old woman, too. No one seemed to believe her. "Never mind. What do you think it means that this refers to Chester's hard work and money but not Richard's?"

"Huh?"

Yolanda read the plaque aloud to him, emphasizing the pronoun. "It sounds like Chester not only paid for but also helped build the courthouse."

"Richard was a judge," Adam remembered. "He'd have had money."

"Yes, that's in here." Yolanda hoisted her backpack around to the front of her body and pulled out the dark blue book. She flipped to a page and read, "Richard Ventimiglia was born in Wisconsin, a graduate of West Point, class of nineteen hundred and one. He then went into the army as a second lieutenant before going back to school. This time he attended National

University Law School, before coming to Arizona—which wasn't a state yet—and settling here and becoming the town's first judge."

"Busy man."

"There's no mention of parents or siblings. That's unusual. Almost all biographies have a family tree."

Adam held out his hand for the book. Reluctantly, Yolanda turned it over. For some reason she felt protective of it. Adam started to skim through the pages, but almost immediately slowed his pace, studying page after page, his brow furrowing.

He was thinner now than when he'd left five years ago. Taller, too. He didn't joke as much, either, but maybe that had to do with his dad's illness and having to make a living instead of living to make art. His hair was the same, though—brown and windblown even when there was no wind. She'd always enjoyed looking up at him even when she hadn't been able to make sense of him. He existed in a world she didn't understand. He'd always done exactly what he wanted to do, taken risks and seemed to love life.

Maybe because he'd never wanted for anything.

"Where did you get this book?" he asked.

"I found it on a shelf in the children's section. It wasn't there earlier."

"What do you mean?"

"I mean it's not a book I cataloged. Until I picked it up from the shelf, I had never seen it before. I think the old woman left it."

"I thought she was looking for a history book."

"She was. At least that's what she said. Now I believe she must have brought this one in with her and then accidentally left it behind."

Adam flipped to the front cover. "No name and no publisher. This is a manuscript more than a book. But someone wrote it and did the drawings so precisely that at first glance, it looks published."

"It's amazing."

"You've read it already?"

"No, just a few pages about Richard Ventimiglia. I had a hard enough time getting through that," she admitted. "The print's small and runs together. Made me wonder if I should get stronger glasses."

"The drawings are well-done and quite detailed, especially for being so small." He closed the book, studying the cover, back and spine. Then he added, "You think there's something in here about Chester."

"I hope."

"I didn't see his name anywhere."

"Really, you skimmed that thoroughly?" Not a chance. Books were her world. She was a master reader and skimmer.

"No." Adam closed the book tightly. "Though I did notice you've got some pages missing."

Yolanda's mouth opened. "You're kidding."

"No. It's actually a common practice. Somebody probably wanted a drawing or two or three." He grinned. "I'm certainly tempted to snatch this book from you and take a few pages. The pictures are not only vintage but also inspiring. Some of the facial expressions are hilarious."

He sobered. For just a few moments he'd gotten excited—more like the old Adam, the one she knew so well—but then remembered something sad.

"Anyway," he continued, "if you go into any library and look at the art books, you'll invariably find many with pages missing. People find a drawing they like and rip it out. Usually nobody notices. I once went looking for an old book that had a picture of Johannes Vermeer's *Girl with a Lute*. I went all the way to Gesippi because the librarian there was willing to hunt down and order the book I wanted. When it arrived, Vermeer's painting was listed in the index but missing from the book."

"It's so odd that you like Vermeer," Yolanda said. What really surprised her was his willingness to track down the book. It showed gumption and dedication.

"Because his paintings are so realistic?" Adam guessed.

"Yes."

"Well, I like all artists who weren't appreciated in their own time. As you don't appreciate me." His words were joking, but his eyes said something else. Something Yolanda hadn't expected.

Not from Adam Snapp.

"Actually, I do appreciate you. Especially right now—you've pointed out two important details. One, the decorative top to the plaque. I didn't realize that even existed. Then you figured out that pages are missing from the book."

She thanked him again and he headed away from her and into the courthouse. Yes, she admitted that she was feeling pretty appreciative of him right now.

Adam Snapp looked darn good from the back.

ADAM FINISHED MAKING his deliveries by ten. It had felt strange, going back to some of his old haunts. The director of the Boys and Girls Club asked him if he'd be interested in teaching an art class on Saturday mornings. The principal at his high school handed over some literature about getting a GED.

His phone rang as he was leaving the Corner Diner.

Another call inspired by the town mural in Wildrose, Illinois. And this time the caller knew exactly how much Adam had been paid, and was even willing to offer a bit more plus expenses for living in the town of Targus, Mississippi.

This time Adam hesitated. His family needed the money, but they also needed him. Right now he couldn't leave. Not until after the surgery, at least. But after that? Would he be more help to his family if he took the Mississippi job?

"Sorry," Adam said, "I'm already employed elsewhere, and it will be at least a couple of weeks before I can even consider relocating." It took a few moments to convince this guy, too. Finally, after Adam agreed to let the man know if the situation changed, Adam ended the call, stored it in his phone and headed for his minivan.

Two calls in one day. It certainly made him reevaluate his current job situation. He could tolerate teaching Tae Kwon Do classes and helping his parents for a while. He was enjoying working with Yolanda on the Victorian; he just wished she'd listen to his advice a bit more. Unfortunately, what she paid wasn't enough to help with his father's surgery.

He blamed himself for being broke. He'd squandered and enjoyed every minute of his time away from Scorpion Ridge. Until he opened his eyes one morning and found it all gone. Along with his girlfriend, new van and all his art supplies.

Adam knew his squandered money had been a huge mistake. Learning the hard way had always been Adam Snapp's way. But it was time to reassess, think about his family, make better choices and find a way to stay in Scorpion Ridge for the next few weeks and still make enough money to help support his parents.

At most, they'd gain ten to twenty new students with this beginning-of-school enrollment push. The students would sign a long-term contract and pay by the month. There'd be no big chunk of change when his father needed it.

It would trickle in, instead.

Luke Rittenhouse, his boss at BAA, would let him sell his art in the habitat's gift shop on commission, but only if it related to animals. Adam had been able to do animals easily. They allowed Adam's quirky side to flourish. Of the five pieces of his that were on sale now at BAA, the bear had real teeth—provided by the habitat's veterinarian—the peacock had real feathers—a simple matter really, he'd just picked them up as he walked the grounds—and the others all had something similar.

They were, however, pieces Adam had completed more than a year ago. Nothing new.

He remembered the passion he used to have. He wanted it back. Maybe he should follow Yolanda's lead, take a community college class and come up with a business plan.

He already had a name when it came to murals, from the more than two dozen he'd done at BAA plus the five he'd painted in New Mexico, California and Chicago. They'd all been collages of small-town history. Each one had boasted a train, a long-dead high-profile town figure and whatever the town was famous for.

They'd been fun, but Adam had to admit his heart was no longer in it. Painting the history of a town he was a stranger to felt wrong.

The places he'd stayed during the few years he'd been away from Scorpion Ridge hadn't been home. They'd been little more than glorified motel rooms. He'd come close to a home in Wildrose. The little apartment he'd shared with Stacey held good memories. He'd seen what it could be like to have someone by his side, someone who believed in him and shared his passion.

He also remembered how the refrigerator was never stocked, how few clothes were in the dresser drawers and that no photos of his family had been displayed.

It had still been a glorified motel room. He'd just not realized it.

Walking up the steps to the Victorian, he wondered if Yolanda felt at home here. She and her mother had lived in a tiny house near the edge of town. It had always looked perfect. He'd only been in it once. He remembered that the furnishings and decor appeared almost staged. Yes, that was the word. It was decorated as if a photographer were about to enter and take a picture.

It didn't seem lived in at all.

Her grandmother's Victorian had never looked perfect, at least not until now. Rosi Acura believed in toys on the porch, bikes in the yard and chalk drawings on the sidewalk. He'd helped her out a time or two with that. Yup, the Victorian was certainly a lot more elegant now than it had been all those years ago.

Back then, the neighborhood kids had thought it was haunted when in reality it was just the oldest house on the block and a bit run-down. The kids had dared each other to take a step into the front yard. Once, when he was ten, he'd run to the front door, rang the doorbell and then hightailed it back to his friends hiding behind a car parked in the street.

Yolanda's grandmother hadn't helped matters. Sometimes Rosi'd open the door and yell *boo*. But then she'd come out with cookies or popcorn and entice the kids into the yard again. Her presence, they pretended, would scare away any ghosts.

Yolanda had spent a lot of time here while her mother worked. She'd sit on the porch, with her nose either in a book or thrust in the air, all annoyed at the silly games boys played.

"You home?" he called, opening the door. In the neighborhood he'd lived in in Chicago, an unlocked door meant a negligent tenant. Here in Scorpion Ridge it meant *come in, neighbor*.

"Hey, Adam." To his surprise, Rosi exited the kitchen. She wore a frilly brown, black and white shirt over black stretch pants. Normal enough attire until you looked at her feet. Black-and-white zebra slippers. BAA had a whole display of wild animal slippers, so these were probably a gift from her granddaughter.

"Yolanda here?"

"No, she's in Phoenix shopping for dormers."

He'd been the one to tell her that the four dormers in her living room were too small for the job they were performing, hence their deteriorating condition. She'd wanted to keep them; he'd urged her to replace them. Guess his pep talk about staying true to the home's history paid off. She should have asked him to tag along, though. She'd have trouble finding the right ones without him.

Rosi followed him to the stairs, but she could no longer climb them. "What are you planning to do today?"

"Doors." He paused at the bottom of the stairs, wanting to get busy yet wanting to talk. Finally, he set the promotional fliers on a table by the front door and sat on the fourth step up, his long legs stretched before him, and glanced at Rosi.

She still looked like she had back when she was hollering *boo* at him. Maybe her face was lined a bit more and maybe she walked slower. Even after all these years, she was the type of woman who took care of people.

She laughed and joined him. "I love this house. Yolanda loves it, too. You're going to fix the rest of it up for us, right?"

"I'm gonna try. Upstairs, I'm pretty sure we're looking at a lot of lead paint in all those doors. I need to see if they're worth saving."

"They are."

That answer was no surprise as this was her house. But Yolanda wouldn't be happy with how much more it would cost to renovate rather than replace.

"How long did you live here?" he asked.

"Since I was sixteen."

"So, we're talking the nineteen forties?"

"Yes. Late nineteen forties."

"I spoke to my grandmother yesterday. She remembered the Ventimiglias. Said the same thing you did, that they weren't very nice. Do you remember Ivy Ventimiglia?"

"I do. I remember those days like they were yesterday. Actually, I remember the past better than the present."

"What do you remember about Ivy?"

For a moment he thought Rosi would withdraw. Instead, she said, "Well, she was a few grades behind me in school. I was in the same grade as your grandmother. Not that Ivy would have associated with us. Me, anyway. I think your grandmother might have spent some time with her. Position, family wealth, heritage, they all meant a lot more back then. Not always for the good."

"What do you mean?" He had an inkling, but wanted her to spell it out.

"Ivy and your grandmother lived here on the hill, the rich part of town. Even if they didn't like each other, and they didn't, they had to pretend."

That was a question he'd have to ask his great-grandmother. To his knowledge, GG liked everyone. "Did you and my grandmother get along?"

"Loretta was larger than life and nice to everyone, even those outside her station. She was also a little wild."

"My great-grandmother, wild?" Adam could believe it.

"Wild and adored. She was homecoming queen."

Adam hadn't known that. "Yolanda's pretty enchanted with the book that got left behind."

"Book? What book?"

"Yolanda didn't mention it to you?"

"I didn't go to dinner with her. Then this morning when I got here she was already gone. What kind of book?"

"It's like a published journal and has all kinds of town history events and even some drawings. This house is in it."

Rosi shook her head. "Journals don't mean anything. Most of us girls kept them back then. And not very much in them was based on fact. Best Yolanda stop thinking about the Ventimiglias. There are none left. Ivy had an older brother but he died in an accident when he was nineteen. Ivy never married."

"You kept track of her? How do you know she didn't marry?"

"It's a small town, even though they moved,

word trickled back. If she'd have married, I'd have heard about it. Weddings were a bit more important in those days, especially for the wealthy. It would have been in the paper, complete with pictures and pedigrees."

"Why didn't Ivy and Adam's great-grand-mother like each other?" In the quiet of the bookstore, Yolanda's voice seemed loud, and both Adam and Rosi startled. Neither had heard the door open and close, yet here was Yolanda, holding a bag of groceries and looking as if she'd been standing there since the conversation began.

"It was a long time ago," Rosi said. "Some say it had to do with Ivy's brother. Maybe a little. Then, too, I don't think Loretta had much respect for Ivy, and Ivy knew it."

"High school's hard on girls," Yolanda said. "There's always a cat fight or two. But they couldn't have moved just because of that. If people moved after every teenage drama, there'd be a For Sale sign on every other house."

"You're jaded," Rosi accused, "and way too practical. Ivy's family made all the calls in this town. And we learned to deal with it. Plus, Ivy's reputation had to be protected at all costs."

Adam was amazed. "You're kidding? Did she do something to ruin her reputation?"

"No, not that I know of. But even associating

with the wrong crowd could cause talk. Ivy was told—no, ordered—who to talk to, where and when. Your great-grandmother was a bit ahead of her time. She used to tell Ivy to grow a backbone." Rosi chuckled. Then she added, "For a while, I thought Ivy and Otis Wilson might get together."

"Otis from across the street?" Yolanda couldn't keep the shock from her voice.

Rosi merely smiled. "His family had position, but not enough to satisfy Ivy's father. Your family—" she nodded at Adam "—lived in the house that's now the Fremont Bed-and-Breakfast. They were Munros. Of course, that house has been remodeled and added onto so much that it's hardly recognizable as one of the grand ole ladies that made up the houses on this street."

Adam needed to ask his grandmother more questions. She'd talked about being a Munro, but until now, how special that was hadn't occurred to Adam. Today she lived in a condo with a view of a golf course and a man-made lake. "But if their relationship wasn't the reason the Ventimiglias moved," he asked Rosi, "what was?"

"Some secrets are better left alone."

"Gramma, you sound like someone on a Halloween show."

"Ask your great-grandmother," Rosi urged Adam. "See if she's willing to tell you anything."

"Don't speak to her without me," Yolanda demanded, "I'm starting to really get into this small-town history."

"Sometimes," Rosi said, "what's dead and buried should stay dead and buried. Loretta knows that well."

"Where did Ivy live?" Adam asked.

"Here. This was her house."

CHAPTER FOUR

UNFORTUNATELY, GRAMMA ROSI had nothing else to say about Ivy. She did, however, have plenty to say about her own family. Yolanda noticed Adam listened intently, but then he'd not heard the story a million times.

Rosi's father had worked for the railroad. He was gone more than he was home. He'd been a smart man, though, listening to the conversations of those who'd had more money than sense.

"My father got a job with the railroad after the black workers went on strike. It was dangerous because it meant he was going against the men who the jobs really belonged to, men who just wanted a living wage."

"Your father was able to make a living wage, I take it." Adam looked around the Victorian.

"My whole family worked hard, some in the field and some in other ways. My father, however, was one to take every opportunity. Because of his personality, as a porter and club car driver, he made pretty good tips. But do you want to know his best skill? It wasn't making people smile. Nope."

Gramma Rosi leaned forward, as if sharing something that shouldn't be overheard. "My father was a great listener. It's a skill most people don't have. He had a family to support during a time when the economy had people running scared. I mean banks had failed, savings were wiped out and the wealthy were no longer counting their money but saying their prayers."

"Gramma Rosi can't remember what she had for supper last night," Yolanda teased, "but get her started on Pearl Harbor, or when television went to color, or the first time she drove an automatic, and she hasn't forgotten one detail."

"Not everyone is as familiar with their family history as you are," Rosi scolded. "I made sure you knew about your great-grandparents." She fixed an eye on Adam. "Do you know the history of the Snapps?"

He shook his head. Loretta had married a Snapp. He was well aware how blessed he was to have an active great-grandmother still living. His mother's family lived in Nebraska and never visited.

"Well, if you want to hear more about Ivy, first ask Loretta. See what she has to say about those long-ago days. She can share more than I can." With that, Rosi turned and headed for the kitchen, muttering something about kids not caring enough about the past until the people who could tell them were gone. She pushed the kitchen door open with both hands. It let out a squeak of protest and creaked as it swung back and forth from her force.

"She's muttering more and more lately. I think she misses my mom," Yolanda said.

"We didn't mention your mom."

"No, but we're asking the kind of questions that she wished my mother would have asked. We're listening like she wished my mother would have listened."

"Your mother wouldn't have listened?"

"No."

"Why not?"

"My mother only had one question she wanted answered," Yolanda said simply, surprised by how easy Adam was to talk to and how willing she was to share.

"And that was?"

"Who her father was."

"And Rosi wouldn't tell her?"

"Not to my knowledge."

Adam stared at the kitchen door, still swaying and creaking gently as if guiding Rosi's entrance into its realm.

"A secret from the past, eh?"

"A big one," Yolanda agreed.

"Was Rosi ever married? We kids all thought she had been. I mean she lived in this huge house and had three children."

"Yes. But her husband was dead by the time I came along. My uncle Juan was named after him. Apparently, he was full of laughter but not much of a provider. My mom never talked about him. Funny, because she's the oldest. You'd think she'd have remembered the most. She seldom talked about growing up here except to say that she hated it. Said there were noises that made no sense and that she felt that just by taking a wrong turn, she could get lost and never be found."

"She had a good imagination."

"No, not really. She just knew how to justify her actions. She didn't like coming here. When she'd pick me up after work, she'd come just inside the door, never all the way in."

"Relatives do that at my house, but it's because they're afraid of upsetting Andy."

"If it hadn't been for me, my mother and grandmother probably would have stopped talking to each other."

"Did they have a fight?"

"No, but Gramma Rosi is a free spirit, and my mother was probably the most conservative person I ever knew."

Adam stopped. "But, she had you when she

was pretty old. I can remember my great-grand-mother talking about it. She thought it was the gutsiest thing Trina'd ever done."

"Gutsy? No, more like an accident. She was only married a short time. I doubt either her or my father worried about birth control. They figured they were too old."

"Your mother always seemed to care about you."

"She did. She loved me. I know that. But at an age where she wanted to put her feet up and watch television, instead she was helping me with homework and driving me to Girl Scout meetings where she felt like an outsider."

"She could have made friends if she wanted," Adam pointed out. "That must have isolated you as much as her."

Yolanda gave a halfhearted nod. Her mother's mantra had been *Men Leave. Friends Leave* hadn't been much more of a stretch.

The kitchen door finally stopped swaying after Gramma Rosi left. She'd had Adam install it because she didn't want the customers to be able to see into the kitchen. It was her grand-mother's favorite room, thus, it was Yolanda's favorite room. It represented laughter and hugs and security.

Rosi's other children, Freda and Juan, came to town when they could. Yolanda especially enjoyed the few Christmases when the family crowded into the room. It was noisy and cluttered and felt like a home.

In this kitchen at Christmas was the only time Yolanda saw what a big family could be.

Every other holiday, Gramma came to them. She was like a breath of fresh air in their little house, bringing color and laughter. Yolanda had wanted her to stay forever. Her mother wiped every round stain left by a water glass, adjusted rugs that maybe had slipped from their perfect setting, and had made it clear that when the dishes were done, the visit was over.

Why?

Yolanda had always wondered, but never more than now.

Adam shook his head, patted her on the shoulder and then he headed for her office. Today was door day.

"Remember to fix that creak in the kitchen door," Yolanda called.

He only nodded.

After he left, Yolanda stood in the center of the living room, comforted by the books and knickknacks and cashier stand.

This was her world. She'd created it. Brought her dream to life.

But even though her mother's will had stipulated that Yolanda use the money to make a dream come true, Yolanda didn't think for a moment that her mother would approve of the bookstore.

Trina Sanchez never advised her to take a risk.

Gramma Rosi understood her dream, though.

Yolanda thought about her mother's house, still decorated in browns and beiges. It was so different than the vibrant Victorian.

Where did Yolanda belong? Who was she more like? Gramma Rosi wasn't the least bit worried about the success of Twice Told Tales. "You'll do fine," she'd said more than once. "People need books." Yolanda's mother would have said, "The population here is not that big. Certainly not big enough to warrant a used bookstore."

The two women who had shaped Yolanda were opposites. Except in one respect—their adamant refusal to share paternal information. Trina seldom talked about Yolanda's father, except to say he had tried. He'd never succeeded, but always, he'd tried.

Rosi's husband, Juan Sanchez, hadn't been Trina's father. Trina was much older than Uncle Juan and Aunt Freda. She'd been grown when they were born. Trina had always wanted to know who her father was. Although by the time

Yolanda was born, when Trina was forty-six, she'd pretty much stopped asking.

Now Yolanda was asking the same thing.

Who Trina's father was.

ADAM HEADED FOR BAA, the minivan nosing its way there as if it had never been gone. Pulling into the parking lot, he aimed for a side road and drove behind the orangutan enclosure and headed into the cabin.

During Adam's absence, Luke Rittenhouse, who owned and managed Bridget's Animal Adventure along with his wife, had rented out the cabin, turning it into a moneymaker. It was probably a good thing Adam was moving to his parents' house. The habitat needed all the money it could get. After changing into old clothes, Adam looked around the tiny cabin. It was two rooms, really. The kitchen and living room were combined, and every inch of wall space was covered with Adam's work. The living room featured cats. The kitchen belonged to birds, the bathroom to amphibians.

It wasn't Adam's best work. He'd practiced in the cabin, so that when he actually created the mural that BAA's visitors would see, it would be improved.

When he'd lived here the first time, he'd wished for more wall space. Now he could only shake his head and wonder what had happened to the guy who'd been so in love with painting.

Adam was very much afraid that he no longer knew how to love.

It only took him an hour to gather his clothes and personal belongings. He'd find out when Luke needed it to be empty, and he'd come back for his art supplies then. In the meantime, he'd see if he could jump-start his muse.

There was no better place to paint animals than at BAA. Aquila the black panther always greeted him as a friend, albeit from his side of the fence. In a pinch, Adam had helped with the anaconda show. He usually ended up helping hold the middle section of the three-hundred pound Rexette. Unlike Aquila, Rexette didn't have a special greeting for Adam. No doubt the snake sensed Adam was secretly afraid of her. The one time they'd put him at Rexette's tail, he'd acted as if they were trying to make him hold a flaming arrow. Finally, Meredith, one of the head keepers, had moved him to the middle.

There he'd stayed.

Maybe it was time to paint Rexette. He felt angst whether he was holding her or not.

After he loaded the van he headed to Yolanda's to pick up the last of the fliers he'd left on the table by the front door.

When he got there she was in the kitchen,

staring at the refrigerator and shaking her head. "When Gramma Rosi lived here, the fridge was always full. I'm lousy at living alone. I go to the grocery store, walk around and convince myself that I don't need anything. Then when I'm hungry, there's nothing to eat," she complained.

"It's the mind-set of the single person. First, you don't want to buy anything because you know it will go bad before you can eat it, especially potatoes. Next, you convince yourself it's just as easy and cost effective to go out. Finally, you find yourself standing in front of the fridge wishing anything like lunch meat, cheese, lettuce, tomatoes, mayonnaise and ketchup would appear so you could make yourself a decent club sandwich."

"Ketchup?"

"Can't live without it."

She raised an eyebrow, clearly not a ketchup enthusiast.

"Why don't you come over to my house? Mom makes meatloaf every Tuesday. There's always plenty."

"No, I don't—"

"My great-grandma Loretta will be there. We can ask her questions about the Ventmiglias. If you don't come, I'll ask anyway. You said you wanted to hear."

She frowned, but he knew he had her.

Strangely enough, he wanted her to be there, part of his family.

For a moment he wondered how Andy would take it. The Snapps rarely invited guests for dinner. She took a moment to run upstairs. When she came down, she'd changed out of her jeans and T-shirt into a simple yellow dress with white sandals. She'd also added a bright yellow hairband.

Too bad he didn't paint people. A picture of Yolanda at this moment could outsell the Mona Lisa.

His parents' house was just a block down and around the corner. His dad's car was still gone, but his mother was home, and through the window he could see GG in the kitchen helping out.

The house represented home. It did. But as Adam walked through the door, carrying his backpack and one suitcase, he still felt like a visitor. Nobody else seemed to notice his hesitation. His twin brother, Andy, didn't notice. He was too interested in Yolanda.

"We went to school together, right?" He followed behind her, a little too close for most people. Luckily, Yolanda just smiled. She didn't try to shake his hand or move toward him, and didn't seem to mind his questions. She hadn't forgotten how to deal with Andy. Adam was impressed.

"Every single year, clear up to graduation." Yolanda was carrying Adam's duffel bag that was spilling over with his personal items: sketch pads, pencils, deodorant. Necessities.

"I remember, you always stood in front of Adam."

"Did I?" Yolanda looked at Adam.

"He's remembering our alphabetical order. You're a Sanchez, and we're Snapps."

"I never noticed."

"Not true," Andy said, neither raising nor lowering his voice. "In kindergarten, he cried because you were taller than he was. You tried to bend your knees to make him feel better. Then in fifth grade, you used to get mad at Adam when he pulled your hair. You had the teacher move you. In seventh grade you were jealous because he was going out with Claire Bender. You had an angry face while we stood in line for pictures. Then—"

"Your memory is good," Adam said easily. "I think Yolanda's starting to remember."

Andy looked pleased, convinced he'd done something important. Unaware that in school it was this kind of chatter, uttered in a serious tone, that had often made people step away from him.

"I wasn't mad because you were going out with Claire," Yolanda protested.

"I don't remember liking Claire that much," Adam said. Big mistake.

"Oh, yes, you did," Andy continued matter-of-factly. "You kept that note she wrote you and you carried it in your pocket. It said, 'Dear Adam, you are the sweetest boy—'"

"I have no memory of the event," Adam said quickly. He'd learned the phrase from his great-grandmother. Sometimes having a brother with an enriched memory was worse than having one with special needs. No matter, Adam had lived and loved Andy long enough to suppress both anger and annoyance.

Yolanda smiled, and Adam realized he'd been rather stupid to think Claire Bender worth his attention. Of course, in seventh grade, Claire had had a few things going for her that the other girls in class didn't. His mother had muttered something about extreme hormones. That much, Adam recalled.

While Adam claimed memory loss, it seemed Yolanda had no such affliction. "I wondered why I never liked my seventh grade class photo. Now I know."

"It was no big deal. In seventh grade going out meant my 'girlfriend' would come to the skateboard park and watch me jump."

Yolanda had never been to the skateboard park. In seventh grade she'd been studying because her mother said she'd need scholarships. When she wasn't studying, she'd been working for Ruth Moore, doing odd jobs around the mini-manse and earning money.

"We'll play UNO tonight," Andy said, not offering to help carry any of Adam's suitcases or supplies, but quite willing to talk. "And eat meatloaf."

That was the thing about Asperger's. It affected everyone a bit differently. Andy didn't like crowds, except the small ones he helped teach at Snapp's Studio. He was a creature of habit, ritualistic almost. But he was fairly social if in his own comfort zone. One of his many doctors said that having a twin brother had made a world of difference in Andy's development.

Adam had played a million games of UNO growing up. It was Andy's favorite pastime. Often, instead of being outside skateboarding, which was Adam's favorite activity, he'd play hand after hand of cards. There was no chance that Andy could skateboard. The act of putting one foot on the board always resulted in a tumble. Even if Adam was holding the skateboard still.

Yolanda didn't seem to realize that she'd been included in the invitation. Still, it was nice to see how easily she got along with Andy. When he'd talked about Andy to Stacey, she'd wrinkled her nose and wanted to know what was "wrong" with him.

Adam had long ago dismissed anything being "wrong" with his brother. Everyone had some sort of idiosyncrasy. Luke Rittenhouse, Adam's best friend and former boss, was deathly afraid of spiders and would leave the room if he saw one. Adam's mother couldn't go to a restaurant or eat at a friend's house without rearranging the silverware, napkin and plate so they were perfectly aligned. Adam's dad teased her mercilessly about it, but he paced whenever anything bothered him. It was why his mother didn't have carpeting in the house.

Still holding on to his duffel, Yolanda followed Adam into the guest room. "This is your room?"

"Up until five years ago it really looked like my room. Now it's the all-purpose room."

"Wow, they didn't wait long."

"Mom always wanted a guest room. She uses it for all her sewing stuff, too. Before Dad quit working for the accounting firm in Phoenix, she'd planned on designing an addition for the house. After he quit we couldn't afford it."

"I always thought you had money."

Adam looked at her, surprised. "Well, we did,

do." But they needed more now. "We did all right."

"We never needed much." Andy joined the conversation, standing in the doorway watching them but not offering to help. Adam set down his suitcase and took the duffel from Yolanda.

"You always had new clothes when school started," she said. "The coolest shoes, and I never saw you without a skateboard or the latest video game."

"You noticed my shoes?"

She blushed and he let her off the hook. "Those were necessities."

"Not if they have designer labels, or if you have a cell phone that tells you the definition for attrition."

He glanced at her, surprised. This was about as honest as she got, and it explained a few things. Like why she'd always looked at him in disdain.

"Yolanda, we were never rich. See this house?"

"I'm seeing the house," Andy commented. "We definitely are rich. We have everything we need."

Andy viewed the world as perfect as long as it was the same. Adam viewed the world in colors and edges and symmetry. The house had never been one he wanted to paint. It was built in the nineteen fifties. The bedrooms, three of them, were just big enough for beds. Everything else was flush against the wall, and growing up, Adam, taller and bulkier than the rest of the family, had often walked sideways just to get around the bed and to his closet.

"Dinner's ready," came a call. His father this time, back from a doctor's appointment.

Andy took charge of Yolanda, leading her into the kitchen and giving her advice as to the type of ketchup she could expect to see on the table and where everyone should sit. It only took Adam a moment to toss his suitcase on the bed before joining them.

His mother had brought in a lawn chair from outside. It was the only seat left unless he took his mother's. He sat across from Yolanda and next to his father. He noted that Yolanda looked at his pale and gaunt father, blinked and then acted as if nothing was different.

Everything was different.

"How's the bookstore coming?" GG asked.

"I'm opening on Friday, Mrs. Snapp. That is, if Adam finishes the doors by Thursday."

"Two days isn't much time," he responded.

"They're just doors."

"They're antiques and deserve more than a slap of paint."

GG smiled and gave him a quick hug. Looking across at Yolanda, she said, "You can call me Loretta. A lecture about doors is what you get when you hire my great-grandson, an artist, instead of a carpenter."

For a moment Adam thought Yolanda would give her famous swallowed-a-pickle look. Instead, she nodded and said, "If we have customers, they can walk around him."

"I can take the doors off their hinges and work in the backyard."

"We should go over your schedule soon, Adam," his mother said. "We'll be leaving for Boston as soon as your father can get an appointment."

"Good," Loretta said.

"Why are you going to Phoenix?" Yolanda asked.

"I'm a candidate for a certain kind of operation," Dad said. "It could add years to my life, but—"

"But we have to act quickly. Now that we know the house and studio will be taken care of, we don't want to wait," his mother said.

"They're not really going." Andy didn't look or sound happy. "Just thinking about it."

"I'll lend you my luggage," GG said.

Adam watched as Yolanda's head ping-ponged between every speaker. She shared the same concerned expression as his mother. There was a difference, though. Yolanda appeared to also be mesmerized by the chatter.

It took a moment for the conversation to die down. His mother put a bowl of mashed potatoes on the table, and his dad said the prayer.

Then Loretta put her fork down and said, "So, Yolanda, this is the first time you've eaten dinner here. Is there something we should know?"

"Only that I didn't buy enough groceries and Adam found me staring into the fridge trying to decide whether to eat a green apple or three slices of American cheese."

"Both sound good," Andy offered.

"I'm surprised Rosi hasn't stocked your fridge. She used to be one of the best cooks around. Everyone wanted to hire her."

Adam couldn't have asked for a better opening. "GG, I think Yolanda's using what's not in her fridge as an excuse to get over here and talk to you."

"Really?"

"We want to hear more about what we discussed on the phone," Yolanda began.

Both of Adam's parents looked up, talk of the operation forgotten. Only Andy continued to eat, undistracted by the conversation.

"My grandma says you and Ivy didn't get along," Yolanda began. "On the phone you said Ivy's family wasn't the kind that encouraged company. I just wanted to ask why you didn't get along."

GG, almost as a second thought, took a bite of meatloaf. She quickly ate a second bite and then a third. "All this because an elderly woman came into your bookstore and spooked you?"

"She did spook me. But after I talked to you I found a book which spooked me even more."

"It's awesome," Adam interjected. "It has all kinds of drawings in it of what Scorpion Ridge used to look like, the people, the places."

"Is it one of those town history books you see at tourist stores?" Adam's dad asked.

"No," Yolanda said. "This book is old. It's dark blue, dusty and has faded embossed gold lettering for the title. I'm sure it wasn't in the bookstore yesterday before the elderly woman showed up. I'd remember it."

"What's the title?" Loretta asked.

"*Stories of Scorpion Ridge, Arizona.*"

"That's a pretty boring title."

Yolanda agreed. "It's handwritten and—"

"So there might not be many copies?"

"Probably none. Plus, the woman said she was looking for books about the history of Scorpion Ridge. That's why I think it was hers. She left it behind."

"So you want to give it back to her?" Loretta asked.

Yolanda nodded. "Yes, but even more I want to know why she said what she did."

Loretta turned to Adam. "There's more to this story than you told me?"

"I only learned of the book this morning when Yolanda showed it to me."

"What did she say, this older woman?" Loretta asked, taking a second helping of meatloaf. Andy was on his second helping, too. Usually Adam's mother interfered before that could happen. Andy tended to keep eating even after he was full.

"She said that the Victorian wasn't really mine."

"Oh, dear," Loretta said. She sat back in the chair, looking a little pale.

"Mom," Adam's dad said. "Are you all right?"

"I will be. It's just that…"

No one said anything, not even Andy, who tended to say the wrong thing at the wrong time.

Loretta pushed away from the table and used the edge to stand up. She'd not looked old, Adam thought, while helping Mom in the kitchen.

She looked old now.

"Was the woman short?" Loretta asked Yolanda.

Yolanda nodded.

"Thin lipped?"

Another nod.

"What color were her eyes?"

"As blue as I've seen."

Loretta shook her head. "Then it seems I gave you misinformation yesterday."

Adam and Yolanda glanced at each other.

"Ivy Ventimiglia might still be alive."

CHAPTER FIVE

DINNER ABRUPTLY ENDED.

Loretta pushed her plate away and said, "I'm not feeling well. I should go home."

The thought of Ivy Ventimiglia being alive had that much impact? Adam didn't like the tremble in his great-grandmother's voice. Her hands always shook, but she managed to get by. Now her hands were shaking so badly that Adam's dad said, "I'll drive you."

Adam's eyes had met Yolanda's across the table. Clearly, they shouldn't ask any more questions about Ivy, at least not now.

His dad didn't hesitate. Meatloaf only half consumed, he was up from the table and holding Loretta by the elbow. "You can stay here tonight."

"No, no, I need to get home."

After the bustle of gathering her purse and a plate of food for her to warm up later, the door soon shut behind them. Only Andy seemed unaffected. A few minutes later Yolanda and his mother started gathering up the dishes. His father's plate was covered and placed in the oven on low.

"UNO?" Andy said hopefully.

Since it was best to keep Andy's routine, Adam nodded and got the cards. But all he could concentrate on was Yolanda and his mother's voices coming from the kitchen, sometimes laughing, and so muted that he couldn't hear what they were saying.

In the end, Yolanda only played through one game of UNO, which she won. Then Adam's father returned and Adam drove Yolanda home.

"Last night before I went to bed, I did an internet search on Ivy," Yolanda said. "I didn't get a single hit."

"I did a search, too," Adam admitted. "I found lots of Ventimiglias, but none that seemed to have any connection to Scorpion Ridge, Arizona. I even searched my great-grandmother's name. She's everywhere, but only because she was a Realtor."

"You'd think if Ivy was back in town and was the lady who showed up at my shop, somebody in town would be aware of it. She's got to be staying somewhere."

"Let's list everyone in town who's around my great-grandmother's age," Adam suggested. "Then we can call and ask them if Ivy's staying with them or if they know where she is."

"Good idea. And I'll hit my gramma up again. She said to come back to her after we talked to Loretta. Rosi definitely knows something she didn't share. I'll also start looking through our family photo albums, the old ones."

"Me, too." Adam thought for a moment. "And we'll need to visit the museum."

"We might find more about Chester there, too." Yolanda clearly liked the idea.

They were almost to the Victorian. To Adam's surprise, he really didn't want to end the conversation.

If he were honest, he'd admit it wasn't the conversation but the woman who captivated him. Yolanda was proving that she did have passion, did have an imagination…and she looked way too appealing in her little dress and simple flats.

Parking in her driveway, he hurried out and around the car, opening the passenger-side door before she had a chance to do it for herself. Then he followed her to the door. She paused, and he could tell she wouldn't be inviting him in.

Too bad.

"Have you read the entire book?" Adam asked, attempting to keep the conversation going.

"No, just skimmed it. The print's so small and close together that I'm having trouble getting through it. I think I'll head to the eye doctor once things settle down. I'll try to read more tonight."

"Let me take it. Maybe I'll recognize some of the names."

To his surprise, Yolanda agreed. She hurriedly unlocked the door, told him to stay put and soon came out with the book.

She held it out to him, and their hands touched. He leaned forward, thinking of kissing those lips that he'd tried to re-create so many times—

She closed the door in his face quite efficiently.

But before the door shut, he saw something in her eyes…muted desire.

Hmmm.

By the time Adam made it home, both his parents were playing UNO with Andy. They always played to five hundred points, and Andy kept score. In his head. And he was always right.

"GG okay?" he asked.

His father placed a card and shrugged. "I walked her in, stayed a few minutes. She's certainly agitated. Maybe this Ivy character isn't worth the trouble."

"I'd agree, Dad, but if Ivy really was Yolanda's visitor, it means Ivy's in Scorpion Ridge, and GG could run into her."

"We'll just wait and see what happens in the next two weeks." Giving Adam a stern look, his dad added, "Don't do anything to upset her."

Might be easier said than done, Adam thought as he headed for the guest room. Shoving his suitcase to the floor, he kicked off his shoes and lay down, finally opening the book and starting to read.

He closed the book at 2:00 a.m., only half-finished. He didn't need glasses, but the print was small and fading, plus the content was dry, more a listing of facts than a journal entry. Finally, he took out a notebook and started making notes about the pages that he either didn't completely understand or that he couldn't quite read.

Later on he'd find a magnifying glass and go back and try again.

Once Yolanda had her grand opening, he'd find a free afternoon and head to Gesippi. He knew a librarian there, Agatha Fitzsimmons, who'd be able to decipher what he couldn't. Not only that, but Agatha might have information about where the book had come from and if there were any others like it.

As he turned out the light and settled into bed, he couldn't stop thinking about *Stories of Scorpion Ridge, Arizona*. It was full of information about heritage and history and even a few town misdeeds. The Snapps were mentioned in the book. He'd known they were an old family. Now he realized just how old. One of his ancestors, Jedidiah Snapp, had shot a man in the leg just for stealing a cow.

Jedidiah hadn't been reprimanded for it, either.

Jedidiah had been protecting his herd, according to the unknown author. Said author also recorded exactly what the cow had looked like, its weight and how well she'd produced.

The book also contained a picture of Jedidiah, and what really caught Adam's attention was how much he resembled his distant ancestor. Here was the hair that never combed down. The bushy eyebrows, too. The only thing Adam couldn't tell from the pages was Jedidiah's height. Adam was six foot. Both his dad and Andy were five-ten.

According to the book, Jedidiah had worked at the mine. Not in it, but as one of the "muckety-mucks." The book's descriptive words, not Adam's.

The Snapps had also owned a good six hundred acres of Scorpion Ridge land. They'd been wealthy, at least until the late nineteen thirties. Too bad some of that wealth wasn't available now. Adam's dad could use it.

But the book didn't say how the Snapps had lost their money.

EARLY WEDNESDAY MORNING, Yolanda's cell phone went off, a tiny chirp chirp that sounded more like birds than a phone. It stopped before she'd edged out of sleep enough to answer. Blinking in the morning light, she tugged the phone toward her and looked at the display. The area code indicated long distance, and the number wasn't familiar.

Assuming it was a telemarketer, Yolanda tried to go back to sleep. She'd been dreaming. Adam had been somewhere in the house, pounding with his hammer. She'd wanted to tell him something. Something about trying to kiss her... But the phone had interrupted her and ended the dream.

And now she couldn't go back to sleep. Rolling out from under the covers, she quickly dressed and headed for the bathroom to wash her face and comb her hair before heading for the kitchen to make some pancakes.

She turned on the radio and told herself to wake up. Get some energy. Smile, even.

Sometimes it felt odd being alone in Gramma's house. She'd always felt alone in the house she grew up in, but not here. It was why after her mother's death, she'd moved in with Gramma Rosi and rented out her childhood home, fully furnished.

Right now, with the bookstore not generating

money and instead gobbling it up, the rent was her only real income. And already the house she'd grown up in looked more lived in than it ever had during her tenure. There were toys in the front yard and fingerprints on the front door.

Had she brought this loneliness with her? She didn't like the idea. Maybe Friday, when the bookstore opened for business, there'd be so many people in and out that Grandma's house would feel right again.

She sat at the old table with a cup of coffee and studied the mysterious number on her phone. She had maybe a dozen friends listed in her directory—she just wasn't the chatty type—so an unidentified caller wasn't that exceptional. So why was it bothering her so much?

After finishing her coffee, she pushed the call-back button. The phone rang and rang. No answering message, no voice mail, nothing.

Odd. The thing with cell phones was that she didn't receive many wrong numbers, not in the last five years anyway, and she'd had her number that long.

After doing the dishes, cleaning her plate and the yellow coffee cup, she walked through the first floor's rooms. Adam could easily finish the doors today. Then she'd be more than ready for her grand opening the day after tomorrow.

Or, the *house* would be ready. Yolanda still

had to buy a few balloons and head to the bakery to order sweets to have on hand. She'd already designed a few fliers and coupons on her computer.

Her dream really was coming true.

Since no one was looking, she danced across the kitchen, holding her empty plate and thinking that life was indeed good—no, *great*. She'd taken a risk and it was paying off.

Except for a strange feeling that she'd prefer to have someone here to celebrate with her— Adam, maybe—and a lingering desire to find Ivy Ventimiglia instead of getting ready for Friday.

Thump.

Yolanda was almost to the sink when she heard the sound. It seemed to come from the kitchen's back door, low to the ground. The newspaper arrived at the front. The country song playing on the radio had twangs not thumps, and Adam wasn't due for another three hours.

Setting the dish down, she headed for the door and pulled away the curtain blocking the window. She saw nothing but the beginning of a sunny August day and the sway of trees and grass. A path led down her backyard, ending at a three-seat rustic cedar swing that her grandmother favored.

Thump.

This time the sound wasn't as loud, but it was still low to the ground and right where Yolanda's feet would be if she exited the door.

Why was she hesitating? Crime was practically nonexistent in Scorpion Ridge. A strange lady smoking in her book stacks was annoying more than criminal. Her words, "This really isn't yours," hinted at loss more than threats.

Yolanda yanked open the door.

The kitten couldn't have been more than four weeks old. It was gray and white, and as soon as it saw Yolanda, it collapsed on its back with its feet in the air as if saying, "I've fallen and I can't get up!"

"Hey," Yolanda said, bending down and scooping the thing and cradling it in one hand. Looking around, she hollered, "Anyone out there? Hello!" No way had the tiny kitten made the thumping noise. Someone, or something, had brought it here and made the noise.

Bringing the cat inside, she wrapped it in a towel and checked it over. No bugs. That was important. And while she could see the kitten's ribs, they weren't sticking out too seriously. "Do you have a mama nearby?"

Instead of mewing an answer, the cat, happily wrapped tightly in Yolanda's blue and white towel, fell asleep. Yolanda dabbed some warm water on a washrag and cleaned its eyes.

Not the perfect scenario, but finding a kitten was much better than finding a stranger with a cigarette and a dire warning.

She didn't want to leave the kitten on the counter—he could roll off—so she carried him into her office and tucked him in the box that held reams of computer paper. Then she headed back to her bedroom, slipped on her shoes and went outside to the garage to search for the mama cat.

The garage hadn't been used in years. Gramma had stopped driving when she'd started saying, "I can see two blocks away, but tell me, is that a car in front of me or a large bear running?"

Years ago Yolanda's uncle Juan had turned what had once been a carriage house into a two-car garage. Yolanda had followed him around while he was doing it, handing him tools, helping to tear down walls and even painting.

The carriage house had been in its original state when they started, with stalls on one side for horses, and space on the other side for a carriage.

Right now the garage held the remnants of the past. There were old lamps in various shades of Harvest Gold and warm green. There were macramé wall hangings and furniture. It had all been here so long, Yolanda wasn't sure what was hidden in the boxes or tucked in all the corners. Maybe she'd find a book or two hidden away when she had time to search.

"Kitty!" She walked into the crowded room, thinking the garage was too hot for a cat to have kittens. "Come out, Mama Kitty."

She hoped to find a mama but not more kittens. She wouldn't be able to leave them in here. She'd been here all of five minutes and already sweat dampened her forehead. In the end she didn't find anything but two lizards, more afraid of her than she was of them, and spiders.

Back in the house, she checked on the kitten—still sleeping—and then headed for her phone.

Katie Rittenhouse, director and owner of Bridget's Animal Adventure, answered on the first ring.

"I've found a kitten," Yolanda announced then changed her words. "Really, it found me."

"How old?" Katie never minced words when it came to animals that might be hurt.

"Four or five weeks, max."

"How does it look?"

Katie didn't need to be more specific. Yolanda, for all that she'd never owned a pet, had worked for Ruth Moore, the original owner of BAA, as a housekeeper. Ruth had had a pet lion named Terrance. Yolanda had also helped out at BAA, usually in the gift shop or running the carousel. She'd never owned a pet, but she'd fed a baby bear, held a giant anaconda and Ollie the orangutan loved her and blew kisses at her.

Then again, he loved all women and only tolerated men, except for Jasper, his keeper.

"Bring it in. We'll have a look," said Katie.

Next thing Yolanda knew she was in her car, kitten still bundled and sleeping peacefully next to her and on her way to BAA. The trip had not been on her to-do list, but BAA's veterinarian would be able to examine the kitten and advise on how the small ball of fur should be taken care of. Luke, Katie's husband, loved cats. Surely he'd take it, and she'd be done.

"You're not what I needed this morning," Yolanda told the kitten. "I open in just two days."

Twenty minutes later she pulled into BAA's parking area. And paused. She'd been here a million times. Her best friend, Janie Salazar, had worked here. Yolanda's mentor, Ruth, worked here still. Adam had worked here, too.

The images on the front entrance, with their 3D effects, were a testimony to his talent. His art made the front entrance seem more like the gates of a circus than a sedate animal habitat.

Only the ticket booths looked ordinary. To the left of the booths he'd painted pirates, wizards, spacemen…all with mirrors where their heads should be so children could look in the mirror and start the adventure before going outside.

The images were a testament to Adam's imagination. The pirates had parrots on their shoulders with real feathers. The cowboys had pop guns that really popped. Each character, be it wizard or spaceman, had some kid-friendly prop.

To the right of the ticket booths was the art representing the animals. Adam's gift was to make things seem 3D. A giant lion seemed to have paws that reached out. One of the elephant's trunks actually squirted water when you pushed a button.

There'd been a whole year as he'd been working where Yolanda had looked forward to working at BAA just so she could see what Adam had created.

Yolanda had known back then that Adam had the talent to do bigger things, make his splash on the world. She'd also known that an artist's life was filled with uncertainty.

Her mother definitely had an opinion about such a life and hadn't liked Adam.

Maybe she suspected that Yolanda did.

Trina Sanchez hadn't seen the need for Adam's work. "Costs money and it's unnecessary," had been her assessment.

Yolanda had pretended to agree with her mother. Somewhere along the line, she'd forgotten that she was pretending and started to believe her mother's assessment.

But now she was changing her mind, and she wished she'd told him how awesome he was all those years ago. Maybe she should let Adam have a little more say when it came to her Victorian. Though, in reality, she'd been the one pushing for the vibrant colors. He'd been the reserved one.

Something had changed Adam. But did she like this new Adam better? He was definitely more conservative now, working for her and his dad. Yolanda couldn't quite separate the word conservative from the word safe, and that just wasn't Adam.

But if Adam stopped being conservative, he'd start taking risks again, and he just might leave Scorpion Ridge again. And it would be a lot harder to let him go this time.

Shaking the gloomy thoughts from her mind, Yolanda stepped from her car and headed for the front entrance. BAA wasn't open for business yet, but the employees had been up and about for hours. The animals had already been fed, the habitats had been cleaned and maintenance would be finished before the first guest walked through the gates.

Yolanda scooted by a peacock and waved at Gloria, who managed the gift shop. She was married to Fred, BAA's veterinarian, and next month they'd celebrate forty-two years of marriage.

Wow.

Yolanda's mom had been married for only a few years before her husband, Yolanda's father, had died. Grandma Rosi had been married a couple of times. Yolanda's mom had refused to talk about the men who'd filled the temporary stepfather role. All Gramma Rosi would say was "Two were nice, one not so much." Then she'd pinch Yolanda on the cheek and say, "You wait for the right one. He's out there. Prince Charming lives."

Trina's advice had been more likely to be "Make sure he has a good job."

"Fred's waiting for you," Gloria called. "He's by his beloved hedgehogs." That meant he was by the petting zoo, where they'd erected a building to house about twenty-five hedgehogs, keeping the males and females separated so that he'd not have a *hundred* and twenty-five.

"I'll call him," Gloria shouted when Yolanda waved. "Let him know to meet you in the infirmary."

Yolanda was well acquainted with the infirmary. A few years ago someone had left a bear, declawed and sick, at their front door. It had stayed in the infirmary for a few weeks. Thanks to the media and YouTube, the bear had made BAA become a household name—at least in Arizona. Yolanda had been one of the many avid watchers as Scoot struggled to survive.

Fred hadn't been able to save him in the end. They still didn't know who'd been responsible.

"I won't give you to someone who'll declaw you," Yolanda whispered to the cat.

She got to the infirmary before the vet and waited at one of the picnic tables just to the right of its entrance. Other than the people working and the animals in the distance, there was nothing to watch. The pen attached to the infirmary was empty; there were no animals recuperating.

Ten minutes later Fred arrived and examined the kitten. Both Katie and Luke Rittenhouse had also stopped by, and at Katie's heels was their daughter, Catherine, almost four years old.

"I want a kitty," she announced as soon as she spotted the cat. Exactly what Yolanda had hoped would happen.

"He's not undernourished," Luke observed, ignoring his daughter's pleas.

"Look at the size of those paws," Katie said. "Fred, count the toes."

"I already did," Fred said. "You've got a polydactyl cat. Seven toes on each of his front feet. Very unusual."

"I'm seven," Catherine proclaimed.

"No, you're not," Katie said, gently. "You'll be seven in three years."

"I act seven."

No one disagreed.

"You think he was abandoned?" Yolanda asked. "I searched the carriage house for the mama cat."

"He might have just wandered off," Fred said. "He's going to be big, probably part Maine Coon."

"You've never had a pet, have you, Yolanda?" Luke asked.

"And I don't want one now. That's why I called you."

Luke shot Katie a look, and she shook her head. "Not a good time for us to take in a cat, especially one that needs to be fed every few hours."

Luke agreed. "Pretty soon we'll be getting up every few hours and feeding Catherine's little brother."

Even Fred, rarely flappable, glanced up. "You're pregnant?"

"Not me," Luke said with a grin.

"I don't want a brother," Catherine added to the conversation. "A sister would be better. We can name her Junie B. Jones."

"That's her favorite book," Luke explained.

"Fred, you want a cat?" Yolanda asked.

"Wife's allergic."

"Can you think of anyone else who works here who might be interested?"

"You might want to hold off a few weeks before finding him a new home. If the mama kitty *is* nearby, you could still find her. Plus, you guessed his age correctly. He's no more than four weeks. He's probably pretty stressed to be separated from his mother. I recommend as little change as possible."

"Oh, phsst. You just think I should keep the kitten."

Luke, not Fred, nodded. "You've never had a pet."

"They are a lot of work and right now—" Yolanda started.

"Right now you're fulfilling a few dreams," Katie interrupted. "Did you ever want a kitten? Ask for one?"

Yolanda looked at the three faces staring at her. Neither Luke nor Katie were Scorpion Ridge natives. They didn't know how she'd been raised.

"My mother didn't have the time or the desire to care for an animal."

"I didn't ask about your mother," Katie said gently. "I asked about *you*. Did you ever dream of having an animal?"

"You're never lonely with a pet," Fred quipped.

Lonely, there was that word again.

"The bookstore opens on Friday," Yolanda protested, but already she was sympathizing with the little guy—no mother, deserted.

"Not one customer would complain if you stopped and fed the kitten while they asked you questions or checked out your books," Luke said.

"And," Katie pointed out, "you'll get more customers. Moms will make a second trip with their children. I'm certainly coming by more often, just to check on... What are you going to name him?"

Yolanda glanced down at the tiny kitten. Fred was holding a bottle, and the kitten suckled eagerly.

"Seven toes, huh? Well, if he were a she, I'd name her Polly, but a little boy..."

Fred handed the kitten over, took a bag from a drawer and started loading it. "Since you're mulling the name, that means you're keeping him. Give me a minute. I can send you home with plenty of stuff. You'll have to use special milk and…" He continued talking, but Yolanda could only stare at the unnamed kitten.

It was the *you'll never be lonely* comment that did it.

"Hey," she said, "since it's going to take Fred a few minutes, have any of you heard of the Ventimiglias?"

Katie gave her a blank look, but both Luke and Fred nodded.

Fred went first. "The Ventimiglias are an old family. I don't know much of their history except that Richard was one of the town's founding fathers and a judge. You should talk to Ruth. Her late husband was the grandson of the first John Moore, who apparently first settled this area along with Richard. They were friends, or partners or something."

"Was John Moore a judge, as well?" Yolanda asked.

"I'm not sure," Fred said. "I do know he was wealthy and a landowner. You'd be surprised at all the land Ruth owns."

"*That's* where I saw the name Ventimiglia," Luke said. "It was when Ruth was transferring ownership of BAA to me. Somewhere back in time, a Ventimiglia owned this piece of property."

Now that was news. It was also something that connected her house to BAA. Both had been owned by Ventimiglias.

CHAPTER SIX

"I TRY TO go to the doctor at least every six months," GG said when Adam showed up Wednesday morning at her condo. "Just as a precaution. And last night I had trouble sleeping. Found myself pacing a lot. My heart raced. I must be getting old."

Something was really wrong. Loretta never referred to herself as old. Adam helped her into his van and gave her a second look. Her silver-gray hair was upswept. Her eyebrows were black, big and exactly like his. Spock would be proud. She was tall, imposing and had a wicked sense of humor. Normally, Adam's dad pulled chauffeur duty. Dad also claimed that GG had a crush on the doctor in Gesippi, which was why she traveled so far and so often.

Today, dear old Dad was in Phoenix, so Adam had volunteered. He'd been wanting to get to Gesippi, anyway. This was the perfect excuse. He'd already called Agatha Fitzsimmons, the librarian, and told her to expect him. He'd do it while GG visited with the doctor.

"I must have paced for two hours," GG said as he held on to her elbow.

"That happen often?" Adam asked.

"No." Then GG launched into an animated account of her morning, only stopping when they got to his van and she realized that it was a bit higher than her own vehicle or his dad's.

"Next time I'll bring a step stool," Adam offered.

"Next time I'll call a cab."

But Adam knew she was joking. Family was everything to GG.

"I remember when your mom drove this van, squiring you kids around. Your stuff fits in here quite nicely." Not a negative word about the flagstone or paints or rags littering the back. But GG had always applauded his artistic talents. She had a dozen of his childhood drawings displayed in her home. All carefully mounted and framed. Every Christmas she purchased an art supply that he truly wanted, from oil colors to artist cloths.

"It serves a purpose," Adam agreed, after he closed her door and settled behind the wheel. "It's almost fifteen years old, you know."

He started the van and backed out of her driveway. Within minutes, Scorpion Ridge quickly faded from sight. When they hit the first curve of the road, his great-grandmother wistfully said, "Used to be a dairy right here. Family's name was Welborn. The father had a Model T Ford truck. All us kids thought that was so cool."

"Looks pretty barren now," Adam remarked. He'd not considered what was out here, past or present.

"The Welborns packed up after both their sons died in the war." She didn't say which war. "I dated the oldest boy for a while. He was handsome. Very handsome," she said wistfully. "One of their grandchildren took up residence at the dairy for a while back in the sixties, but that didn't last. The place was already inhabitable."

Now it was invisible, Adam thought, wondering how he could paint it, *if* he could paint it. He would use the white, gray and black hues that matched a September storm.

"Too much change. Back then, we had a doctor right in Scorpion Ridge. He was related to the Welborns and did house calls. Wish Doc Thomas did that." GG easily changed the subject.

"House calls all the way from Gesippi?" Adam asked. "That would get tedious."

"He could come to Scorpion Ridge two days a week. I told him he could use my house as a home base. I'd make him my famous lasagna."

"What did he say?"

"That lasagna gives him heartburn. But he was kidding. If he'd just diversify his clinic, then I wouldn't have to drive all the way to Gesippi."

Adam was only fifteen minutes into the sixty-minute drive. "And if Doc Thomas were to embrace your idea, you could see him twice a week." He rather liked the idea of his grandmother having a beau.

"I love the way you think." GG tapped her fingers on the windowpane. "But really, it's you we should be talking about. You say you and Yolanda are just friends, working together... So how come you're not bringing a young lady over to meet me? For a while I thought you'd met somebody in Illinois. You talked about a girl you liked. What happened to her?"

Adam wasn't crazy about this change of topic. "We were too different," he said. Although, in truth, they had been very similar, willing to do whatever it took to get ahead in the art world. She'd just taken a bit more than she deserved.

"Different is good," GG said.

He opened his mouth to say, "Not in this instance," but the van's engine starting to cough. Adam took his foot off the gas. Yeah, that should do the trick. Except the cough turned into dry heaves, and the van died without even noticing that the gas pedal wasn't in use.

"You run out of gas?" GG was taking this much too calmly.

"No, I filled up before I came to get you." He tried starting the engine. Nothing. It was August in Arizona and their van had just broken down. Air-conditioning would too quickly become a distant memory.

Glancing at the odometer, Adam frowned at the number—over three hundred thousand—and reminded himself that at least the van was paid off.

"Come on, baby," he cajoled as the vehicle coasted to the side of the road. Since it was on a slightly downhill slant, he was grateful the brakes still worked. He was a good forty miles from the outskirts of Gesippi.

Opening the door, he hopped down onto the hot dirt and headed to the front hood. Raising it, he stared at the car parts that meant nothing to him. He created art. He didn't work with soulless car parts smudged with grime. He brought pictures, and now homes, to life. No ignition needed.

His great-grandmother opened her door and started to step out. Adam hustled over. "Roll down the window and stay put. I'm calling for help."

His father was in Phoenix, gathering items at the big box store that the family used at home and at work. He was too far away for Adam to bother.

His mother was at Snapp's Studio with Andy, and a class was already in session. Andy had been in a mood this morning, and his mother handled him best—which was the main reason Adam had volunteered to drive GG to the doctor.

If he called his mom, she'd need to find another adult to stay with both the class and Andy.

He pushed on his phone's internet and searched for the number to Tucker's Auto. It was the only tow-truck place in town. Luckily, the Tuckers knew his family and would tow without upfront payment. Adam didn't have the money.

He paused a moment before punching in the number. He'd need to take care of the payment, too, make sure Tucker's Auto didn't bill his father.

It took just a moment to make the arrangements.

Returning to the van, he scavenged in the back and found an old but clean T-shirt and poured water on it. Then he passed it to his grandmother. "Put this on your face and lean back. I don't want you to overheat."

"I lived in Scorpion Ridge before air-conditioning was affordable. Don't worry about me."

Right… Adam had no idea when air-conditioning had become the norm, but he suspected it was a bit older than GG. He called his mother to catch her up. She hesitated and then offered to close the studio and come fetch them. "Your brother's in the back room rearranging all the uniforms."

Which meant he was upset. Adam looked at GG, but she took the phone and said, "Don't be silly. Adam's already called the tow truck, and I still have time to get to Gesippi."

His mother, obviously aware of GG's crush on the good doctor, merely said to call if they needed her.

Thirty minutes later, GG was asleep and Adam was looking at his phone. The class at the studio would end in just five minutes, so his mother could easily come rescue them before they melted into puddles, never to be seen again.

That gave him an idea for a painting.

Wow, two ideas in one day. If this kept up, he just might pick up a brush and be able to paint something.

Three cars passed them, none driven by someone he knew. He tried Tucker's twice more but only garnered a "We're trying, but there's a few people ahead of you." Adam spent the next ten minutes playing games on his phone and gathering errant food wrappers, receipts and even three different socks from the floor of the van. He'd not cleaned the car thoroughly in a while, and he wasn't happy with how much he'd let slide lately. He needed to make some decisions. At twenty-five years old, it was time. He knew he couldn't work forever at his father's Tae Kwon Do studio, just as he'd never make it in a cubicle working nine to five.

There had to be a way to combine business and pleasure.

He was enjoying bringing Yolanda's house back to its former grandeur. More than he'd thought possible. Flipping houses was a big art in America right now. Whole television shows were dedicated to the craft.

There were plenty of houses in Scorpion Ridge that needed a little TLC.

But were there people to buy them?

First of all, could he manage to buy one, flip it and make a profit? But could he even think that far ahead when his father was in crisis right now?

He looked at his sleeping great-grandmother. Maybe he should remember this the next time she overexerted herself. He could just take her fifteen minutes from town, make sure it's during the hottest part of the day, pull over to the side and do nothing. Then she'd get all the sleep she needed.

He checked his watch. If his day hadn't gotten hijacked, he'd be with Agatha Fitzsimmons learning more about the Ventimiglias before returning to Yolanda's house. Part of his enjoyment in working on the renovation, he acknowledged, was Yolanda. She surprised him. She'd made it clear all along that she was disappointed in his choices: living in BAA's night watchman's cabin, dropping out of school and then leaving town to go paint murals.

She was all about paperwork and business hours. He was about creating art and going with the flow.

Though recently she was begrudgingly starting to admit that she respected his art. He liked that. And she'd been right about not dropping out of school. He intended to right that wrong.

He was so lost in thought he barely noticed the approaching car, not until it stopped, parked and she got out: Yolanda.

She'd filled out in the years he'd been gone. Instead of being a stick-thin girl with pretty hair, she was now a pretty girl with glorious hair.

"You need help?" she asked once he stepped out of the driver's side, tossing his phone on the passenger-side seat.

He closed the door behind him. "The van coughed twice, coasted to the side and won't start again. I've looked under the hood. Nothing's leaking that I can see. I don't care about the van at the moment, though. Can we move GG to your car where there's air-conditioning?"

"Absolutely."

"I've called Tucker's. They should be here any minute," Adam said as he opened the passenger-side door and gently rubbed his great-grandmother's shoulder.

She didn't open her eyes or move. For a moment Adam felt a stab of panic. He should have called his mother to come. He should have stood in the middle of the road and stopped one of the two cars that had driven by earlier.

Of course GG would say, "I'm going to be all right." Grandma types always said such things.

Yolanda raised an eyebrow and said, "You have water?"

"Two bottles. I gave her mine to drink, and I used hers to dampen an old shirt. She's still got it on top of her head." He gently removed it, and her eyes opened.

"Hey, GG, wake up."

"Tow truck here?" she asked groggily.

"No, Yolanda's here. We're going to move you to her car and the air-conditioning." He helped her down, and both he and Yolanda walked her to the Ford.

Yolanda opened the door and scooped up a towel then moved aside to let GG sit.

The towel moved.

After years of working at an animal habitat, moving towels didn't faze him. But Yolanda had never been one to care for ailing animals at home. A small gray, furry head peeked out of one corner, and Yolanda waited for Adam's reaction.

"A cat?"

"Just a baby."

"What are you doing with it?"

"It showed up on my doorstep. I've just come from BAA. Fred gave it a once-over and told me how to take care of it."

"You've never had a pet."

Yolanda sighed. "That's because my mother was allergic."

"Or so she claimed," GG quipped, reaching for the towel, removing it and then cradling the kitten in her arms.

Yolanda didn't respond. Maybe she'd suspected that her mother's allergies were fabricated, too.

"This is more adventure than I've had in years," Loretta commented.

"You want me to call Mom? She said she'd come."

ADAM HEADED BACK to the van to gather GG's purse. Yolanda followed, walking around his van, peering in the windows, a look on her face he didn't recognize. "I didn't realize how much room you had in this car. How often do you go to Phoenix?"

"Right now I go when Dad needs me to. We go to Costco and stock up on bottled water, toilet paper and such."

"Hmmmm."

"Why?"

"Next time you go on a weekend, I'd like to come with you."

"You want twenty-five cases of bottled water and a hundred rolls of paper towels?" He didn't want to burst her bubble, but getting her bookstore going would take a while. It had taken Snapp's Studio four years to break even, and that was with both his dad and mom pouring their hearts, time and money into it.

Except for her Gramma Rosi, Yolanda was pretty much alone.

"I want to go to garage sales and thrift stores. I can find books, keep my stock up and sell them for a profit. Would you be willing to take me with you?"

"I'm not sure how much time I'll have before I have to be back, and I don't want to rush you." Although oddly the idea of scouring through garage sales to find hidden gems with Yolanda sounded like fun.

She frowned as if realizing she hadn't thought the idea through—not typical for Yolanda at all.

"It would be only a couple of hours. But never mind. It was a bad idea." She turned, blue-black hair swaying as she walked away from him.

"We could try it once," he offered, wanting her back.

She didn't acknowledge him.

YOLANDA SCOLDED HERSELF for even considering taking their relationship beyond work on the Victorian and solving the Ventimiglia mystery.

Maybe she should have offered to pay him for his time, like she did with his renovation work. Or make a trade. Should he ever become homeless, he could sleep in the carriage house. No, that was catty and undeserved.

He, seemingly without a care, followed her to the Ford and folded himself into the small backseat. "Can you turn the air conditioner up higher?" he queried.

She obliged only because Loretta nodded.

About the time he appeared to get comfortable in the too-small area, a tow truck appeared on the horizon.

"Yes!" He unraveled himself much like an accordion and burst out of her tiny car, running toward the tow truck. It skidded to a stop. When the door opened, one leg appeared. A tall blonde, definitely female, and wearing a Tucker's Auto shirt, climbed down and said, "So, you need a tow."

Yolanda got out of the car and went over to stand next to him. "I guess you've not met Melissa, Adam. She's Don's granddaughter."

"And she can tow cars." Adam stated the obvious in an awed tone before moving forward to shake Melissa's hand and introducing himself.

Melissa gave Adam a business card accompanied by a smile that didn't seem suitable from a tow truck driver in the hot Arizona desert.

Loretta, still holding the kitten, exited the car and came to stand next to Yolanda. "Melissa's the one who wanted to be a movie star," she whispered. "She didn't like Hollywood much, I hear."

Together they watched as Melissa took Adam's keys and climbed into the driver's side to do something to the brake. "You want anything else outta here before I hook her up?" she asked him.

"Just my backpack."

While he retrieved it, she climbed into the tow truck and came back with some paperwork for Adam to fill out.

Yolanda should just leave. They didn't need her, and there was no point standing here as if she was watching a show. She stepped forward and put a hand on Adam's shoulder. "I'm taking off. If you want, I'll take Loretta home. You've got everything under control here and you'll be able to stay with the van."

"Nothing's under control," he countered.

No sooner had he said the words than the tow truck lurched a little, then a lot, before suddenly backing up on its own.

"I told them it was shifting out of gear!" Melissa ran for the driver's side.

She swung inside just as it slammed into Adam's van. Melissa stopped the tow truck, but now Adam's van was moving, heading for the street.

Both Adam and Yolanda reacted at the same time. Adam sprinted and grabbed the door handle while Yolanda hurried to push herself against the front fender. Since the van wasn't moving fast, their combined effort worked. The van stopped.

From the tow truck, Melissa muttered a few choice words. Adam let go of the handle and walked to the back of his van to survey the damage. Yolanda followed. It looked as if someone very strong had tossed a bowling ball into the back hatch.

"Don't worry, my dad will take care of the damages." Melissa went about hooking his van to the tow truck. Then paperwork followed.

After that, Melissa drove away, Adam's van getting smaller and smaller.

Adam followed Yolanda to her car. He seemed a bit dazed. "My van," he murmured more than once.

She didn't point out that the van was on its last legs. Adam and that van were a bit like Fred—no, Shaggy—and the Mystery Machine from Scooby Doo: a bit funky.

"When do you think I'll get it back?"

"You'll have to ask Melissa."

"I can't believe her tow truck hit my van."

"If we don't hurry," Loretta reminded them, "I won't make my doctor's appointment."

Doctor's appointment? "Where are you heading?" Yolanda asked.

"Gesippi. Her appointment's at two. We have just enough time."

Taking one last look at the dearly departing van, Adam paused only a second before asking, "Can you drive us?"

"To Gesippi? That's forty-five minutes away, plus a wait and return. That could be hours. My store is opening in less than 48 hours. And you're supposed to be working on the doors."

"We can reschedule my doctor's appointment," Loretta said. "My heart's not racing anymore, and I'm sure the fact that I couldn't sleep had to do with age and not something serious."

Adam smiled, and Yolanda knew she'd be driving them to Gesippi.

Lately, she couldn't get away from Adam.

Not even in her dreams.

But did she want to?

If only he were a nine-to-five kind of guy with a portfolio and a Dave Ramsey way of thinking.

"I can't believe I'm driving you to Gesippi." She walked to the driver's door and looked back at him. "I've a dozen things to do today."

"None more important than family."

As she climbed behind the wheel, she wanted to say "you're not my family" but just then Loretta spoke up, "You've got to give this little guy some kind of book name since he's going to live in a bookstore."

"I've a million things to do." Yolanda waited while Adam returned to the cramped position in the backseat.

"My knees and spine appreciate the offer to take us to Gesippi but suggest next time you buy a vehicle, you get something longer." He grinned at her, back to being as easygoing and carefree as ever.

Never mind that his great-grandmother was heading to the doctor because of a racing heart plus lack of sleep, that his dad was going to have surgery soon and leaving him in charge of his special needs brother and that he had to finish all the doors in her house in less than two days.

But apparently, he had all the time in the world to joke about cars!

Just when she thought Adam Snapp was growing up, becoming the man he could be, he proved her wrong.

"Adam will do a great job on your doors. You should see the doggy door he installed for my next door neighbor." Loretta practically beamed.

Repairing old houses and installing doggy doors was not a full-time job, though. Her mother hadn't been wrong about the need for the head of the house to look toward the future and not just the present.

Unfortunately, in a town the size of Scorpion Ridge, the men in Yolanda's age group were few and far between. The fifty-two guys in her high school graduating class had either married, moved or...were dreamers like Adam.

"Maybe while we're there we can stop—"

"—at this great diner," Adam interrupted. In the rearview mirror, he shook his head. Too late, Yolanda remembered Loretta's reaction to the idea that Ivy Ventimiglia might be alive.

Was it the reason for the racing heart and lack of sleep? Based on Adam's interruption, yes.

"I was just going to suggest that," Yolanda finished.

The car fell silent. Perhaps it was the sound of the engine or the motion, but almost immediately, Loretta's eyes closed, and the sleep she claimed she didn't get last night came.

Yolanda glanced in the rearview mirror, but Adam was busy burrowing in his backpack, his lips a thin line of concentration. He looked the way he usually did when he surveyed an almost finished piece of art. She'd give him a minute before she interrupted him.

Until a month ago, she had never been to Gesippi or met Agatha Fitzsimmons. When she'd seen an article in the paper about the historic courthouse and the library that had been in its basement for decades, Yolanda had paid attention. She wished she'd visited sooner, when the library was open and vibrant, before budget cuts changed the "open ten until six" sign to a dearly departed epitaph.

Agatha had been a wealth of knowledge for Yolanda, and the older woman had promised to come to Scorpion Ridge to visit the bookstore.

Adam finally settled back, an aged blue book in his hand. Her book. No, not her book, but the one the elderly woman—who may or may not be Ivy Ventimiglia—had left.

Ivy's book.

He, without her having to tell him, had kept it in a small plastic bag.

"Loretta's sound asleep," Yolanda informed him. "I take it you're hoping we can stop by and visit with Agatha Fitzsimmons."

"I called her before I left the house this morning. If anyone can tell us about this book, it's Agatha," he said. "Plus, I know she didn't sell off every book when the library closed. What if there's another one about Gesippi?"

Yolanda's footpressed down on the accelerator. "Did you ask Agatha if anyone called her asking about such a book?"

"No." Adam carefully replaced the book in the bag. "That's yet another trail to follow."

"I'm amazed you knew this library existed," Yolanda said. "My mom used to drive me all the way to Phoenix for library books."

"Loretta's Red Hat group has members from all around. Agatha is a member."

"How long has your great-grandmother been a Red Hat?"

"Almost twenty years, almost from the time the organization started. My mother was so excited because they knew what to get GG for every holiday. She's got red hats, red hat pins, red hat stationery and my brother even painted her a picture with red hats."

"I didn't know Andy could paint."

"He tries."

Yolanda changed the topic. "Do you really

think her rough night and her visit to the doctor have to do with us questioning her about Ivy?"

"You saw how quickly she stood up from the table when we realized Ivy might still be alive. She's never before asked to be driven home in the middle of dinner."

"Are you sure there's not a drawing of Ivy in that book?"

"I haven't gotten to the end. That's something else I want Agatha's help with. There are a few pages with words so faded I can't make all of them out. I copied a few key words, and I'm hoping she can fill in the missing information."

Yolanda drove the remaining miles without asking any more questions. Adam's great-grandmother couldn't be asked any more questions. And Gramma Rosi had clammed up as soon as she'd heard about Loretta taking it so seriously.

Scorpion Ridge's mystery had gotten deeper.

CHAPTER SEVEN

LUCKILY, THE MEDICAL clinic was empty, not even a receptionist up front. Adam had never been here and was a bit surprised that his grandmother's doctor practiced out of a house. Just when Adam thought he'd have to shout, "Hey! Is anybody here?" a man way too close to his grandmother's age came out of a back room, a big golden retriever by his side.

"Zeus, we have company," the man said. Then a smile lit his face, one that made him look a bit like Santa Claus. "Loretta, I was beginning to think you weren't going to make it."

This man was a doctor? Adam had seen plenty of doctors. Having an autistic brother meant a childhood filled with medical professionals, not just a pediatrician, but also gastroenterologists, sleep specialists and such. None of them had worn bright green tennis shoes or a T-shirt advertising The Grateful Dead.

"My great-grandson and I were rescued by an angel. That's how I got here. Doc Thomas, this is Adam and his…" GG paused.

"Friend," Adam supplied.

"Boss," Yolanda said.

To his credit, Doc Thomas didn't so much as snicker. "Come on back, Loretta. I'm ready. Zeus, stay."

Adam followed, noting how each of the bedrooms functioned as examination rooms. In front of him, GG gave the doctor a blow-by-blow account of breaking down in the heat and the long rescue. Behind him, he could hear Yolanda explaining to Zeus that the kitten she held didn't really want to be disturbed, especially not by a big, wet nose.

Loretta was ushered into a room at the rear of the house. Adam took a seat next to the door. His great-grandmother had always seemed larger than life to him. When he was really young, she'd scared him. Then one Halloween when his parents couldn't leave his brother, she'd taken him trick-or-treating.

She'd dressed up, and they'd gone to every house in town. She knew everyone, and he'd had more fun than he'd ever remembered having on Halloween before. After that, they did something together at least once a week. Something fun. It was exactly what a boy with a special needs brother wanted.

She allowed him to be the center of attention, for one night a week.

"I know what I weigh," GG told the doctor. "It's the same as the first time you ever weighed me. I'm not getting on your scale."

"Oh, but I got a new scale two days ago and need to see if it works," Doc Thomas said, handing her a glass of water. "You'd be my first."

"Hurrumph."

That easily, the man got her weight, followed by her blood pressure. Adam's cell vibrated, and he checked his text messages. His mom. He quickly texted back that everything was going fine. His mom followed with a list of things he should share with the doctor.

Great, this would definitely get him on his great-grandmother's good side.

Questions were asked, forms were filled in and finally Doc Thomas pulled up a little stool and said, "Loretta, how do you really feel?"

"Dad's been telling her to slow down," Adam tattled. "He thinks the last house sale she handled was too much for her."

"Oh, pooh," GG said. "The last six months I've only sold one house. It was my cousin Linda's. You remember her. She always made you eat sweet potatoes at Thanksgiving. Can't believe she finally decided to sell and move in with her children. Handling the sale gave me something to do."

"And Mom says that organizing events in

your condo community, volunteering at the museum and putting together the church bulletin are also too much for you." Adam read right from his phone.

GG rolled her eyes. She might be suffering a setback, but she was still great-grandma, full of piss and vinegar. "I'm mad at myself for getting all upset at dinner. And it really shouldn't matter after all these years."

At the worst possible time, before Adam could press for more details, Doc Thomas said, "It's not your heart. You have the heart of a sixty-year-old. Your blood pressure is up. That's about it."

"High blood pressure shouldn't keep me awake all night pacing. Why couldn't I sleep? Usually when I'm upset I eat chocolate and watch television until I can't keep my eyes open. That didn't work last night. The chocolate didn't taste right, and television was more annoying than soothing. What I really want to know is why was my heart racing?"

"Ever have panic attacks?" the doctor asked.

"Never."

"Then I think you just had your first one."

"How do I make sure I never have one again?" GG asked.

"Get rid of whatever is upsetting you." Doc Thomas smiled, patted GG on the shoulder and continued. "If, as you said, it shouldn't matter, then don't let it."

She nodded, no surprise, but to Adam's amazement, she looked at him with a deep, probing and somewhat guarded expression. Even the doctor's gaze followed.

"What?" he said. "I haven't done anything."

It seemed as if both GG and the doctor waited for a full minute but really only seconds clicked by. Then the doctor turned back to GG, advising her to slow down, let others do more with her and for her.

It was true. Adam hadn't done anything. He had, however, asked quite a few questions. About Ivy Ventimiglia, who Rosi Acura said had some sort of feud with his great-grandmother. Surely, though, Loretta wasn't having a panic attack over teenage angst from almost seventy years ago.

Part of him wanted to drop the query, tell his grandmother that he'd never bring up Ivy's name again, but if it had indeed been Ivy who'd surprised Yolanda at her bookstore, then it was better to be sure and be prepared. Because if just the mention of Ivy's name inspired a panic attack, how would GG react if Ivy suddenly reappeared?

And she just might!

Suddenly, the quest was a whole lot more personal.

"I want you to lay back and rest," Doc Thomas said. "You were out in the sun a long time, and upset. I'll come check on you in thirty minutes, see if any of your vital signs have changed." He glanced at Adam. "I don't want anything else upsetting her. Why don't you two kids make yourselves scarce for a while?"

"We can do that." Adam started to excuse himself but stopped. "GG, I can stay here with you."

"No, I'm going to be fine. Feel better all ready."

Adam went out to the living room-turned-waiting room. Yolanda sat with the kitten cradled in her arms and the golden retriever at her feet. It was a good look for her, made her seem more of a vulnerable human being instead of the totally-in-control-at-all-times woman who made him want to be better.

"How's Loretta?" she asked.

"Probably okay. The doctor doesn't want her to do anything that worries her."

"So we probably shouldn't ask any more questions."

"Not of my great-grandmother," Adam agreed.

"Or of my grandmother, either."

"Funny how they're closing ranks," Adam

remarked. "They both know something they're not willing to share."

"Maybe it's best to let sleeping dogs lie," Yolanda said.

"I'd agree, but you're the one who had Ivy Ventimiglia show up and make an unsettling comment. In case she returns, we need to find out what happened all those years ago—" he looked down the hall to the room where his grandmother lay "—so we can keep them safe."

This time Yolanda nodded.

Heading for the front door, he opened it and let her walk out first—under his arm. "We've just enough time to visit Agatha."

"Let me see if Loretta wants to mind the cat. She seems to like him."

When she returned—without the kitten— Adam held out a hand, which Yolanda took. Her fingers were small in his, warm, just the right size. She wasn't someone who gave her trust easily. Her mother had seen to that. Suddenly, Adam wanted to earn her trust.

It took all of three minutes to find Agatha's house. "I've always been surprised by how many Victorians Arizona has," Adam said. "Adobe is understandable. Brick, too. But Victorians?"

"My gramma always said that the Victorians in Scorpion Ridge were built to show off the residents' wealth. Now that we know the Ventimiglias lived in my house first, that makes sense."

"My family has always owned this house," Agatha said a few minutes later, ushering them through the door. "My grandfather brought my grandmother, his new bride, to this area before Arizona was a state. He built this house to make her feel at home. She was from a wealthy Eastern family. I've never even met that branch of the family. They wouldn't, at least during my grandparents' time, visit Arizona." She leaned forward. "Too afraid of Indians."

For the next few minutes, while Agatha fussed over the kitten, Adam examined the intricate woodworking in the house, his fingers suddenly itching to work with terra-cotta, decorative trim, patterned shingles.

Maybe murals didn't have to be his only specialty...

Agatha led them into her living room and motioned for them to sit down and got right to the point. "You have some questions for me?"

"Wow," Yolanda said, clearly still in awe of the decor. "Your house is so different than mine."

"They cannot be that different," Agatha said. "They were built at the same time by the same architect."

Adam noted Yolanda's surprise. It had only

taken him a few minutes of studying the design and the architectural details to notice the similarities.

"How do you know that?" Yolanda asked.

"I'm ninety-two," Agatha said. "When I was growing up in this house, it was a much smaller world, and with no television, our parents told stories, shared family histories." She leaned closer. "In other words, we actually talked to each other. None of this Facebook, texting or tweeting."

Adam watched as Yolanda scanned the room. The rug was old but well-kept. Two columns flanking the doorway, white and gold, welcomed people into the room. An oversize fireplace, with a mantel that reached to the ceiling, filled one whole wall. Vintage plates and clocks took up most of the display area. Built-in bookcases lined three of the walls, filled with what looked to be well-loved hardbacks as well as overflowing paperbacks. Agatha had not one but two old pianos. Scattered between the couches and chairs were old carousel horses.

"You have a lot of books," Yolanda said.

"Lifetime's worth."

"My grandmother, Rosi, does, too, but she kept them up in the attic."

"Rosi?" Agatha asked. "You mean Rosi Acura?"

"Yes, she's my grandmother. She's giving me her house. I should have come here before we restored it," Yolanda breathed.

"I didn't realize when we met at the library book sale that you were Rosi's granddaughter. I heard she went into a retirement center. I didn't put two and two together. I thought you were just the new buyer."

"You know Rosi?"

"Of course. Scorpion Ridge is bigger than Gesippi and there was nothing exciting happening here when I was young. So on Saturday nights the Gesippi kids would head to Scorpion Ridge for barn dances and such."

"How did you meet my grandmother?"

"She was a housemaid and then cook assistant for the Ventimiglias."

"So you know Ivy, too?"

Agatha's eyes opened wide. "Now that's a name I haven't heard in a while."

"WE KEEP HEARING THAT," Yolanda said. She was trying to imagine her grandmother as a housemaid and cook in the house she now owned. It was a hard concept to wrap her mind around. Especially since her grandmother had said that she didn't know the Ventimiglias well, not well enough to talk about.

"I wonder why she didn't tell me she was their housemaid?" Yolanda mused.

"Once her family moved into the Ventimiglia place, I suppose they wanted to forget how hard they'd had it before. Think about it, honey, your grandmother's family was poor, had been for generations, and suddenly they were living on the same street as the Moores, the Snapps and such. Your grandmother was smart. She only focused on the future."

"How do you suppose they came to own the house?" Yolanda asked.

"Rosi hasn't said?" Agatha looked curious.

"She doesn't respond well to questions about the past," Yolanda admitted.

"That was a hard time. It was during the war. I always wondered if the Ventimiglias had lost all their money. Plus, the son died shortly before they left. Maybe they lost their desire to stay where there were so many memories."

"That doesn't explain why Gramma Rosi's family had enough money to buy the house."

Agatha shrugged. "I'm not sure."

Adam chose that moment to open his backpack. "Maybe there are a few things you are sure of. Yolanda and I have this book…"

While he searched for it, Yolanda described the elderly visitor to her bookstore.

"That could certainly be Ivy," Agatha agreed.

"She was a small thing, with the brightest blue eyes, and very sharp-boned."

"And you think she could still be alive?"

"Lots of us are still alive. Did you know of the people turning sixty-five this year, one out of every ten will live past ninety-five?"

Yolanda and Adam looked at each other. This is what they got for questioning a librarian.

"If there are no more Ventimiglias, why did she come back?" Adam said.

"She said she was visiting relatives," Yolanda reminded him.

Adam frowned. "I forgot that you told me that. But everyone keeps saying she has no relatives. Then again, no one seems to have heard of Chester."

"I don't remember there being a Chester," Agatha said.

Adam quickly filled her in about the plaque on the courthouse wall.

"'His hard work and money,'" Agatha said wonderingly. "I'm not sure if Richard Ventimiglia worked hard or not. My father always said that Richard had gotten rich off the backs of others."

"I thought he was already rich," Yolanda said.

Agatha left the room for a moment and then returned with a book. Flipping to a page, she relayed what Yolanda and Adam already knew.

"He was a graduate of West Point, went into the military and then got a law degree."

"Scorpion Ridge wasn't big enough for a lawyer," Yolanda said.

"Big enough for a politician, though, and judge." Agatha closed the book. "What does the book say?"

Adam answered, "Let me find it." He started taking out papers and pencils and even a bag of red licorice.

"The book is written as if the author was a fan of Richard's," Yolanda said.

"Or," Agatha added, "afraid to write the truth."

"He wasn't a very big man," Adam remarked.

"People, overall, were shorter back then."

Yolanda stood. "So far, this hasn't gotten us any closer to understanding why Ivy's back, or even if the mysterious visitor *was* Ivy. How about friends? Could there be a good friend she's staying with?"

"If that were the case," Agatha said, "it would be a male. She didn't have any real girlfriends."

Yolanda nodded. "Both Loretta and Gramma Rosi say she was mean."

Agatha considered that for a moment. "Mean? I suppose she became mean. It would be hard to exist in that family without learning how to assert yourself."

"Got it!" Adam pulled out the book from his backpack. "I know exactly where the paragraph describing him is." He flipped halfway through the book, paused and then read, "'Richard Ventimiglia spent his days at an office in the courthouse, making decisions for the good of the town, and nothing was decided without his approval.'"

Agatha reached for the book and lovingly stroked the spine before checking the dark blue cover to read the title. *Stories of Scorpion Ridge, Arizona.* "Oh, my, this is not one I've seen before." She opened it up, thumbed through it for a moment then pointed at a drawing and said, "The details are exquisite. I remember dancing upstairs in this house. It had a ballroom. Was a shame when it burned down. Oh, and here's the first courthouse. The one they rebuilt didn't come close to the elegance of this one." Glancing up, she spoke sternly to Adam. "You, young man, need to re-create these, make them bigger, leave out no details. We'll put on a historic display at city hall. There are people who have no idea about our past. This is a treasure trove."

To Yolanda's surprise, Adam seemed taken with the idea, but all she could think was there'd not be much money in such a venture. Gesippi was broke. Scorpion Ridge was very careful with its money. Re-creating old drawings just so people could look at them wasn't something Mayor Janice Kolby had budgeted for.

Adam found the drawing of Richard Ventimiglia and read the caption next to it. "'He had a loud voice and always wore a white shirt and black suit. It made a rustling noise when he walked, overpowering the sound of his heels.'"

"He certainly made an impression on someone."

Yolanda drew Agatha's attention back to the inside of the front cover. "It says that the book belonged to Chester, but I don't think he wrote it. We believe that Ivy left this behind the day she visited my bookstore. But she said she was looking for another book, maybe similar to this one, that had different information in it."

Carefully, Agatha went through the pages. "Really, you think there's a companion book? Wouldn't that be grand."

"We don't know. But the elderly woman sure was searching for it. She also said something peculiar. She said that the house didn't really belong to me."

"Well, if it was Ivy, at over ninety she could very well be remembering the past and thinking the place was hers."

"But she didn't mention it until the end of our conversation. If she was senile, why didn't she demand that I get out and complain because her stuff's all gone? She was mostly just annoyed because she couldn't find the book she wanted."

"You showed her everything you have?"

"No. She was smoking a cigarette. Inside! I wanted her to leave." Yolanda closed her eyes and remembered all that she'd done since Ivy's visit. She'd looked at all the books she'd placed in the history section. She'd opened every sealed bag. Granted, there was still a trunk of books upstairs, but Yolanda had briefly gone through it weeks earlier. None of the books inside resembled the one Ivy had left. Yolanda needed to go through the trunk again. Maybe the companion book wasn't identical.

If there *was* a companion book.

Did her Gramma Rosi, who denied ever seeing such a book, have a private stash somewhere? The guest bedroom upstairs was housing all the stuff Rosi couldn't bear to part with but hadn't been able to take to the retirement center.

And what if the old woman came back to look for it while Yolanda wasn't there?

Suddenly, Yolanda felt vulnerable, and she stood. "Adam, you should call and see if Loretta is ready."

"Why? She'll call when she's finished. She likes visiting with her doctor."

"We all like Doc Thomas," Agatha agreed.

"I want to go home and look some more."

Nodding, Adam reached for the book and his backpack.

"I'll call around," Agatha offered. "See if I can find out what happened to Ivy and if she's come back."

"Don't call my grandmother," Adam advised. "I'm worried talking about Ivy is what inspired her to visit the doctor today. She couldn't sleep last night."

"She was sweet on Ivy's big brother for a while."

Both Yolanda and Adam froze.

"We mentioned the brother last night, right?" Adam queried.

Yolanda nodded. "We did. I did. Gramma Rosi said he and Loretta didn't get along."

"Didn't she say it was Loretta and Ivy who didn't get along?"

"Right. You suppose she didn't know about Loretta and Ivy's brother?"

"Housemaids knew everything in those days," Agatha interjected.

So many questions, Yolanda thought, and the people with the answers were just providing more questions.

Just then Adam's cell sounded. Figured, Billy Joel's "My Life." Adam excused himself and went down a couple of steps to take the call.

"I'm surprised to see you two together," Agatha said. "But it makes a whole lot of sense."

"We're not really together. He was on his way here to take his grandmother to the doctor. His van broke down. I happened along and gave him a ride."

Agatha's face scrunched up, as if she were considering Yolanda's words and not quite believing them.

"Really," Yolanda protested. "Adam and I have known each other forever. Right now he's working for me, helping me restore my Victorian."

"You seem to get along perfectly," Agatha observed.

"He was the natural person to help me with this mystery. He was there, working on the saloon doors in my office, when Ivy stopped by. Then there were pictures in the book. Who better to show them to?"

"And you think that's all Adam is about?"

Yolanda looked down to where Adam stood on the sidewalk, smiling and talking on the phone to his great-grandmother. She thought about her mother's advice on men: "Marry someone who makes good money so you'll never do without and you won't have to work hard all your life."

Then she remembered something Gramma

Rosi used to say: "You can judge a man by the way he treats his mother."

In Adam's case, it was about the way he treated his great-grandmother, mother and brother. It was hard not to see the good in a man who'd play a million games of UNO just to make his autistic brother happy.

What would such a man do to make her happy?

Maybe get a traditional job?

Maybe the bigger question was, could *she* make such a man happy?

Adam ended his call then, and Yolanda was saved from having to defend her singlehood any longer.

"GG's going to be fine. She's ready to go home."

Yolanda followed Adam to the door, stopping just before she exited. "You said Ivy became mean, being in that family. What do you mean?"

"It was a man's world back then and not all men were, are, created equal. Her father was a hard man. Him, she could survive. But her brother was spoiled, never had to work or take responsibility for anything he did. It makes for an ugly home life."

"And this was well-known in the community? My grandmother would have been aware of all this?" Yolanda asked.

"Your grandmother would have been well aware, but social station meant something back then. From the time she was seven and entered service, Rosi was trained to be neither seen nor heard in the Ventimiglia family."

Yolanda was aghast. "You mean she went to work that young?"

"You'll have to ask her, but that's the age many began working. I imagine she did what the seven-year-old who worked in our house did, polish the silver and such."

"What was the brother's name?" Yolanda asked. Maybe she'd read about him in the book and hadn't realized.

Agatha frowned, deep in thought. "It was a family name, not something simple like Mike or Joe. Maybe the mother's maiden name? I've got some old diaries and record books. Let me look through them. I'm sure he's mentioned. I remember when he died because it caused an uproar."

"How did he die?"

"He fell into an old well. Drowned. They didn't find him for a few days. He was in line to inherit, the only son."

Adam stopped at the door. "It's not that easy to fall into a well. What happened?"

"Some say he had too much to drink and fell in. Others say he was pushed."

"What do you say?" Adam asked.

"I say I don't think he was looking for a drink of water in a well when his house had electric pumps and running water. I doubt if he knew there was such a thing as well water."

Adam's cell phone rang again—Loretta wondering where they were.

"On our way," Adam told her.

"One more question." Yolanda dragged her feet even as Adam guided her to her car. "You said you'd never heard of Chester, yet his name is on a plaque on our courthouse. It says he built it."

"Built the new one or the one that burned down?" Agatha asked.

"The original. When did it burn down?"

Agatha scrunched up her face, thinking. "Sometime in the nineteen forties. Quite a few people believe the fire was set on purpose. And the town didn't have the money to rebuild it properly. That's why the new one is such an eyesore. The first one, though, was a classic."

An hour later, after stopping at the drugstore to get Loretta a prescription and to pick up a few things for Adam's mother, they finally pulled into Loretta's driveway.

"I really appreciate this," Loretta said, giving up the kitten she'd cradled the whole trip home. "It's been quite a day."

Yolanda had to agree. On the drive home she kept looking in the rearview mirror at Adam, who was all curled up and uncomfortable in a too small area, yet he never complained, even when the kitten chose his lap to sleep on.

Once Adam helped Loretta inside her house, he returned to the car and said, "Drop me off at the studio? Mom says they desperately need me to teach a class that starts in ten minutes. If you don't mind, could you also take the milk home for me and put it in the refrigerator? I'll give you a key to the house."

"Can't you just put it in the refrigerator at the studio?"

"No, Andy gets out of therapy at four. He'll get home before I'm done. He'll pour himself a glass of milk, drink half, take his shower and then come to the studio."

"Can't he…" Yolanda paused, remembering Andy and his quirks. Before Adam's return, she'd seen Andy at church, but he'd sat with his parents, didn't go to class and the moment the final "amen" sounded, Andy had gone to his parents' car and waited for them.

Away from the crowd he couldn't control.

"I'll do it."

But when she went to Adam's house to put the milk in the refrigerator, she noticed the photos in the living room of Adam and Andy as they grew up. The photos reminded her that she'd known Adam all her life, from little boy on the playground who, at age nine, didn't think she should play soccer because she was a girl, to teenager who leaned over way too often to ask her questions about homework he should have done himself the night before, to employee at Bridget's Animal Adventure, whose oversize hands would gently cup a sick baby bear and help feed it during the midnight hours.

One who took cement walls and made them *Wizard-of-Oz* worthy.

She needed to get a handle on him. She liked thinking about him being this happy-go-lucky, free-spirited boy who always landed on his feet. Lately, though, she was seeing him as an amazingly talented adult man who pitched in when his family needed him.

Conflicted. That's what she was.

Leaving Adam's house, she hurried to her house to settle the kitten in before any accidents happened, and finally headed back to the studio to pick Adam up.

But as she headed for Snapp's Studio, her thoughts took another twist.

She should avoid him at all costs. And not because she didn't respect him. After everything he'd done for her this last week, helping her with the mystery and the bookstore, he'd gained her respect and maybe a little more than that.

Subtle attraction.

But she knew him too well. Right now he was shouldering his responsibilities in Scorpion Ridge but what if an offer he couldn't refuse came along? Or, an even better thought, what if his father got better and Adam wasn't needed?

He would leave, and this time he might not come back.

Adam was just locking up when she pulled into the studio's parking lot. He pushed his unruly brown hair out of his eyes and headed for her car.

"Hey," he said, getting in, as if she picked him up routinely.

She said "hey" back, trying for a flip tone and nonchalance. It must have worked because he talked about his Tae Kwon Do class and Andy's plans for the competition coming up this Saturday.

Used to be all he talked about was art. She rather missed that.

"Want to come in?" he asked when they pulled up in front of his house. "I know we'll be playing UNO tonight. Andy's still grumbling about you winning."

UNO sounded so much better than going home to a big, empty house, but the grand opening was looming. "No, I've some things to do around the bookstore. I open in less than forty-eight hours."

"Anything I can do?"

"No, it's all stocking. I'd have it done in the time it would take to explain."

Adam nodded and stepped from the car. Coming around to the driver's side, he waited until she rolled down the window.

"I really appreciated what you did for me today. GG's pretty special. You made a day that started all wrong end perfectly right."

She'd done that?

Before she could respond, he leaned down and kissed her. Right on the mouth, his lips firm and questing, warm and giving. Anyone could drive by, or his family could come to the door and witness. But she kissed him back, all the while thinking *stop*! and reminding herself that she didn't live alone. She now had a cat.

She had no desire to kiss the cat.

And every desire to keep kissing Adam.

Standing, he gave a cocky grin and said, "I'll see you tomorrow."

Yes, she'd see him tomorrow. What she really wanted, though, was a lifetime of tomorrows, and he wasn't that kind of guy.

CHAPTER EIGHT

THURSDAY MORNING ADAM rolled out of bed ridiculously early and settled at the kitchen table: a bowl of cereal to his left, his Mac laptop and a spiral notebook plus drawing tablet and necessary art supplies to his right.

For the first time in a long while, he felt good. Maybe it had to do with Yolanda Sanchez. He'd meant to give her a chaste thank-you kiss but it had instead turned into a taste of pure temptation.

The urge to draw surged through him, and he felt free. That shouldn't be the case; after all, he was back in Scorpion Ridge, worried about his father and without wheels.

He shouldn't be feeling happy, but he was.

The book was propped up in front of him, and he shook his head trying to get Yolanda out of it so he could concentrate.

At first, the book had intrigued him because of the drawings. He'd not understood Yolanda's quest to find its owner. Now he was as curious as she was for a number of reasons.

He wanted to know more about the Snapps, more about Yolanda's family and more about the Ventimiglias, not just Chester and Ivy, but now Ivy's brother, who seemed not to have a name.

So he started at the beginning of the book, and in his spiral notebook he recorded the first date mentioned: 1884. Throughout, four primary families were mentioned: the Ventimiglias, the Moores, the Snapps and the Welborns. That name had meant nothing yesterday, but now thanks to his great-grandmother, he knew where they'd lived and a bit more.

He separated four sheets from the tablet and labeled each with a family.

The Snapps were mentioned, in detail, in three different places. A third of the way into the book, there was an image of Jedidiah Snapp. Making his first rough draft, he re-created the drawing of his…what? Great-great-grandfather? Bringing the man's face to life was easy. In some ways Adam was drawing himself.

He started with just a basic outline. Then he formed the eyes—they had the same shape and held the same expression that Adam's dad wore when he was being serious, which was pretty much throughout Adam's childhood. Dad was even more serious now.

Jedidiah's clothes were different from either Adam's or his dad's, and his hair was shorter.

But as Adam enlarged the image, he noted the cheekbone structure was the same as his. Deftly, Adam used his eraser and smudge stick on the teeth to show both highlights and shadows.

It had always been the details that Adam loved about art. His home had been full of routine, and nothing was allowed to be out of place. Adam had to cater to Andy or there might be an outburst. In art, though, Adam was the one who could control everything. He could arrange the canvas any way he wanted. If he wanted to portray chaos, he could. The canvas was his.

It wasn't until after he'd left Scorpion Ridge and was on his own that Adam started dabbling with realism.

The minutes flew by as he continued drawing, reading and recording a timeline. Jedidiah's wife was a woman named Amelia. She was only mentioned once, and the drawing of her showed a woman standing not quite next to but more behind her husband, somewhat in shadow. Halfway through the book, he got to a section that described the land they'd owned. A few minutes of research on the computer and he discovered that the Snapp land had been where BAA was now.

Wow, Luke Rittenhouse and Ruth Dunbar would get a kick out of that information.

The book didn't say how the Snapps had lost

the land or how the Ventimiglias acquired it, as Adam knew they had because Luke had seen their name on the title records. The internet didn't bring up a bill of sale, either, so Adam had no date to add to his timeline. What he did find was a red-boxed message stating: Data lost in courthouse fire.

He stopped reading and reached for the cereal he'd not touched. But he was interrupted before he could bring the spoon to his mouth.

"I didn't know you could draw like this." His father stood in the kitchen's entrance staring down at Adam's drawing on the table. "Everything I saw you draw seemed to be so cartoonish."

Adam wasn't sure what to say. He'd been drawing all his life. He'd started with recreating *Star Wars* figures, advanced to creating his own comic books and then made a living both with murals on BAA's walls and weekends spent as a caricaturist.

"It's what I do best," Adam finally said.

"Your grandmother said you were making a good income as a muralist. She said your last mural brought in twenty-five thousand dollars."

"It did, for six months' work."

His dad sat at the kitchen table, carefully pushing the laptop aside and pulling the drawing close to scrutinize. "Can you paint portraits?"

"I used to paint all the *Star Wars* figures, remember?"

"They're in the attic." Adam's dad looked a bit uncomfortable. Pointing to the line drawing Adam was doing, he asked, "Who is this?"

"It's our relative Jedidiah Snapp." Adam held up the book. "Yolanda found this and now it's a bit of a mystery. We both think it's why GG got so upset at the table the other day."

"Our family history got Grandma upset?"

"No, it was the Ventimiglia history that got GG upset. Some of their story is in here, but a lot of the Snapp story is in here, too. Starting in the late eighteen hundreds and going up to—" Adam checked his timeline "—about nineteen twenty-nine so far."

Adam's dad switched his gaze from Jedidiah's likeness to the book. "What did you find out?"

"We went from rags to riches to rags again."

"That hasn't changed." Dad flipped through the pages while Adam finished his cereal. After Adam took his bowl and spoon to the sink, his father tapped the book's thumbnail of Jedidiah. "You captured it perfectly."

"Not yet, but I will."

"Mom's got most of the old photos, but she's

a Snapp by marriage. I'm not sure she would be able to shed much light on Jedidiah's history."

"And you don't know it?"

"I believe Jedidiah would have been my great-great-grandpa. Long dead by the time I came around."

"Is anyone alive who might remember something about him?"

"If Loretta wasn't already upset, I'd have her take you through the museum's archives. You'll get a lot of information there combined with what Loretta can tell you."

The museum was on Adam's list of things to do today…with Yolanda. He'd already called Thelma Sheldon, one of the museum's guides. And after getting a go-ahead from her, he'd texted Yolanda his plans. She'd not responded yet. He wished he'd thought to invite her to breakfast. She'd be amazed that his family once owned BAA. He really needed to stop by and visit with Ruth Moore, who'd owned the land BAA occupied since before Adam was born. She was too young to have hung around the group of Scorpion Ridge residents Adam was currently researching. But her husband had been a Moore.

The Moores weren't mentioned in the journal much, and only one of them had been depicted.

The drawing showed a stern man sitting behind a desk and counting money.

That matched every description Ruth had shared of her husband.

Adam sat next to his father, close, together as they'd not been in a long time. With an artist's eye, Adam took a moment to really look at the man. His father had always seemed so together, sure of himself, strong. This morning he was moving and thinking slower than usual. He'd not even mentioned what had happened to the van yesterday.

"Dad, you feeling all right?"

"I'll make it through the day."

"I'll fix you breakfast," Adam offered. His father started to protest but then nodded. While Adam cracked eggs, added milk and cheese and cooked up an omelet, his dad went through the book, but kept going back to the drawing of Jedidiah.

"It's uncanny," he finally muttered.

"How much I resemble him?"

Adam's dad shook his head. "Yes, that, too, but even more just how well you re-created the likeness. It almost looks alive."

"Do you know Agatha Fitzsimmons over in Gesippi?"

"No."

"She's a librarian, about GG's age. Yolanda

and I visited with her yesterday. She said I should enlarge and paint the pictures in the book and put together a display at the courthouse. I think she's wrong."

His father started to protest, but Adam didn't stop.

"I think they should be pencil drawings, like the originals."

"Is there money in that?" Adam's father was nothing if not practical, just like Yolanda.

"Yes, there could be numbered prints made of each one and sold. Plus, the original could go for four digits."

"You're kidding."

"I thought—" Adam set a plate in front of his father "—that GG told you I was making a good living."

"Then why did you come home?"

Adam added a glass of orange juice and a fork. "You asked me to. You needed me, right?"

His father looked at the food, back at the drawing and then at Adam. "I didn't think you'd come."

"Really, Dad? Whenever you needed me, I was there. I walked Andy to school. By the time I was ten, I knew what a functional behavior analysis was, and how to be a part of sibling therapy, and that we'd have pancakes for breakfast every morning because Andy loved them."

"I always appreciated how devoted you were to Andy."

"I taught him how to button his shirt."

"I didn't remember that," his father admitted.

"I wouldn't let anyone pick on him at school. Ever."

"I do remember that, especially the two times you got suspended."

"Whenever you asked me to do something, I did it."

"Did we ask too much?"

Adam didn't answer for a few minutes. He'd not been expecting to have this conversation today. Usually, his dad woke up at seven, fixed his own breakfast and by seven-thirty was heading off to the studio, where he worked in his office doing a few side accounting jobs.

Adam's mother, on the other hand, had Andy duty in the morning. Andy woke up at eight, on the dot. Highly functioning, he showered and dressed—though he always left a mess in the bathroom—and came to stand by the stove to watch his mother make pancakes. He expected the food to be on the table at eight-twenty, and he didn't eat cold pancakes.

Adam couldn't remember an instance where his mother had failed to keep the schedule. She'd learned early on that meeting Andy's simple expectations made the day go smoother. But she'd always offered to make Adam something else. He refused, claiming he liked pancakes.

Once he moved out, pancakes were off his breakfast list completely.

"You didn't ask too much," Adam said, finally. "But you might have listened too little."

Dad took a bite of the omelet, chewed a moment and then countered with, "I'm listening now."

They were having the conversation Adam had dreamed of having for years. The one where he told his dad that art was a passion, a career and life.

But with his dad being sick, watching Andy and working at the studio was the only passion that mattered now.

"It's going to be okay, Dad."

Someone tapped on the back door. Adam got up and opened it. GG beamed up at him, pushing her way in and said, "I'm feeling much better." Almost immediately, she hesitated, "Oh, I've come at an inopportune moment. You two are finally talking."

Neither man answered.

"I'll just go. Pretend I never interrupted."

Adam's father pushed the plate away. He'd eaten maybe three bites. GG tried not to frown. That's what Adam noticed first. What he noticed next was the time.

"Andy gets up in five minutes. You might as well stay."

Looking at the clock, she nodded. "I was in the mood for pancakes. I think I'll start them and let Mom sleep in a bit more."

Adam recognized an opportunity when one fell in his lap. "I just made Dad an omelet. How about I make you one?"

Her face brightened, and she nodded. She, too, had eaten a million pancakes with Andy. "I didn't know you could cook."

She sat her giant black bag in the chair next to her son and settled in. Immediately, she picked up the drawing of Jedidiah so she could see it better.

"How on earth did you manage to do this? It resembles one of the photos I have in the trunk your grandfather brought back from Germany." She leaned in closer. "No, it's somewhat different. He's older here, a bit more sour-looking."

"Jedidiah Snapp," Adam said, breaking more eggs and mixing once again, taking milk and cheese from the fridge. "I enlarged a drawing from the book Yolanda found at her store. I don't think I got the mouth quite right. Something about the teeth. Maybe you could bring me the photos. Are there any others?"

"Only three or four of Jedidiah. They didn't take as many photos back then. They're all pretty dark. Were there any other Snapps in the book?"

"There's a drawing of his wife, Amelia, but she's standing behind Jedidiah, smaller than him, and I can barely make her out. The book recounts Jedidiah's life, that he worked in the mine as some sort of supervisor and that he shot a man for stealing a cow." Along with the omelet, he started the pancakes for his brother.

"I think I have one good one of Amelia. She outlived him." GG chuckled. "The man Jedidiah shot was a Ventimiglia cousin. Sure made life interesting. I met Amelia right after George and I married. I'm not sure the woman knew how to smile. But then, she had four children and only two lived past infancy. Your grandfather and his sister. She didn't approve of me. I can tell you that."

Adam's father looked interested. "That's a family story I haven't heard. Why would anyone not approve of you?"

"She said I was too uppity, probably because the Munros—my family—had a bit more money than the Snapps. Plus, I dated one of the town boys before I married George. Wealthier than him, or at least he pretended to be."

An alarm sounded in the back. Any minute, Adam's mother would be waking Andy.

"When did you start going out with George?" Adam asked.

"He came home from college and I was at loose ends..." Loretta's words tapered off, almost as if she'd forgotten what she wanted to say first, but Adam wasn't fooled. They were venturing back to a time she didn't want to talk about.

A time that had given her an anxiety attack just two days ago.

Loretta leaned forward, edging the book toward her. "This is the book Yolanda found? *Stories of Scorpion Ridge, Arizona.* The book she thinks Ivy Ventimiglia left behind. What's in there about my family?"

"Your family?"

"The Munros."

"With everything that's going on, I keep forgetting that is your maiden name. Not much, but I could check again. I don't remember any drawings of the Munros."

Loretta looked annoyed more than anything. "Figures that if the Ventimiglias are involved, they'd leave the Munroes out."

Adam had to smile. This was the Loretta he knew and loved. "Something I thought interesting, GG, is that the Snapp family used to own the property where BAA is located. That information is in the book. But I've looked online at property titles and there's no trail of a sale. I asked Luke, and he remembers seeing the Ventimiglias name on some of the old paperwork, but not ours, not the Snapps."

There was a pregnant pause, and Loretta's eyes narrowed before she slowly said, "I wasn't aware that the Snapp family used to own the land BAA is on."

"According to the book, we did."

"I think I need to read the book."

"That would be great. Both Yolanda and I would appreciate any insight you can share about the contents."

"I wonder if all the information in that book is true. Who wrote it?"

"Chester Ventimiglia's name is on the inside cover, but the handwriting is different than what's in the book."

"I've never heard of a Chester."

"All this talk isn't upsetting you?"

"A bit," she admitted.

"Really?" Adam leaned forward. This time his father did, too.

Loretta took a deep breath and rolled her eyes. "I'm almost embarrassed by that silly anxiety attack. I mean, who cares about what happened so many decades ago? The past is dead and buried. Sharing it doesn't mean digging it up, does it? And if Ivy's back, I need to know why she returned after all these years."

Adam and his father glanced at each other. His dad shrugged, but Adam shook his head.

"Well, Robert, you never knew this, but I was engaged to Wood for a year."

"Wood?" Adam asked.

"Woodhull Ventimiglia. Ivy's big brother. Woodhull was his mother's family name. He hated it, especially when people called him Woody."

Adam almost fell off his chair. Engaged was more serious than the 'Sweet on' Agatha had suggested. Yolanda would love this. He'd managed to get the brother's name and another family connection.

A connection to his family.

"What happened? Why did you break it off?"

"Why do most young people break it off? He got involved with another girl. Then he died. George was a better kisser, believe me. Only thing I ever regretted was not getting to live in that gorgeous house. It was to be my wedding present from the family."

"Morning." Adam's mother came into the room. "Well, this is a treat. Breakfast ready and all the family around the table." She gave Loretta a kiss. "What's the occasion? And who's a better kisser?"

"No occasion, really." Loretta pushed the book away from her. "And I was just sharing that my husband was a great kisser. I'm sure Robert picked up the trait. As to why I'm here, I feel better and decided to stop by and see my favorite son and his family for breakfast. I didn't expect anyone but you and Andy to be here."

"I'm your only grandson," Adam's dad pointed out. It was something he didn't point out often as it reminded him that he'd barely known his parents. They'd died when he was in elementary school. GG and her husband had raised him.

"And I live here now, too," Adam added.

Andy came in, headed for the stove and carefully took a plate, a fork and four pancakes, stacked perfectly, before sitting down. If Adam's mom hadn't snatched the drawing of Jedidiah aside, the plate would have gone right on top.

"Who's this?"

It took about five minutes, but she got the whole story.

"GG's going to bring over a chest that has more photos in it. I can improve upon Jedidiah's likeness before I actually draw the final version." The thought of going through the chest, matching black-and-white history to the book's drawings, was enticing enough, but add in doing it with Yolanda at his side... Suddenly Adam couldn't think of anything he'd rather do.

"That isn't a final?" his father asked.

"No, this is just my outline."

His father said the same thing he'd said earlier, only now it was more a statement than a question. "I didn't know you could draw like this."

Something changed in his father's expression, a slight nod, almost an awakening. This moment, as his father fingered the image of Jedidiah, Adam figured the man finally realized who his son was and what his son was capable of doing.

It occurred to Adam that Yolanda had always appreciated his talent, just not what he had chosen to do with it.

It also occurred to him that her opinion of him was starting to matter.

YOLANDA STOOD IN the middle of the children's section, perfectly put together, and thought to herself, *I'm not ready.* She wanted another week to reconsider her choices.

The bookstore opened at eleven the following day. Since she'd accomplished nothing yesterday except for tooling Adam and his great-grandmother around and acquiring a cat, she had everything to do today. If she were sensible, she'd spend the entire afternoon making sure her ancillary items were displayed and priced. She had T-shirts and mugs with Twice Told Tales on the front. She also had plenty of stationery and writing utensils for sale.

Instead, once she was certain she could do nothing else in the children's section, she went to horror. The decor was a bit bland. Adam had given her a few suggestions, but when she got excited about the idea, he backed off. She wasn't sure if it was because he didn't want to paint or because he didn't think he'd be around long enough to finish the job.

Men leave. Something else her mother had drilled into her.

Yolanda hated the idea of Adam leaving. She enjoyed being with him. Checking her watch, she realized he'd be here in just under an hour. They were supposed to go to the museum together. Yes, his irresponsible ways were starting to affect her. No way should she be leaving her business the day before it opened.

"Come here, Gulliver," Yolanda called.

Loretta had been right. Since the cat would be living in a bookstore, he'd needed a literary name. She'd settled on Gulliver because from almost the moment she'd saved him, the kitten had been traveling. First to her doorstep, next off to the vet and then all the way to Gesippi, and tonight she planned on taking him to the group home where Gramma Rosi lived.

Halloween masks! That's what she'd put in the horror section if she couldn't convince Adam to paint.

Gulliver, of course, still hadn't responded to her request. At four weeks not only were his antics more slapstick than polished, but he also had no clue that he even had a name.

Leaving the horror section, she headed to the attic. There were a few more books up there. Yes, she could tell herself that she was fetching them, at this moment, so she could have them for sale on Friday. But honestly, she was heading to the attic to see if there was indeed a companion book to the one Ivy had left behind.

Adam had called this morning to confirm the plans for their museum visit, and he'd been full of news. In the midst of recounting all the new information, he'd made her laugh by saying, "One thing for sure, I'm glad GG married into the Snapp family instead because I'd have hated writing the last name Ventimiglia on every school paper. I'd have missed recess."

He didn't know how to have a typical phone call or leave a dull text. Something was always going on.

The stairs creaked behind her. Down at the bottom, Gulliver mewed, too small to jump up the step and stay with her. "I won't be long," she said over her shoulder, wishing she had a guard dog as well as an undersized kitten.

Gramma Rosi had not updated the Victorian, ever. Yolanda suspected that Rosi's last husband had done a bit, but not much. It grew dim at the top of the stairs. The attic had one light, an open bulb with a string switch. The light circled out but didn't reach the corners.

The minute Yolanda stepped into the attic, dust greeted her and she sneezed. Which, of course, simply spread the dust even more. Years of her family's history scattered the room. Broken furniture seemed the favorite junk to collect. Next to that were kitchen appliances. Yolanda could only hope that the old appliances could be deemed retro and that Adam could fix some of them to sell on eBay.

Adam. There he was again, invading her thoughts. Too often lately, he'd forced his way into her life. Or worse, wormed his way into her mind and kept her from thinking rationally.

Heading to the left side of the attic, where the books she'd not managed to sort yet waited, she crouched down, opened the first chest and gasped.

The chest was empty.

CHAPTER NINE

CROSS-LEGGED ON THE FLOOR, dust filming her fingertips, Yolanda took a deep breath. This trunk should not, *should not* be empty. Someone had entered her home, without permission, and taken what was hers. Prickles of fear tiptoed up her spine. Then the Sanchez in her, proud and strong, kicked in.

She'd been home all morning. This had happened yesterday or earlier.

She called Adam first, upset more at the lost information in the books than at the lost income she could have made selling the books. She realized she sounded slightly frantic, which was unusual for her.

"I didn't take the books from the chest," she insisted. "I'd remember. I was looking forward to going through them." Scanning the attic, she saw nothing else out of place. It was as if someone had come up the stairs, taken only what they wanted—her books—and left. If they'd left footprints on the dusty floor, she'd obliterated them.

She sniffed the air, wondering for a moment if there was a hint of cigarette smoke or if her imagination wanted to find what wasn't there. Truly, though, she couldn't imagine the frail older woman making it up the stairs, let alone carrying the heavy books *down* the stairs.

"I don't care about the books," Adam said, surprising her. "I care about you. If someone was in your attic, they could still be there. Call the police."

"We don't know when the books were taken," Yolanda pointed out. "Could have been yesterday or…" She started to say last week, but she was certain the theft had taken place between Monday, the day Ivy showed up and left behind *Stories of Scorpion Ridge, Arizona*, and today. Four short days.

"Doesn't matter," Adam said. "Go outside, sit on the front porch where people can see you and call the police."

"I'm not worried. The only sounds I've heard all morning were Gulliver's antics."

Gulliver had a tendency to run into walls and furniture when he wasn't sleeping. She'd also heard a book's occasional whisper, begging her, *read me*. Opening a bookstore at the same time as becoming an amateur sleuth had a way of stealing any free reading time, and Yolanda was definitely starting to feel withdrawal.

In the background, she heard someone calling Adam's name.

"Are you at work?" she asked.

"Was," he answered, "I was at work. And when I get to your house, you better be outside."

"All right," she said. "I'll be waiting for you." Hitting the disconnect button, she headed to the stairs, taking each step carefully, wanting to be quiet, listening for sounds that didn't belong, looking for signs of an intruder. She glanced left and right, trying to ascertain that everything was in its rightful place. The only thing wrong was the feeling of vulnerability that kept her company.

Once she made it outside to the porch, she tapped the numbers for information and got the number for the police department. Scorpion Ridge didn't have their own force. Instead, the neighboring town of Adobe Hills policed their area. Yolanda made the call , then punched in her Gramma Rosi's number.

"Who'd want any of the junk in the attic?" Gramma said after hearing Yolanda's tale. "Most of it needs to be thrown away."

"They didn't disturb the junk," Yolanda reiterated. "They didn't even carry off the trunk, only the books that were in it. I'm sure it has to do with the book Ivy left behind."

Gramma Rosi was silent for a moment. Then

she said, "That book again, and all your questions. Thelma Sheldon called me yesterday and said you and Adam were visiting the museum today because you had all kinds of questions. She wanted to know why I didn't tell her I had pictures of the old courthouse."

"Why would Thelma care?"

"She worked there as a secretary when she was just sixteen or so. Her daddy was the mayor."

"Really? What was her last name?"

"Rasmussen. Her daddy was a classmate of Richard's at West Point. They moved here when Thelma was six."

"Figures," Yolanda said. It didn't surprise Yolanda that her Gramma Rosi knew the exact age Thelma had been when she moved to Scorpion Ridge. Lately, Rosi knew more about the past than the present—except apparently when it came to the Ventimiglias.

Gramma Rosi let out a huff. "Thelma will talk your ear off, that's for sure."

"Every time we show the book to someone," Yolanda said, "they get all excited. And we keep finding out more about our history. Or, even better, not finding out about our history. Nobody's heard of Chester. The woman, we're sure she is Ivy, mentioned his name, and it's on the plaque at the courthouse. But otherwise, it's like he never existed. He's not in the book, just his name on the inside cover. Agatha didn't recall meeting him. Neither does Adam's great-grandmother, although she got as upset as you did. We had to take her to the doctor yesterday."

"Wha… Slow down. When did you talk to Agatha? And is Loretta all right?"

"Loretta's fine, just having problems sleeping. We visited Agatha yesterday. She lives in a Victorian, too. I have some great new decorating ideas, and I want a piano! I didn't realize you knew Agatha. She wants Adam to re-create the drawings from the book and put on a show at City Hall."

The sound of air whistling through teeth came across the line. "I probably should ask, is there mention of me in that book?"

"Not one word that I can find."

"Hmmm. Maybe I need to read this book, as well as check for what's missing in my house," Gramma Rosi said. "I'm coming over."

My house? Not that Yolanda cared, but it was now supposedly Yolanda's house. Yolanda got to her feet and started to pace. She should beg off going to the museum with Adam. She had way too much to do today, and now with this theft and Gramma Rosi coming over…

However, the only way to get her life back into order was to figure out what Ivy wanted and why she wanted it now. Maybe then Yolanda could get her and Adam's relationship back to being strictly professional.

Instead of a close relationship with someone she was starting to count on.

Even sitting on the front porch, waiting for the police to show, and talking to Gramma Rosi on the phone didn't take her mind off what Adam had said. *I don't care about the books. I care about you.*

"Everyone knew the Ventimiglias," Gramma Rosi said, interrupting Yolanda's thoughts and reminding her that now was not the time to be daydreaming about the handyman. "Look, Adam was right to tell you to stay outside. I'm coming over."

"I'll come get you—"

"No, Mr. Teasdale will drive me."

He was the man who managed the group home. Lately, he'd been squiring Rosi around. Probably because Yolanda was too preoccupied to do it. One more priority that she was neglecting.

"Okay, see you in a few minutes. But I think—" Too late. Gramma Rosi had already hit the off button. Yolanda had time to pace from one end of the porch to the other. Then Adam, looking out of place in his mother's Cavalier, showed up, still wearing his white Tae Kwon Do uniform. He only made it to the bottom porch step when the sheriff's Range Rover parked behind him.

"Gramma Rosi will be here any minute," Yolanda told the men.

"Good," the sheriff said, coming up the steps. "She might recognize what's missing more than you would."

Yolanda doubted it. She'd first met Sheriff Rafael Salazar at his mother's diner. He'd been a busboy while she'd been kicking her feet in a booster seat and spreading cracker crumbs all over the floor. Years later when she was just out of her teens, she'd run into him at BAA. She'd sold tickets. Sometimes dangerous or injured animals were dropped off at the front gate, and Luke called Rafe. Rafe had once helped Luke and Jake Farraday, from Game and Fish, capture a python, now named Rexette and a prime draw.

Last year she'd attended his wedding. He'd married into the BAA family, marrying the owner's sister-in-law. Very fitting. And his wife had been Adam's protégé. She, Janie Salazar, now taught art at Adobe Hills Community College and had a gallery. "Tell me what's missing," Rafe said, giving her a slight hug.

Yolanda led them up the stairs to the attic so they could see the opened trunk. It looked small now that she had two men with her.

"You're sure you didn't empty the trunk yourself?" Adam asked.

Yolanda ran down the steps, grabbed her notebook off the kitchen table and came back up. "No, I didn't check it off my list of things to do."

Both men looked at each other. "She's a list-maker," Adam said.

"How many books were inside?" Sheriff Salazar wanted to know.

"Maybe twenty to forty."

"Can you tell me any titles and how much you think the books were worth?"

"I couldn't say. They've probably been packed away for decades. I've been dividing the books into three categories—throw away, everyday and rare. Most of the chests had three or four that I'd consider rare. The everyday was stuff like Bibles or *Gone with the Wind*. Offhand, the value might be between fifty and a hundred dollars."

"Anything else missing?" Sheriff Salazar asked, glancing around the room. "Maybe jewelry or antiques?"

"No, nothing else has been moved, and I know the books were in this trunk the last time I was up here," Yolanda told them. "I'd been working in the attic on and off for two months. This was the last trunk. The books in here were in poor condition. I knew they'd take the longest to go through. That's why I saved it for last. Today."

Adam didn't blame Rafael for giving the attic another noncommittal glance. It was full of old furniture, suitcases, trunks and even two old lawn mowers.

"Nothing else is missing," Yolanda insisted.

"You checked downstairs, too? Jewelry, money, electronics?"

"My grandmother took her personal jewelry when she moved to assisted living in town. I have maybe five dollars in my purse. I own a laptop, still in my office, and a Kindle. It's in my purse."

"No Xbox," Adam said morosely.

Rafe, to his credit, didn't act sympathetic, at least not to Adam.

"Can you think of a reason why someone would take the books up here when you have thousands downstairs?"

Yolanda looked at Adam, one eyebrow raised. He nodded.

"Well…"

An hour later, Sheriff Salazar finished his third cup of coffee, handed Yolanda back the copy of *Stories of Scorpion Ridge, Arizona*, and said, "I find it interesting that the four families mentioned are all anglo. I mean, why aren't the Acuras and Salazars mentioned?"

"My grandmother was a housemaid for the Ventimiglias," Yolanda said.

"That's mentioned in the book?"

"No, Agatha Fitzsimmons told us."

"Amazing. Maybe I should visit Agatha. My family came early on, maybe just before the courthouse fire. I believe one of my great-uncles helped rebuild it. He was a laborer." In the end, Sheriff Salazar wrote a report, but with only a vague description—books, dusty, old—and no titles, it was a futile effort and they all knew it.

"I really will try," he promised.

Before he left he praised Adam on some of the Victorian's improvements, questioned why on earth Kool-Aid-orange saloon doors were being used for Yolanda's office and then introduced himself to Gulliver, who promptly collapsed on the man's foot, paws in the air as if saying *go ahead, arrest me. You won't find handcuffs the right size.*

When he finally drove away, Yolanda stood on the porch watching as his Range Rover disappeared. She half wanted Adam, standing by her side, to step closer, offer comfort, take her in his arms… But if he did, she should step away.

Adam wasn't right for her.

Men leave.

"I called you away from work," she apologized.

He looked down at his white master's uniform and shrugged. "I've never been comfortable being a *gyosannim*."

"What?"

"A Tae Kwon Do instructor. After you called, Mom called Mr. Chee to take over my class. It probably ended ten minutes ago, and right now they're going over his new schedule. He'll be taking on more responsibility."

"I didn't realize that was an option."

"Dad originally thought that bringing me on would save money. But it won't save them the kind of money they need, and Dad recognizes now that it's not what I want to do."

"I didn't realize it was so serious."

"Dad's surgery is under his insurance, but…" Adam stopped, seemed to regroup then said, "It's not nearly enough to cover the bills."

"After your dad gets better, they can start sav—"

"He won't get better."

Yolanda stepped back so she could look him full in the face. She saw sorrow, acceptance and something else: maturity.

"The surgery buys him time, that's all," Adam said. "At the most…five years."

Yolanda didn't hesitate; she wrapped her arms

around him. He felt strong, solid, warm. Her chin tucked into his shoulder, and she closed her eyes.

She didn't say sorry. He knew.

"At our breakfast table this morning, I realized that I can make more money doing murals and caricatures than what the family would save by having me, instead of Mr. Chee, take my father's place."

"What?" She stepped out of the embrace, feeling a little empty and lost. "I'm not following."

"I came back home to not only help with Andy while my dad has his operation but to also take Dad's place at the studio until he got better. At least that's what I thought. However, it's going to be a more long-term assignment, and I can contribute more outside the studio."

"So you figured you'd just be in Scorpion Ridge for a short while and then leave again?"

"Yes, but maybe I just didn't want to consider that my dad was really sick enough that he needed me here."

Yolanda nodded. Her mother, just last year, had gone to the doctor with a headache that wouldn't go away. Six weeks later she was gone.

Six weeks was no time at all to say goodbye.

"He's lucky to have you," she said.

Adam sat down on the front step. "Growing

up, you assume your parents can manage and handle everything. And my parents did. They managed to make me and my brother's life the best it could possibly be. I mean, my dad walked away from corporate America so he could open a studio so my brother had a place to not only work, but also to feel necessary."

Yolanda settled down next to him and wrapped her arms around her knees. "Gramma Rosi said your dad was one of the smartest men she knew."

"Wish I'd have understood that sooner."

Yolanda didn't tell Adam what her mother had thought about him.

"Dad also handled money well," Adam continued. "He has a portfolio, life insurance and had enough money saved to live on for six months."

All things Yolanda's mother had pushed for.

"Nothing, though, can make up for what my parents are spending on Andy and my dad combined right now. We're hurting. He's been dipping into his portfolio, borrowing against the life insurance and now the emergency fund only has enough to live on for two more weeks."

"And you had no idea it was that bad?"

"Dad only told me the true diagnosis about three days ago. I had no clue about the details of the money situation until this morning."

"I think it's wise that you're going back to your art if it can help."

"Let's just hope I can paint—and I'm not talking flipping houses and refinishing doors. I'm talking full-out murals like I used to do."

"You can do it, Adam. It's always been your dream."

He looked back at her Victorian, and she wondered if he was contemplating *her* dream. It was coming true, but would it last?

She'd been thinking about people leaving—her father, mother, Adam, but maybe she should have been more worried about what happened when you woke up from a dream to discover it was temporary.

HE HADN'T MEANT to dump on Yolanda. But this morning's conversation at the kitchen table—complete with bank statements and bills lined up in front of him—had opened his eyes. His family was in danger of losing both their home and business. And soon they would lose his father. Adam had some control over the first two: home and business. The only contribution he could make to his father's situation was to make his last years worry-free.

"I'm going back to work full-time," he told Yolanda.

"You *have* been working, here and at the studio," she pointed out.

"And I've been making about a tenth of my earning potential, all because I've been licking my wounds and telling myself that I didn't have what it takes to make it as an artist. I was lying to myself. For over two years, I was making it."

"In the five digits, right?" Yolanda asked.

"Yes."

"Adam, that's amazing. Why did you stop? Did the offers stop?"

"No. I've had two offers out of state in the last month. Plus, Huckabee's Ostrich Harem wants a mural, too."

Her face twitched. He liked that side of her. The side that wanted to be all serious but recognized humor.

"He's been open to the public a little over a year and wants to cross-promote with BAA."

"Luke might consider it," said Yolanda.

"I'll tell Huckabee when I see him."

"So you're taking the job."

"Yes, maybe. I called and left him a message. He hasn't called back yet. That makes you," he admitted, "the first one I've told." Saying the words made his decision feel concrete, made him want to take back the maybe. There were too many maybes in his life right now.

Maybe the surgery would help.

Maybe he could take care of his twin brother without disruption.

Maybe he could rebuild his career.

Maybe he should make Scorpion Ridge his home base.

"I'm a little hesitant to tell my father, though. What if I stand in front of a bare wall and nothing comes?"

"Pshaw," Yolanda sputtered. "*You* come up with nothing? I'd like to see that. I've heard you muttering about how I could use my wall space better at the bookstore. Remember that idea you came up with of a caricature of me on my office door, complete with a shellacked book and fake glasses?"

It was exactly what he needed to hear.

"When are you going to Huckabee's?"

"I'm hoping to set up an appointment for next week." Adam checked his watch. "Speaking of appointments, don't forget the one I set up with Thelma Sheldon. We'll do the museum tour and figure out if there's anything we're missing in the Ventimiglia timeline."

"There's plenty we're missing," Yolanda said. "I spoke with Gramma Rosi this morning."

"You tell her about the break-in?"

"That's why I called her. It's also why she's on her way. I'm surprised she's not here. No doubt she found someone to talk to. She can't make it from the front porch to the car without encountering a friend. Thelma might be the perfect guide. Gramma said that she worked in the courthouse when she was younger, and her father was best friends with Richard Ventimiglia."

Adam didn't get a chance to respond. A baby-blue Cadillac drove up, parked a good two feet from the curb and a white-haired gentleman opened the driver's-side door, ran around to the passenger side and helped Gramma Rosi to the sidewalk.

She wasn't smiling.

And she was a woman who always smiled.

The driver left his car in the street and stayed beside Rosi as she walked toward her house. "I want to check to see if anything else is missing," Rosi said after giving Yolanda a kiss on the cheek and nodding at Adam. "I've lots of photos and keepsakes I've left behind."

"Want me to park your car?" Adam offered Anthony Teasdale. Now that the man was closer, Adam recognized his fifth-grade teacher. The man was a good twenty years younger than Rosi but looked the same age. Probably teaching decades of ten- and eleven-year-olds had a lot to do with that.

"What's wrong with the way I parked the car?"

Adam glanced back at the two feet of pavement that separated the passenger side of the Cadillac from the end of the sidewalk. "Nothing," he answered.

Rosi and Yolanda took off up the steps, with Adam and Mr. Teasdale following. Yolanda had an arm across her grandmother's shoulder and was busy assuring Rosi that nothing was missing. Rosi was grumbling that the police hadn't stayed around long enough for her to arrive.

"The sheriff himself came," Yolanda said, "and filled out a report. But he got a call and was needed somewhere else."

It took a good half hour before Rosi was convinced that everything in the second story was in place. She didn't even want to go up to the attic. "I wouldn't know where to start. Besides, lots of stuff up there isn't even ours."

"Really?" Yolanda jumped on that. "Then why is it up there?"

For a moment it didn't appear that Rosi would add anything else. But Mr. Teasdale sidled up beside her and said, "Rosalee, tell them what you told me as we were driving here."

"The Ventimiglias moved out very quickly. They left quite a few things behind. My father moved most of it into the carriage house and into the attic. Over the years, I'm pretty sure we've forgotten what's theirs and what's ours.

Makes me wonder if Ivy really is back and looking for something that is hers."

"Why wouldn't she just knock on the door and ask for it?" Yolanda asked. Adam was thinking the same thing.

"The Ventimiglias didn't leave on the best of terms with Scorpion Ridge, and there's some bad blood between our families."

"Why?"

It took Gramma Rosi a few moments to answer. "It offended the Ventimiglias that our family went from working for them to owning what had been theirs."

"That makes no sense. They left the town, nobody remembers—"

Rosi held up a hand. "Enough people remember. Plus, Ivy grew up in this house. Rightly so, she'd feel resentment. What happened was through no fault of hers."

"What happened?" Yolanda asked.

It was Mr. Teasdale who answered, "The stock market crash of '29 set Richard back, and the family fortune was never the same."

Adam frowned. Mr. Teasdale was a good twenty years younger than Rosi Acura. "How do you know all that?"

"My father was the town historian for about twenty years," Teasdale said. "I remember him talking about the Ventimiglias at the kitchen table. They were quite a family. Royalty, really, when it comes to a small town like Scorpion Ridge. They were the family that made all the decisions, many quite bad."

"Like?" Adam asked.

"Richard Ventimiglia, quite frankly, could be bought. His decisions weren't always based on the greater need, more on the greater greed. Also, he made promises that he never kept, like improving schools and instituting fair practice in labor for non-whites."

"Yet he remained in office?" Yolanda was amazed.

"He had power. It's a hard thing to fight," Mr. Teasdale said. "Here's something you probably haven't heard before. More than one man thought that Richard Ventimiglia was responsible for the courthouse fire."

Gramma Rosi nodded solemnly. "My father did."

"All the marriage certificates, wills, court records, deeds and tax records were lost."

Adam suddenly understood.

"So the companion book that Ivy was looking for might really be something that belongs to her?"

"Could be," Gramma Rosi agreed. "I wonder what could be in the book that makes her want it now?"

"You know," Adam reminded them, "we're not certain there is a book, outside of the one she left behind."

"She said she was looking for it. She offered to search through the inventory I'd not yet shelved," Yolanda reminded him.

"Then why leave this one behind?" Adam pulled his backpack from the floor and opened it, quickly retrieving the book Ivy'd left.

"Any chance she didn't leave it?" Mr. Teasdale said, taking the book from Adam and opening it. For the first time Adam felt concern. It was a very old book and not everyone was familiar with how to treat it with respect. He needn't have worried. Mr. Teasdale handled the blue text almost reverently.

"No one else was there besides Adam and me," Yolanda interjected. "Gramma Rosi was outside. She couldn't have made it inside and back out again in the short amount of time I was away from the children's section. And there's no way I would have accidentally left it in there. Plus, it was on the floor."

Almost in sync, their eyes scanned the room. Yolanda had plants, shelves, small tables and floor lamps. Nothing was out of place. Nothing was on the floor. The only object that didn't act as if it belonged was Gulliver, who—as if he sensed an audience—skidded into the base of a floor lamp, making it wobble, and then jumped on the bottom shelf and tried to hide between two books.

"I took inventory from four other chests," Yolanda said. "I wrote all the titles down. If I can find her again, I'll return them all to her."

"This book is awesome," Mr. Teasdale said. "I can't believe the artwork."

"Agatha Fitzsimmons wants me to enlarge many of them and then put on a show at City Hall," said Adam.

Mr. Teasdale glanced up, his eyes wide and a smile spread across his face. "Have you been to the museum? Some of these photos look like old photographs we've spread through the main room."

"We have a private tour—" Adam checked his watch "—in thirty minutes. Thelma's taking us around."

"She'll do a good job. She knows lots of town history. Take the book. I think you'll be surprised by the detail and will enjoy doing a comparison."

"I'll hate parting with this book," Adam admitted. "It's been a step back in time and art. And it's full of mystery. We've a Chester who nobody's heard of, yet his name is on the courthouse wall. We've a Richard who wasn't a nice guy. We've an Ivy who seems to be able to disappear. And we've a Woodhull who died mysteriously."

"Oh, my," Rosi said, sinking down onto the step of the staircase and staring up, her gaze turning to Adam and then at Yolanda. "Nothing good will come of you two digging around that particular grave."

CHAPTER TEN

ALL GRAMMA ROSI would say after that was that, yes, Woodhull's body had been found in a well, and yes, the family had moved soon after.

Yolanda remembered something that Loretta had said—no one had been unhappy to see the Ventimiglias leave. What a sad legacy.

"Tell Thelma I said hi," Gramma Rosi said, a semblance of her natural humor resurfacing, as Mr. Teasdale opened the front door for her. "She'll have some interesting info on Richard, the father. He was her godfather, fat lot of good it did her."

Yolanda and Adam followed Rosi and Mr. Teasdale to the car, almost like an old married couple saying goodbye to their relatives. Again, Yolanda felt the strange feeling of "togetherness" with Adam. She was almost as disturbed by it as she was the intimacy Mr. Teasdale and her grandmother seemed to share.

In a daze, Yolanda grabbed her purse and followed Adam to his mother's Cavalier, grumbling, "I can't believe I let you talk me into taking the afternoon off. I open tomorrow. Do you hear me? *Tomorrow.*"

Adam walked to the passenger side and opened the door for her. "And for the last week all you've been doing is arranging books, re-arranging books and worrying that you need more books. I'm curious about this book and its mysteries."

"You're going to try and do the art display at the City Hall," she accused. "That's why you're curious. You don't need me along."

He paused, half in the car and half out. "If you don't want to go, stay behind. I thought you were interested."

Yolanda made a face. Never, in her whole life, had she felt such a loss of control. No one was acting as they should, not her grandmother, not Adam and not herself.

If she was honest, it was herself that she was most concerned about. Still, she got in and closed the door.

As Adam started the car, he didn't deny her accusation about wanting to do an exhibition. "It's a whole new venture. I've been thinking about how to stay in Scorpion Ridge and do what I love. This might be the answer."

"For now. But the project will only last a few months. And you're good at painting murals," she pointed out, "and they make money."

"Yes, but to earn money I'll have to go out of state and live a vagabond existence. I didn't realize until I was sitting across from my father this morning, seeing just how sick he was, that I don't want to travel the world at the expense of family."

"All you talked about growing up was getting away. You couldn't stand the restrictions your father put on you."

"That was the talk of a teenager who resented…" He stopped talking, an expression on his face she couldn't read, one way too serious for him.

"Go on," she urged.

"I resented Andy. Every piece of our life revolved around him. I thought it so unfair."

His expression contorted for a moment, but finally his forehead smoothed out and the easy grin she expected wedged back into place. "I also," he said, "if you recall, said I wanted to live on a yacht and sail into the Bermuda Triangle."

"You were joking about that one."

"I wasn't then," he said, sounding very serious for one Adam Snapp. "I now understand my dad was right. Andy, in many ways, made our family better. I wasted time and energy thinking life was unfair. People grow and change. You certainly have. I always pictured you in a pinstriped suit running a lawyer's office or something."

"I was going to be an accountant, but then my mom died and I inherited both her money and Gramma Rosi's house. Mom's will stipulated I had to do something I enjoyed with the money."

"And who was supposed to approve of what you *enjoy*? A lawyer?"

"No, Gramma Rosi. I think it's what made her decide to give me the house. We were sitting there talking about dreams. Seems I didn't really have any. She kept insisting good grades and a well-paying job weren't dreams but realities. She asked me to list three things I truly loved. I said books, Bridget's Animal Adventure and church."

Adam looked at her strangely. "That's what you love? What about going out with friends, getting a new car, or, since you love animals, going to Africa on a safari?"

"Be practical."

"If that's being practical, I'm glad I'm not."

"Gramma said that BAA was doing just fine, but that we could give a donation to the church, and that if I loved books so much, why not go back to school and major in library science or open a bookstore. I chose the bookstore."

"Still believe you made the right choice?"

"Well, it's certainly enabled me to go out with

a friend." She peeked over at him, wondering if he realized that she'd never been one to hang out with the other kids after classes let out. She'd always been working at the mini-manse, or the zoo, or some part-time job in town. She'd never seen the need for a new car. She drove the old Ford her mother left her. It was gold, four door, and got good gas mileage. Going to Africa on safari—the thought about took her breath away.

Her best friend, Janie Salazar, the sheriff's new wife, had gone to Africa and painted. She came home all aglow and ready to settle down.

"Africa might be fun," Yolanda allowed.

Adam might have had a few more things to say, but instead he pulled into a gravel parking lot that boasted three cars. Yolanda recognized one as belonging to the curator. She wasn't sure about the other two, but the Scorpion Ridge Museum was behind the Corner Diner.

Thelma Sheldon was waiting for them at the front desk. "It's not often enough," she said, "that locals take the time to come explore their heritage. I'm glad you're here."

"We've a bit of a motive," Yolanda said. She looked at Adam, and he produced the book. "We're trying to find out a bit more about Ivy Ventimiglia and her family."

Yolanda paused. Everyone they'd mentioned the name Ivy to had paused to murmur something along the lines of "now there's a name I've not heard in years." Not Thelma. She merely said, "About time someone took an interest in that story."

"We heard you had a personal connection to the Ventimiglias."

Thelma nodded. "Richard Ventimiglia borrowed money from my father the week before they moved. Of course, my father had no idea they were leaving town. We didn't hear from them again, and my father claimed he worked ten years longer, way past retirement, than he wanted to, because of the monetary setback."

"Must have been quite a bit of money," Yolanda remarked.

Thelma only nodded.

The Scorpion Ridge Historical Society Museum was in a turn-of-the-century adobe house. The first room they entered had at one time been a bedroom. Now it held a desk for the museum volunteer, a glass case where fragile and aged china was on display and a shelf with books. There were three books from a local author who wrote romance. They had nothing to do with Scorpion Ridge's history and everything to do with the people of Scorpion Ridge looking out for each other. There were also two nonfiction books about Scorpion Ridge. One was more or less a travel guide—places to see and stay. The other was a history text called *Scorpion Ridge Today and Yesterday.*

Yolanda took one of the dusty copies from the shelf and read the copyright date: nineteen seventy-nine. From the "real" today's standpoint, the book was about Scorpion Ridge and just yesterday.

"Have you read this?" Yolanda asked Thelma.

"Twice."

"Does it talk about the Ventimiglias?"

"Or the other founding families?" Adam added.

"There's a whole chapter on the Ventimiglias. You're in there, too, Adam. Or at least your ancestor Jedidiah is."

"The cow story." Adam nodded.

"Ivy said she'd come here looking for the book," Yolanda remembered.

"Not on my watch," Thelma said. "I'd have recognized her. I work Tuesday and Thursday. Adam, your grandmother—"

"Volunteers on Monday and Wednesday," Adam finished for her. "You're closed on Sunday. Maybe she came on a Saturday. Who's on duty then?"

"That would be Samuel Teasdale."

Yolanda and Adam looked at each other.

"That's how Mr. Teasdale knew you were a good guide, Thelma," Yolanda said.

"And," Adam added, "that explains how he knew some of the drawings in the book matched photographs on the wall."

"Samuel said I was a good guide?" Thelma looked quite happy with this.

"Mr. Teasdale wouldn't have recognized Ivy," Yolanda said. "She was way before his time."

"And you believe Ivy was here, in the museum?" Thelma went from happy to almost excited.

"It's possible," Adam said. "She's searching for a book about Scorpion Ridge history. One that might look a bit like this one."

He turned his backpack around and dug out the book. Thelma took it and started carefully skimming through the pages, sometimes stopping and squinting, other times appearing a bit perplexed.

"I recognize this one!" She held up a page where a horse and buggy were parked in front of what seemed to be a saloon. A man was standing by one of the wheels, wearing a top hat and leaning on a cane. "That was the minister at the old Scorpion Ridge Church."

"In front of a saloon?" Adam grinned.

"He went in there once a week and usually escorted about four of five of his flock from the room. My dad said the saloon owner once sent someone to beat him up. I can't remember the minister's name. I do remember that he wound up converting the man who'd been sent to beat him up. Oh, that was quite a story, quite a story."

"Be interesting to see that happening today," Adam said.

"And look at this one." Thelma held the book so they could see. "It's the front of your house, Yolanda. There's Richard and his wife. Ivy's sitting on the front porch step. Their son is by the front door."

"You'd think they'd pose together," Adam said. "There's no sense of togetherness. It's as if there's three different events happening. You have a photo of a husband and wife. Then you have a dreamy-daughter photo. Clearly, she's in another world."

"Ivy did dream."

"Then you have Woodhull." Adam leaned forward, studying the photo. "He's angled away from the others as if he can't be bothered with a family photo."

"Woodhull was what you call a black sheep." Thelma frowned. "He was older than me and used to tease me mercilessly until I hit my teens. Then he stopped."

"Why?" Yolanda asked.

"I begged Ivy to tell me, and she said he didn't think I was pretty enough to mess with."

"Idiot," Yolanda said.

"He went with your great-grandmother," Thelma told Adam. "She was about the prettiest girl in the town."

"You have any idea why they sold their house to Yolanda's great-grandparents?"

"That surprised the whole town, but lots of those old houses were being vacated. Their owners couldn't afford them. We lost our house about that time, too."

"Which house was yours?"

"Oh, it's long gone. Maybe it's in the book." She flipped over a few more pages before shaking her head.

"Could you take us around the museum?" Adam said. "We're most interested in the Ventimiglias, especially Ivy and her father."

"Strange that Ivy would show up now." Thelma led them into a long room that must have once been the living area. To the left was a trunk much like the ones in Yolanda's attic.

"Oh, these," Thelma said after Yolanda mentioned the resemblance. "Everyone owned these when I was young. Otis Wilson sold them in his store. This one came from the ruin of the courthouse fire. There were deeds and such in it. The only papers to survive."

Yolanda was interested, but Adam seemed to hang on every word.

"Like home ownership papers?" he asked.

"Yes."

Thelma went on, pointing out an old black stove that took up one wall and the photos on the wall behind it. There was an old table, scratched and sturdy. Candlesticks and lanterns took up most of its surface. A few school desks were pushed against the other walls. Old readers were opened on top. A few ink wells and feather pens rested in a deep ridge toward the top.

"This served as a school in the late eighteen hundreds," Thelma said proudly. "Scorpion Ridge has never been a ghost town."

"I thought Scorpion Ridge was founded in nineteen fifteen?" Yolanda mentioned.

"Oh, the Ventimiglias and Moores sure did change it from a one-horse town to a thriving community, but that was a few years after Arizona became a state. There were a few farm families hereabouts before that, not that the Ventimiglias or Moores recognized or gave credit to them."

The second bedroom of the house had more to do with the history of the town's founding fathers. Sure enough, at least judging by Adam's reactions, some of the photos matched drawings from the book.

Yolanda took the room in quickly, moving from old Bibles, to calling cards, to old cameras. Adam never left the old photos and old oil paintings, and Thelma didn't leave his side. After about ten minutes, it became clear that one painting mesmerized them more than any other.

"That was the school that took the place of this one. It was three times the size because the town had more commerce by then." She looked at Yolanda. "Though it was still mostly farming."

Yolanda figured that should mean something to her, but it didn't. She moved close to the painting. It depicted an old-fashioned high school, two stories, with tall windows and four white pillars in front. Its front lawn held at least thirty people. She recognized Richard from the previous painting. His wife, too. Ivy was there, but again, off to the side. Just down from her were at least ten other young ladies, a gaggle that Ivy clearly didn't belong to.

"That's GG," Adam said, pointing to a pretty blonde with ringlets and wearing vivid blue. She was in the center of the gaggle.

"I'm right here." Thelma indicated a short, brown-haired girl to the left of Loretta. "It was November, and we were putting on some play. It was a huge event for the town. Remember, we didn't have movie theaters or video games. My father was going to give a speech before the play. Mr. Ventimiglia had provided lemonade and sweets. Everyone came."

"Is that Woodhull?" Yolanda asked, her finger almost brushing a dark-haired young man leaning against a tree. He wore a loose white shirt, brown pants and large black boots. He was staring at the young women, maybe Loretta specifically.

"That's him." Thelma looked at Adam. "He had the lead in the play. I don't even remember what it was."

"He's not dressed up," Yolanda said.

Thelma laughed. "One of the church ladies painted this, just for fun. She was pretty good. Did most of the paintings we have here. Of course, she might draw a dress you'd long outgrown or make your hair style the wrong decade. Do you recognize him?" She pointed to a chubby boy standing to the left of Woodhull. He held a glass of lemonade and something else.

"A cookie," Thelma answered the question before Yolanda could ask. "That's Otis Wilson."

"My neighbor," Yolanda exclaimed. "He's always coming over to my house and foraging for food."

"We always said Otis had one hollow leg that he kept trying to fill with food." Thelma gazed at the picture and smiled. "He looked up to Woodhull, ran around with him some. Otis, though, never stood up for himself. I think he admired the fact that what Woodhull wanted, Woodhull got. Otis had feelings for Ivy, I think, but her family never would have allowed the match. Once Ivy moved away, he stopped smiling." Thelma squinted at the painting. "The only reason I know this is supposed to be the night of the play is the lemonade glasses some people are holding. That, and the principal is standing at the door welcoming people. It was the only night he acted welcoming."

"Is it a fairly accurate depiction of what the townspeople looked like?"

"Spot on," Thelma said. "The colors are perfect. Loretta's favorite dress was this blue one. I'm wearing the gloves that I thought made me look so grown-up. Woodhull always wore those black boots. They had three-inch heels so he'd appear taller. See, he would have been about Yolanda's height. My, though, he thought he was big."

"People don't like to talk about him." Yolanda adjusted her glasses and bent to examine the image of Woodhull more closely. He seemed like an ordinary guy. Someone she could sit down next to and have a conversation with. "Why? I mean, I realize he was unkind, but really, both my Gramma Rosi and Loretta seem to want to avoid his name. What did he do?"

"Funny," Thelma said. "It's been decades since all this was brought up. It's not a story I tell when we do tours here. It's sad history, best not shared."

Adam nodded. "The Ventimiglias' history had been all but forgotten until Ivy showed up here last Monday. If she wants to make sure her family is not portrayed in a negative way, why make waves?"

"And why come to my house?" Yolanda said. "It hasn't belonged to her family in more than fifty years. Gramma said it might have to do with the fact that she worked there when she was young."

"The people in your family always were hard workers. My, my, it was like you were grown up at five."

"Gramma started working when she was seven."

"And worked that same job until she was fifteen," Adam remembered.

"Which was about the time when your great-grandparents purchased it from the Ventimiglias," Thelma added.

Adam looked perplexed. "If Rosi's father had money for the house, he'd have had money before the purchase, enough money so his young daughter could quit working."

"People didn't take money for granted back

then. It wasn't like now when you can quit Mc-Donald's and start the next day at a Burger King. Plus, there was no unemployment. When you're raised knowing that money is hard to come by, you keep thinking that way even when you have money."

"But," Adam pointed out, "Rosi's not in this photo. Is that because she didn't go to high school?"

Thelma's eyes crinkled. "Many kids in those days dropped out young and went to work. Your grandmother was one of them, Yolanda. You remind me of her, you know. When she was younger."

"Too young," Yolanda said in a soft voice. It surprised her, this sudden insight into her grandmother. "All she could talk about as I was growing up was how proud she was that I stayed in school."

"Yolanda, honey," Thelma said, "I think you were the first girl to graduate in your family."

"My mom didn't graduate? She talked about it."

"She made it all the way to eleventh grade. So did her sister."

"Freda quit school, too?"

"She ran away to Hollywood. Said she was going to be a star. We all believed her. Boy, could that girl act."

"I've met Freda," Adam said, "and can totally imagine her on the big screen. But why did Yolanda's mother quit school?"

"I don't rightly know," Thelma admitted. "She ran away. She didn't come back to Scorpion Ridge until fifteen years later. She worked here in town for a while, cleaning. She was contracted to clean City Hall, which is how she and I became acquainted. I worked there, too, at the time."

"She never told me any of this," Yolanda said, trying to picture her mom years younger and struggling to make ends meet. Maybe that's why saving had become so important to her. To Adam, Yolanda muttered, "Mom didn't like it when I started working for the Moores. She said there was no room for advancement or betterment there."

"Didn't Ruth help send you to school?"

"Yes."

"Not all bosses or Moores are like Ruth," Thelma said. "Your mother knew that, probably more than anyone."

"I'm pretty sure," Yolanda admitted, "that my mother hoped my dream would take me out of state, or at least out of Scorpion Ridge."

Thelma nodded. "She sure wanted to get away herself, but if I ever brought up what happened in the years she was gone, she'd walk away. Then she quit one day out of the blue, no notice or anything. She got a job working for Ruth Moore, married your father and a few years later had you. Sure surprised all of us. She was over forty when you were born. I never did find out why she left Scorpion Ridge or why she came back."

"What was your best guess?" Adam pressed. "Did she have any girlfriends she might have confided in?"

"Adam!" Yolanda scolded. "Thelma said she didn't know."

"No, she said she wasn't sure. There's a difference."

But Thelma would say no more.

ALL IN ALL, Adam surmised, the trip to the museum had been informative. As they headed for the front, Yolanda purchased one of the history books and he considered what they'd learned and what they hadn't.

"Any chance there is a print of the painting of the high school? I'd love to have one."

"No, it's one of a kind. Sure brings back memories looking at it, but also makes me feel a bit like living history."

"The papers that were in that trunk. Are they here in the museum?" Adam asked.

"No, they'd be at the courthouse."

Adam nodded and went on. "Is Chester Ventimiglia featured in any of these paintings or photos?"

"Chester," Thelma repeated. "I don't believe I've heard of him."

"Maybe he was a relative of Richard's?"

"It's possible, but my father always said Richard won every argument because he'd never lost one since he had no one to argue with."

"I'm an only child," Yolanda said, "and I know how to lose arguments." She shot Adam a look, one he correctly interpreted.

"No wonder I have such a hard time arguing with you," Adam agreed. "You think you know how to lose. If you really lost arguments I'd not have painted those saloon doors Kool-Aid-orange."

"It's a pretty color," she defended.

Adam took the books from Yolanda's hand—including one of the romances—and added them to his backpack. "What about how Woodhull died? And what did he do to make so many people dislike him? You never answered that question, Thelma."

Thelma rested her elbows on the front desk, suddenly looking tired. Adam started to say "Never mind" but she interrupted. "All I've heard is that he took what he wanted, and because he was young, he wasn't very good about hiding his sins. As for how he died, the town was divided on that. Half thought he'd been pushed or dumped into the well. Half thought he'd been drunk and fell in."

"What do you think?"

"My father made a good point at the time. The town of Scorpion Ridge no longer used well water. There was no reason for him to be near that well."

"Was it on a main path?"

"No, it's behind Tucker's Auto. Pretty sure it's still there, all boarded up."

"Your father have any idea who might have wanted Woodhull dead?"

Thelma gave a sad little grimace. "Word was he'd gotten some girl in Gesippi pregnant. There was talk of a forced marriage and rumors of him refusing to take responsibility. But nobody knew who the girl was, and no one we hung around with had a baby nine months later."

"When did he die, Thelma?"

"I believe it was 1944, or thereabouts."

Adam did some quick calculations and realized that Thelma had indeed known someone who'd had a baby nine months later. But it wasn't a girl her crowd would have hung around with. Adam just couldn't prove it yet, and he wasn't sure wanted to.

CHAPTER ELEVEN

THE PROBLEM WITH growing up, Adam thought, besides realizing that all the adults you'd thought were perfect really weren't, was that responsibilities became so important and time sensitive that using a skateboard to get from point A to point B became impossible. He'd rarely managed to utilize his board since his return. There'd been days, just six years ago, when he'd skateboarded from his house to BAA.

It had taken him over an hour, and he'd loved every minute of it.

But back then, he'd had hours to spare. He decided how to spend his hours. And he'd had no bills or responsibilities.

That was a luxury he no longer had, but he really wanted an hour on his skateboard today so he could think about everything that had happened without distraction. Just him and the board, no cell phone, no six students following his every move, no Yolanda looking kissable. No father looking thinner.

"What are your plans today?" his father asked as he walked into the room.

"I'm going to BAA. I want to talk to Luke about the mural at Huckabee's. I also want to see if he's discovered anything about the Snapps owning the land, or how the Moores got it. After that, I'll teach the ten o'clock class. I'm really starting to get back in shape." He flexed a muscle. "When that finishes, I'll head over to Twice Told Tales and tell Yolanda what I've found."

"Why don't you just invite her along?"

Adam wanted to, but today was her grand opening, and if he waited, it might be a week before he could find time to talk to Ruth.

"Her store opens today." Adam checked his watch. "In three hours, she switches the sign to Open and then there's no turning back."

"Maybe I'll drive over and see what she has in stock. Since I'm not able to work much, I have time to read." His dad chuckled. "I guess there's always a positive."

The alarm sounded. Any minute Andy would come into the kitchen. "You want me to stick around and help?" Adam offered.

"No, I like making breakfast."

As Adam headed for the back door, he glanced at his skateboard leaning against the patio wall. One thing for sure, skateboards weren't meant for two. Maybe he didn't miss it at all.

A few minutes later his mother's car bumped over a road the town kept promising to pave. BAA wasn't open to the public yet, but Adam knew the code to one of the back gates. He let himself in and went looking for Luke Rittenhouse, who'd been his friend for well over a decade.

Before they'd worked together at BAA, they'd met at Snapp's Studio. Luke's little sister had had Down Syndrome. Luke had driven her to a special class for children with disabilities. Adam had been there with his twin brother. At their first meeting, Adam had been angry and refusing to participate, letting his father know that Tae Kwon Do was Andy's thing, not his. Luke, still in high school and much more supportive of his sister than Adam had been with his brother, had taken Adam under his wing.

And then when Adam and his father had their major falling-out, Adam had moved into the caretaker's cabin at BAA and started working.

In some ways Luke had saved Adam.

And was still saving him.

Peacocks screamed; they were everywhere. A large cat offered the morning a yowl, but Adam couldn't identify who the culprit was. He'd never been as good at "Guess the animal that made the noise" as the other employees at BAA. A rabbit followed him to the snake house.

It was always best to look for Luke there first. Nine times out of ten, you'd find him.

Sure enough, BAA's director was with his anaconda, Rexette, changing the water and substrate.

It took Adam maybe two minutes to negotiate a space with Luke for a weekend caricature business.

"Sure, do it. Our visitors loved it when you did that before, and now that you've built a name, it'll be even better. We'll put some of your artwork on display. How's the flagstone painting going?"

"Not at all. It's not what I want to do."

"You want to be renovating Yolanda's place and drawing caricatures?"

"No, I want to be doing anything that earns me money. My dad's sick, sicker than most people realize. I'm thinking about taking Willy Huckabee up on his offer to paint a few murals for him. He offered me the same fee as what I was paid for the Wildrose job."

Luke let out a whistle. "I'm sure glad I got you when you worked for room and board."

"Things were easier then," Adam agreed.

"How sick is your dad?" Luke asked, emptying the small pool that Rexette loved to lounge in. When Adam didn't answer, he said, "Silly snake's getting water blisters, he's in here so much."

Adam looked at the snake. It took four people to lift him from the box and do the snake show. His favorite food was frozen rat. He, if in a bad mood, would try to bite the hand that fed him: attacking head-on or from the side. His life span was roughly thirty years. He had about twenty years left. Fifteen more than Adam's dad had.

"Honestly...my dad's dying. He's scheduled for surgery, but even if that goes well at most he'll only have an extra five years."

For a few moments, the only sound was the hiss of ventilation. The smell of snake and man. Right now the snake house was empty. In a few hours, it would be full of visitors.

"Then I'm glad you came back," Luke finally said. "I always knew you had it in you."

It wasn't the response Adam wanted. He wanted Luke to mutter a bad word, rare but possible, or say how unfair life was, or shake his fist at God. All things Adam wanted to do but hadn't yet. Adam started to turn, walk away, wallow in the self-pity that had been threatening to boil over but had been subdued by too many commitments.

Luke made it worse by adding, "You'd better hurry up and get married and give the man a grandkid. That'll make him happy. What are you waiting for? I've never seen Yolanda happier."

"Yolanda's happy because she's opened a bookstore and fulfilled a dream. It has nothing to do with me." Even as Adam said the words, he wondered if they were true. Amidst everything he was going through, job insecurity and Dad's illness, Yolanda was the bright light in his life.

"Yeah," Luke continued, "I hear you were the first to respond yesterday when her place was broken into."

"She called me—"

"Called you before she called the police."

"I was closer!"

"I also hear you two had a private tour of the museum with Thelma."

"We're trying to figure out who the book belongs to. By the way, have you found out any more about the Ventimiglias owning the land BAA is on?"

"I asked Ruth about that." Luke finished repositioning all of Rexette's belongings and motioned for Adam to follow him out of the room. Luke led Adam to the next enclosure. This one held a crocodile monitor. Eight feet long and growing, this one, named Ginny from New Guinea, lived in an enclosure four times as tall as Rexette's. The enclosure held a tree, a rock tower and stairs. The monitor enjoyed climbing.

"She's semifriendly," Luke said, "but I always put her in a handling cage before I go in. I want to keep my fingers." Before he stepped in, he pulled his cell phone from his back pocket and punched a number. After a moment, he said, "Ruth, I'm in the snake house. Adam's here with me. You want to come talk to him?"

Adam couldn't hear Ruth's response, but soon Luke said, "Okay," and disconnected. Turning to Adam, he said, "She's over at the clinic. Why don't you head over there?"

"Thanks, I always appreciate your help." Adam turned to leave, but Luke called him back.

"You're strong, both physically and mentally. Your father is very lucky to have a son like you."

"I caused him a lot of grief when I was younger."

"Then cause him a lot of happiness now that you're older and wiser."

Wiser? Adam could only hope.

He was halfway to the veterinarian clinic before he thought to check the time. As much as he wanted to hear what Ruth had to say, he didn't want to miss his ten o'clock Tae Kwon Do class. Quickly, he called his mother—already at

Snapp's Studio—and asked her to have Andy get things ready for the first class of the day.

"Don't worry," she said. "Your dad's here, too, and if you're a few minutes late, he can direct Andy in leading the class. It's been done before."

But not often, Adam knew. Andy was quite capable, unless something went wrong. Then he shut down. They made sure to always have someone there in case that happened. Today it would be Adam.

Ruth Dunbar was sitting in a chair feeding a lamb. BAA had several of them, not just because of their connection to BAA's name but because Ruth just plain liked them. "This one's allergic to her mother's milk. We're trying cow's milk."

"If it grows up to be a sheep that moos, I'm blaming you," Adam said.

"You never change," Ruth accused. She got up and put the lamb in a little pen outside. "I'm really hoping this one becomes a pet. That would be great fun."

"Meredith won't allow it," Adam said, referring to the head keeper who believed that animals were happiest in their natural habitat. She was of the opinion that only those who had no chance of surviving in the wild belonged here.

She also thought that the horses and sheep belonged on farms.

"She's too busy planning a wedding to care," Ruth scoffed. Coming back into the clinic, Ruth leaned against a counter and looked at Adam. "You've opened quite a can of worms, you know."

"Just trying to figure out what's going on."

"When Luke mentioned that the Ventimiglia name was on the deed of BAA, I about fell over. I had no idea. I headed into town and went to the courthouse. Looks like you're going to suffer from the same historical destruction as I did. You did know the courthouse burned down in the forties?"

Luke nodded. He'd heard more about the fire in the last week than he had his whole life.

"When I signed over the habitat and minimanse to Luke, I found out the old courthouse fire destroyed the original deed, but no one was too fussy about it then because no money was exchanging hands between Luke and me. Until you brought it up."

"Okay," Adam said slowly, figuring he'd not like what came next.

"I owned," Ruth corrected herself, "I *thought* I owned the property between the habitat and that ostrich compound. But when I went to the courthouse a few days ago, I found out that the town only has a deed that was reconstructed a good two years after the fire, and it does not have a signature! Can you believe it? So now I have a lawyer helping me through census reports and taxes to prove the land is mine. Unfortunately, that's where Luke saw the name Ventimiglia. It's on the reconstructed deed, something about a tax lien."

"So that land might belong to the Ventimiglias?"

"Since Luke told me about your quest, I've made copies of everything and am going over all the documents. It seems that crook Richard Ventimiglia put a lien on the land, saying John's father owed back taxes. If there's one thing I can tell you about the Moores, it's that they took care of what they owned and their money. They'd not have neglected to pay taxes."

"So the Ventimiglias own it," Adam said again.

"Apparently, they might. Good thing there's none of them left. My lawyer figures the Moores' ownership is grandfathered in. He's also looking into what else Richard Ventimiglia did all those years ago."

"And you were going to tell me this when?"

"As soon as I had something solid."

"You have anything solid now?"

"Since you're here and wanting to know, the

lawyer discovered something else. It seems your family owns the old Ventimiglia home."

Adam almost laughed. He stopped just in time. Nothing, nothing was funny about this.

"You mean the Victorian I'm restoring?"

"Yup," Ruth said.

"It has a lien?"

"No, there's a record of a transfer of title from one Woodhull Ventimiglia to one Loretta Munro."

"Yolanda's house," Adam whispered.

"Maybe not," Ruth said. "Could be your great-grandmother's house. She was supposed to marry Woodhull. That might be why the house was deeded to her."

"But Yolanda's family has been living in it for decades. They bought it from Richard. What they've paid in taxes alone has paid for the house over and over."

"It seems Richard did a bit of double-dealing and deeded the house twice. He probably did a deed to Yolanda's family, but later, pulled it and filled a different one. It was easier, for the men in power, to get away with such dishonest practices. Add to that a fire. Well, now you'll have to meet with an arbitrator. That's what I'll need to do if we find a Ventimiglia relative still alive."

Adam knew indeed one was still alive. Maybe more if Chester had really existed.

"And the arbitrator will do what?" Adam kept his voice steady, but his mind was probing a dozen scenarios, none of them good.

"Find a solution that meets the needs of both parties in dispute."

Adam didn't want to be in dispute with Yolanda. He had better things in mind.

"Can we just sign the Victorian over to her?"

"That's up to Loretta. Your great-grandmother is a Realtor. She'll know the worth of that Victorian."

"Which is?"

"At the least, five hundred thousand dollars. And with all the work that's been put into it over the last six months, more like eight hundred thousand."

"Even in this rinky-dink town?" Adam was amazed.

"People from California love to buy winter homes."

Adam was aware of that, and so was Loretta. When she found out she owned the Victorian, she'd be sad for Yolanda and her family, but she'd be thinking about her son and the hospital bills. She couldn't just turn her back on five hundred thousand dollars.

Perhaps she'd offer Yolanda something fair, but not enough to replace a dream.

Adam didn't know what was fair. All he

knew was that he was responsible for much of the work that had ratcheted the price up. He'd helped improve a dream that his family might very well destroy.

THE SUN SPREAD rays of gold across the front lawn. Yolanda couldn't have asked for better weather for her grand opening. Everything looked crisp and new and inviting. A small crowd waited outside the bookstore. Most of them were friends of her grandmother's. All of them were readers.

Yolanda made a mental note to put a few more chairs and benches on the front porch. Hopefully, there'd be many a morning when readers would gather in wait. Adam would be here in about an hour, after he finished teaching a Tae Kwon Do class. She'd tell him her idea... he could paint the chairs to match the pillows she'd buy.

After making sure Gulliver was tucked into his bed by the desk where she'd be working, Yolanda unlocked the door and poked her head out. "Come on in."

"I've been looking forward to seeing what you and Adam have done," Thelma said. "I hear he's quite a craftsman."

As soon as they entered, the women—as well as two men—scattered. They ohhed and ahhed over the colors, though most didn't appear to appreciate her orange saloon doors. Could Adam be right that the color just didn't work?

"Well," Yolanda said to Gulliver, hiding from all the noise under a chair, "it's our first day, and we've got lots of customers."

Two grandmothers were in the children's area exclaiming over Junie B. Jones and wondering what the Minecraft books were. Five women were in the romance section already arguing about which was better: contemporary or suspense. All asked her where the large-print selection was.

"I'll have that next month," Yolanda promised, already rethinking bookshelf space.

Willy Huckabee, who owned the ostrich farm just outside town, sat cross-legged in the history section. Around her mother's age, he was probably the youngest patron.

She touched his shoulder. "Can I help you?" He'd snuck by her. He was a huge person, so she was a bit surprised.

"No, I'm just trying to figure out if there's anything in Scorpion Ridge's history that will help make my ostrich farm more successful. I mean, some idiot brought camels to the desert. Why aren't ostriches appreciated more?"

Yolanda wasn't sure she quite got the connection, but she left him in peace. A few minutes later Gramma Rosi arrived, greeting everyone as if she were the hostess of a grand party. Sales started soon after, and Gramma Rosi shooed Yolanda away.

Walking from room to room, Yolanda handed out her first-day dollar off coupon. Adam arrived after that, gave an appreciative whistle at the crowd—or maybe it was at her—and disappeared into the kitchen.

He was working there today, repainting two of the walls that had suffered some dings after her new appliances were installed. She hurried after him to tell him to be careful. The man who'd delivered her appliances had managed to break a glass covering from the chandelier. Then he'd knocked one of her favorite yellow coffee cups from the kitchen table. It had shattered into a hundred pieces. When she'd moved into Gramma Rosi's house, she'd had three of those mugs. Now one remained. The third had disappeared with the mysterious Ivy.

Glancing around the kitchen, it looked as if everything was in place. "Just making sure. I cleared the counters last night, like you asked."

"Easier to repaint a whole wall than to make a repair. You can always tell the difference."

She'd started to argue but remembered that they had leftover paint. Besides, she wanted him here today. It was only yesterday that she'd discovered the empty trunk.

The kitchen's swinging door was still swinging when Adam returned, motioning to her. She stepped over Willy Huckabee, who seemed to be skimming through every book, and looked at what Adam was pointing at.

Make that *who* Adam was pointing at.

Otis Wilson stood in her kitchen, his nose in the refrigerator, going through the contents. "Not much here," he complained.

"He's right," Adam agreed.

"If you wouldn't keep dragging me places, I'd have time to go grocery shopping." Yolanda gently backed Otis away from her fridge and closed the door. "You can't keep walking in uninvited," she told Otis. "Please stay in the bookstore area, and let me know you arrive." She softened her voice. "I've got doughnuts." She led him to the front door. After settling him in the rocker, she took out her cell phone and called his son to come get him.

Otis's son was the man who often proposed to Yolanda, although he was already married. He also wrote for the town's twice-a-week newspaper, and just might now have to write a favorable column of Twice Told Tales. Yolanda handed Otis two doughnuts.

"I thought there'd be a free breakfast," Otis

complained, as she settled down beside him and arranged a napkin in his lap. His hands were shaking, but his eyes were bright. "Her grandmother always fed me."

Yolanda hadn't heard Adam come around the side of the house.

"Rosi doesn't live here anymore," Adam reminded the elderly man.

Otis harrumphed, "This house was never really hers anyway."

Yolanda gasped. The statement took her right back to the morning Ivy Ventimiglia had come by. "What do you mean? My great-grandfather bought the house," Yolanda said indignantly.

"Trying to come up in the world, he was," Otis agreed. "And not by the best means."

Luckily, Otis's son came up the steps just then. He rolled his eyes. "Dad, how did you get all the way here?"

"I walked. Did me good."

Then, as if he'd not just told her that her ancestors were undeserving, Otis sweetly thanked her for the doughnuts.

"It's just town people," Adam soothed, but Yolanda thought he looked distracted. This wasn't the Adam who had so recently kissed her; at least ten times today she'd touched her lips remembering. And wishing for more. Maybe he already regretted their intimacy.

"Last mural I did," Adam said, "in Chicago, almost got canceled. Everyone on the committee had some piece of history they thought had to be portrayed. Most of them were selfish, trying to paint the town and their heritage as something it wasn't. Man, did they bicker. I did almost fifty thumbnails before they approved the final."

"How long does it take you to do a thumbnail?"

"About three hours."

"You spent almost a month just getting a thumbnail they could agree on?"

"I did. Sure made me miss Luke. He just nodded at me and advised that I not go too outlandish."

Yolanda remembered the bench Adam had designed and painted. Situated right outside one of the food kiosks, it actually made a fart noise when a person sat down.

"Yolanda, I've a question!"

"Coming." Turning to Adam, Yolanda said, "When did you get so wise?"

"Around the time I started getting closer to you." He said it much too seriously. Yolanda's heart, already torn by what was sensible compared to what was desirable, broke a little.

Conflicted. She was definitely conflicted. When she'd believed their relationship was strictly platonic, it had been safe to befriend him. Now that friendship was turning into something else. And all she could think of was her mother saying, "Men leave."

The rest of the morning passed in a blur. Willy Huckabee purchased three books. Two had to do with Scorpion Ridge; one had to do with animals.

Adam's great-grandmother swooped in, checked out what her friends were purchasing, made sure everybody admired Adam's work and swooped out again.

"She's afraid you'll ask her more questions about Woodhull," Gramma Rosi surmised.

"That's not it." Yolanda watched Loretta get into her car. "She said the other day that she wants to know why Ivy is here just as much as we do."

Gramma Rosi just shook her head.

Sure enough, later in the morning Otis Wilson's son came back and took a few photos of her grand opening for the paper. Just before noon, Adam sauntered into the main room carrying take-out pizza that Yolanda had ordered for all of them. She tried to give him some money from the cash register, but he waved her off.

Gramma Rosi promptly sat down with some of her friends on the porch to eat and chat. For dessert they had the brownies Rosi'd baked to help her granddaughter out. Yolanda didn't mention that no "real" customers would get a taste, since Gramma Rosi only gave them to her friends.

The bookstore continued to be busy, as a few people came during their noon break. All said they were glad to have a bookstore in the neighborhood. Most purchased at least one book.

Somewhat aghast, Yolanda shared with Adam, "You were right. Except for romance, I've sold more horror than anything else. What's wrong with people?"

"Maybe we like to be scared." Then he added, "Better to be scared by things that aren't real. Being scared in real life doesn't stop on page three hundred and twelve with the words 'The End.'"

Yolanda thought about yesterday. The feeling she'd had when she realized the books were gone and that somebody had been in her house. She'd like a "The End" for that story.

"Maybe you like to be scared."

Then, because Gramma Rosi remained with her friends, Yolanda took over the front counter, though Gulliver garnered much more attention than she did.

She'd been planning to close at six, but her place still had customers, so she simply sat on the stool behind the cash register and watched her dream take wings.

What a great day. She'd talked books with Mr. Teasdale, who claimed writers were changing history. She'd pored over a devotional with Thelma Sheldon, who thanked them again for visiting the museum.

"It's been a long time since I really looked at that painting," Thelma remarked.

"Was that play put on before or after the courthouse burned down?" Adam asked.

Thelma smiled. "Oh, that was before. The courthouse burned a year later, just a few days after Ivy and her parents moved. I just want to cry when I think of what the museum might have on display if we hadn't lost so much during that fire."

Adam glanced across at Yolanda and muttered, "The people of Scorpion Ridge are still losing things because of a fire that happened back in the nineteen forties."

Thelma gave him a confused look as she left Twice Told Tales. By seven-thirty, only a few people remained. Mr. Teasdale came and picked Gramma Rosi up. Next, Adam carried out a box of books for a young mother who had gotten carried away in the children's department.

Then it was just the two of them.

"I'd better go," Adam said. "I promised Dad I'd go on a bike ride with Andy tonight."

"Adam, what's wrong?"

"Andy thinks he's out of shape. Dad used to go bike riding with him—"

"I'm not talking about Andy. I'm talking about today. Something's bothering you, and you might as well tell me. Did you find something out? Something I should know?"

He hesitated, and Yolanda watched as his eyes moved around the room, taking in her books, the cashier stand, the bright orange saloon doors that she'd soon allow him to repaint any way he wanted.

"Want to go get something to eat?" Adam finally suggested. "It's been a while since that pizza. Plus, I didn't manage to snag either a doughnut or one of your gramma's brownies. I always do better talking when I have food in front of me."

"Are we going to the Corner Diner?" Yolanda asked.

"It's that or the sandwich shop."

Yolanda thought for a moment. "There's a new Italian place on Third Street. Just opened a week ago. Want to try it? My treat."

"Sounds good."

"Let me run upstairs and change my clothes and freshen up. You want to do the same?"

Adam looked down at her clothes, somewhat surprised. "Neither of us is dirty."

Yolanda laughed. "Give me a minute."

Running up the stairs, she felt almost giddy, but really, this wasn't a date. This was just two people who worked together going out after work. For the purpose of information-sharing. Surely if this were a special evening, he'd have gone home, changed into something a little nicer, combed his hair.

She'd not left any lights on upstairs, and she'd not been back up here since early this morning. The evening sky was just beginning to cast soft gray shadows along the floor. Yolanda got to the room she'd claimed. It had been hers as a child when she came over. Eventually, she'd move to the master, but it still felt too much like Gramma Rosi's.

Opening the door, she stepped in, telling herself not to overdress, not to act overeager; after all, this was Adam Snapp: Mr. I Don't Care.

Her feet froze just past the doorway. About thirty books lay strewn on the bed. Slowly she moved toward them, trying to remember if she'd left books there this morning but knowing she hadn't.

The smell of old paper, mildew and dust wafted to her nose, and she sneezed. It turned into a half scream as she realized what she was looking at.

The books from the trunk.

Returned.

ADAM WASN'T SURE whether to be relieved or annoyed at the reappearance of the books. One thing for sure, telling Yolanda that she might not be the owner of Twice Told Tales wasn't going to happen tonight. She had other things to worry about.

Plus, soon after they'd arrived at the restaurant, they'd run into Janie and Rafe Salazar. They'd invited the couple to join them, and after Yolanda filled Rafe in on the returned books, Adam had been forced to pick up much of the conversational slack.

Yolanda's forehead was still pinched in worry, and so far all she'd done was push her spaghetti around. Next to her, Janie was talking about Crisco, a bear at BAA that was about to become a father.

"You keeping the cub?" Adam asked.

"Absolutely, and we're having a name-the-cub contest and expanding the bear habitat. We'll probably need a new mural."

Adam tried to smile.

"Don't worry, Luke can pay," Janie said.

Getting paid was a good thing. Adam had taken the time to talk to Willy Huckabee this morning while the man had been perusing the history section. He'd still been interested in a mural, and what he offered to pay would cover Mr. Chee's salary for a year. Adam had set up an appointment to talk concepts with Willy on Tuesday.

He still had to figure out how he was going to fit the mural into his already busy schedule. Tomorrow Adam was escorting a few of his dad's students to a Tae Kwon Do meet in Mesa, Arizona. Starting the following Saturday, Adam would be back at BAA, doing caricatures. When it started cooling down, he could make two to five hundred dollars there on a good day. Not as much as what he made mural painting, but enough to help out at home. Plus, two other Scorpion Ridge families had offered to hire him for renovations.

He'd have to work for Yolanda a lot less, and at a time when she needed him a lot more.

Finally, Janie was able to get Yolanda to talk about what was bothering her—the mysterious return of the books.

"I once had," Rafael said, in his best sheriff voice, "a kid who stole five Snickers bars from the convenience store feel so guilty he took them back."

"And he confessed?" Yolanda asked.

"Yes and no. The store owner didn't catch him stealing, but he caught him returning them."

"Maybe that's what happened here," Janie suggested.

"Stealing Snickers bars is an impulse crime,

usually," Rafe said. "Going up to an attic, walking to one specific trunk and taking the contents is premeditated."

"I didn't see or hear anyone going upstairs," Yolanda said. "I even called Gramma Rosi. She didn't notice anything unusual, either."

"Just be glad the books were returned."

"But were they *all* returned? I never went through those books. Maybe whoever stole them found the one he or she wanted and gave the rest back. I wouldn't be able to say whether one was missing."

"We might never know," Adam said. "But think of it this way. Your bookstore has lots of empty shelf space after today. Now you can restock with the returned books."

"Most of what was on the bed were old books. About half need repair. A few I'll just throw away. There were some that will fetch a nice profit, though."

"Any good art books?" Janie asked Adam.

"Not really. Maybe a coffee-table book or two."

Janie grinned. "Any by Jimmy Murphy?" Jimmy was Meredith's fiancé. He was a photo journalist who'd recently had a glossy, oversize book published.

"I've five copies of his book," Yolanda said. "They're right by the cash register and are full priced because they're new. I think I sold one today. That they're autographed sure helped."

In the end, Rafe paid the bill. Or rather his mother did, as she owned the Corner Diner. She insisted, calling it her gift to celebrate Yolanda's grand opening. Adam left the tip. One big enough to make the waitress smile.

It was just past nine when Adam walked around his mother's car to help Yolanda from the passenger side.

She was unique, a lady, something he hadn't appreciated enough until now.

It was late August and the heat of a summer day was changing from broil to warm.

He followed Yolanda up the path, then up the stairs, but his eyes never left her body, noting her graceful shoulders, the curve of her right cheek, the way she moved as if contentment were a dance step he didn't understand.

But he could paint it, and he would, just as soon as things settled down.

He'd show her right here, on her porch. He'd paint her in red, with white stripes, the colors bringing out the vibrancy of her hair and eyes.

She paused in front of her door, and he stepped back, giving her space—although what he really wanted to do was push her against the door, cup the graceful cheek that taunted him just now and give her the kind of kiss that promised forever.

But she was Yolanda Sanchez, and she would want more than he knew how to give. And now wasn't the time to complicate things with romance. He had enough maybes on his plate.

As she unlocked the door he said, "If you get scared or anything, go ahead and call me, but I don't think you have anything to worry about."

She nodded, looking unsure.

"I'll sleep on the couch if you want me to." It would be agony, but he would do it.

"No. I'll be fine."

He kissed her on the forehead, not quite where he really wanted to aim. She went inside, and as soon as he heard the click of the lock, he headed back to his mother's car.

With any luck, his van would be ready in the morning. He'd fill it with five students and be off to Mesa for the day.

Tonight, though, he wanted to draw.

Andy was already in bed and snoring when Adam walked through the door. Checking his watch, Adam saw it was almost ten o'clock. That was early for Andy. He usually stayed up to watch the late-night shows. He enjoyed commentaries and things like *Man on the Street* or *Stupid Pet Tricks*.

The sound of the television came from the living room. Adam paused in the hallway to listen to his parents' voices. They were discussing his father's health.

His mother was saying, "We need to work on getting you well first. Then we'll start working on your bucket list."

"And if I don't get well?" his father protested. "Then what? I just stop living? Consider this the number two item on my bucket list."

Adam peeked through the door to the living room and watched as his mom rested her head on his dad's shoulder. Growing up, he'd taken it for granted that all parents were like his: working together, hitting bumps, grumbling, figuring things out, working together again.

Like he and Yolanda had been doing all week.

"What's number one on your bucket list?" Adam asked.

His mom sat up. Clearly, she'd not heard him enter. His dad merely said, "Making sure your mom and brother are all right."

A decade ago, Adam would have stormed out, feeling once again that he was somehow on the outside looking in on his family, only around to fill in for others. A few years on his own had fed the hunger of becoming his own man.

"Don't you want to make sure I'll be all right?" he asked.

Robert Snapp slowly stood, and Adam stepped

back, trying to mask his expression. More than anything, Adam wanted to see his dad granite-hard again, with his blond military haircut and shoulders so strong he could lift two five-year-olds, then ten-year-olds, then fifteen-year-olds, at the same time and run across the front yard yelling for his wife to open the front door so he could deposit both boys on the living room floor and wrestle with them until the boys were out of breath.

"You," his dad said, hair gone, shoulders half their original size, "will be all right. I grow prouder of you every day."

Adam's mother scolded, "Honey, that's not what he needs to hear." Turning to Adam, she added, "What your father's trying to say is, Andy will never be all right, and the thought of leaving me alone to deal with Andy bothers your father."

"You won't be alone," Adam said. "I'm here."

"See," Dad said, "you're already all right in my book."

It was a compliment, one that Adam needed more a decade ago, but somehow, hearing it today was good enough.

He left his parents to their discussions and went to the kitchen for a snack. His mother had moved his drawing supplies to a side counter-top. He retrieved them, sat down and pulled

Stories of Scorpion Ridge, Arizona, from his backpack.

His rough-draft etching of Jedidiah and his wife were finished. Amelia looked more real now that he'd added details from a few photographs Loretta had passed on. What Adam really wanted, though, was to have a likeness of Richard, Ivy and Woodhull.

Taking his yellow sketchbook and sketch pencils, he settled back at the kitchen table and opened the book, skimming a dozen drawings before deciding on the one he wanted to re-create tonight.

As with Amelia, Richard's wife didn't seem to have a role. In every drawing, she was looking down at her feet. It would be impossible to draw her in detail. He'd get the part of her hair or the top of her hat right. He could re-create her shoes better than her face.

Ivy was a little easier. She always managed to place herself to the side, almost as if she didn't want to be included in a family picture.

Adam smiled. His family, at least until he'd hit fifteen, had had a portrait taken every year. Every time, they'd posed with Andy and him flanking their parents. There'd been one with the two boys sitting while their parents stood. There was one taken outdoors with both boys lying on their stomachs, heads up, chins cupped, while their parents sat cross-legged amidst them. In most cases the Snapps could be captured all together inside a hula hoop.

Not so with the Ventimiglias. Woodhull was never in the perimeter, and Ivy was always ten strides to the left or right.

But he could make out her face. It was thin, with full lips and a small nose. Her forehead was always covered with a wisp of hair. She must take after her mother in looks because both Richard and Woodhull were dark-haired. In a way, Adam wondered if Richard had made sure his wife wasn't pictured right beside him so that no one could comment about the fact that she was taller than him. Taller than her son, for that matter.

Hmmm. Adam riffled through the book carefully, noting Ivy was in at least five drawings. She sat in all of them. He needed one of her standing to truly gauge her height. His best guess was that she was as short as her father and brother.

After about an hour, his mother came in and stared over his shoulder. "There's something about them that looks familiar."

"Not possible," Adam said. "They left in the late 1940s."

"People wore so many clothes back then that all you can see are part of their faces."

That was true in the case of all the Ventimiglias and of Amelia. Jedidiah had a clear head shot. Adam got the sense that convention had not applied to the old man.

"Where's Dad?"

"Asleep."

"On the couch?"

"No, in the recliner. It's better for his back, he says."

"What was the second item on his bucket list?"

She sighed. "A trip to Paris."

"Are you going?"

"Yes. He really wants it."

"Good."

She both nodded and shook her head, a skill only women seemed able to master.

"I can help with finances."

"Adam, no, you don't have that kind of money."

"William Huckabee has commissioned me to paint a mural. He offered me over twenty thousand dollars."

"No, you save your money." She wagged her eyebrows, something else he could never do. "Someday you'll meet a nice girl, get married, buy a house and settle down. You'll want that money."

Adam wanted to argue, but it would be wasted words.

The girl he wanted to settle down with lived in a house that might really belong to him.

And he'd have to paint a lot of murals to come close to its asking price.

CHAPTER TWELVE

SATURDAY MORNING, ADAM was the first one up. Although he really wanted to spend the early hours drawing, he ate a hurried breakfast and then grabbed his skateboard.

Used to be, his skateboard had felt like an extension of his feet. During the last four years, as he set up temporary lodging in one city after another, the skateboard had been his second-best friend, after his art and before he met Stacey.

But there was nowhere better to board on an early morning than Scorpion Ridge, Arizona. This early, the sun didn't blister; instead, it caressed.

It took him a good fifteen minutes to make it to Tucker's Auto. His van waited outside, parked and washed. Inside the garage, some sort of drilling was taking place, sounding more like they were digging a hole to China rather than fine-tuning delicate machinery.

No one was sitting in the front office because they didn't open for another hour. Adam went into the garage and searched for whoever was making all the noise.

He ended up at a yellow Volkswagen that appeared new on the outside and trashed on the inside. Sort of like his van, but he had art as an excuse. It looked as if someone had taken a hatchet to this vehicle.

"Excuse me," he said, bending down.

Incredibly long legs came out from below the driver's-side door. Jeans that must be painted on and a tucked-in gray shirt with a Tucker's emblem over the left breast came next. Then blond hair tied in a ponytail shoved under a Tucker's Auto cap. Melissa Tucker.

"Hey, Adam. You here for the van?"

"I'm driving five students to Mesa for a competition, so I was hoping to pick it up early."

She rolled the creeper so it was free of the Volkswagen's underbelly and gracefully stood. A smudge of oil was on her cheek. He'd been noticing cheeks a lot lately. Funny, even though he acknowledged her beauty, he didn't feel a bit inspired to paint Melissa.

A hefty charge card bill later, Adam's skateboard went in the back and he was on his way home. He'd be picking up Andy at home and then heading to the studio for the students. But first he needed to clean out the back so the kids had a place to sit.

Remnants from Illinois still loitered on the floorboards. A few thumbnail drawings were in a red folder labeled "Possibilities." A menu from Adam's favorite take-out restaurant was tucked in a cup holder in the back. Under the rear seat was an old T-shirt. Way too small for Adam and advertising a band he'd never heard of.

Stacey's.

He paused, waiting for the emotions to wash over him. He expected regret, betrayal, anger. They didn't come. The shirt was just a shirt. And Stacey, well, she was just a girl. That was it. A girl who knew how to act like a woman but not how to love like one. What had he seen in her? Now he couldn't remember.

"You ready?" Andy waited at the end of the driveway, practically standing on his toes in excitement. Any other social situation and Andy would still be in his bedroom, convinced that staying at home was better than going out.

"I just need to throw away a few things. Then I'll get my bag and we'll head to the studio."

"I packed your bag." Andy held up Adam's backpack.

Adam let out a breath and counted to ten. No doubt the original contents of his backpack were strewn across the guest room. But getting mad at Andy was an effort in futility, and truly, Andy had been trying to help.

Quickly, he went inside, straight to his room and organized the belongings Andy had tossed onto his bed. Yolanda's book was on his pillow.

His mother was in the kitchen clearing the table. "Want some pancakes?"

"Sure, but I'll take them to eat while I'm driving."

His mother checked the clock on the wall, peeked out the window at the van where Andy's bobbing head was clearly visible and nodded. "Good idea."

"Where's Dad? I'm sure he has some last-minute advice."

"Still in bed and don't wake him. He had a rough night."

Adam now knew that every night was rough. "This is the first time I've gone to a competition without him."

His mother nodded. "Then we'll just pray that it's the last. Your father hates not going."

Once he'd returned outdoors, he opened the back door, tossed his bag on the seat and checked to see if he had everything. Andy had packed two water bottles, a bunch of pencils, a camera—one that hadn't been used in ten years—and a book. Competitions usually took the whole day. If the Snapp luck held, they'd arrive in Mesa at nine, sign in and their first event wouldn't be until hours later. There'd be lots of sitting around, and the book would come in handy.

"Good job," Adam told his brother. Andy nodded, opened his iPad and started watching a movie he'd seen a hundred times. He didn't move when Adam jumped behind the driver's seat and headed the van toward the studio.

Half an hour later, all five students were in the van in various stages of being either sleepy or over-energized. They all knew Andy, though, and even the over-energized ones kept their excitement contained.

One mother accompanied Adam. He appreciated her presence because it meant he didn't have to entertain the kids. She organized Slugbug games and Find the Fifty States on License Plates as he drove. It had been a while since he'd been to a competition. He'd earned his black belt by the age of twelve and had gone to third degree right before he'd quit at age fifteen. He had known the forms without thinking about them, and a fifth degree black belt master had said Adam was a natural.

But all that felt like a lifetime ago, or something that had happened to someone else, though there were moments when Adam wondered how much he'd have enjoyed the sport if it hadn't been his family's life.

Today's competition was in a school gym.

The group from Snapp's Studio was right on time. The mother herded the kids in to get weighed.

Adam had forgotten the smell, the feeling, the sights of a competition. The youngest competitor looked to be about four. The oldest he pegged around sixty-four. And even after almost a decade away, the staff and competitors remembered Adam.

Soon he was doing what his dad had been doing for years, judging both forms and breaking. When his dad had dragged him here as a kid, the day had been excruciatingly long. Not today. It went by quickly. Adam was impressed by his dad's students. They had grace, agility and clearly knew the foundation of their levels. A few students were obviously placed in incorrect ranks. Adam marked down a green belt who had the skills of a yellow. Then he listened to the kid and his instructor whine about the injustice.

Andy earned a silver. So did all the other Snapp's Studio competitors. They were all pleased and talked all the way home about getting gold next time.

It was after eight when the van finally pulled up in front of Snapp's Studio. Most of the parents were already there waiting for their offspring. Only one student was left hanging. Andy paced, not appreciating the delay. Andy had an award to put on his shelf, and he wanted to go home and do it.

It had been a long time since Adam had had to deal with one of Andy's moods. Andy began touching the passenger-side door, first lightly then with more and more force.

"Andy," Adam said, "I'm going to unlock the studio. Go on inside and sit in Dad's office. We'll put a movie on his computer."

Andy's iPad had long since lost its battery life.

Adam didn't want the little boy left waiting for his parents to be scared, and Andy could be threatening when his temper took over. Adam kicked himself. He should have taken everyone inside and settled Andy the minute they got to the studio. It used to be second nature for Adam to anticipate the best course for Andy.

"Okay," Andy agreed. "I want to watch *Who Framed Roger Rabbit.*"

The only flaw in the plan, Adam realized a short time later, was that Andy refused to move from the computer until *Who Framed Roger Rabbit* ended.

Too bad, because Adam really wanted to stop by Twice Told Tales and check on Yolanda. He'd texted her five or six times during the day. She'd responded twice. Both texts had been brief, telling him that the bookstore was full and she'd talk to him later.

Funny, he wanted later to be now.

THERE WERE TWO boxes of books on the front porch when Yolanda opened her door on Sunday morning. Since the Twice Told Tales sign had gone up, people often dropped off their excess books. But most knocked on the door and came in with their box, talking about having too many books and not enough room.

Twice in the last six months, Yolanda had stepped on to her front porch and found surprises. Last time it had been a whole collection of Louis L'Amour novels. To Yolanda's delight, two had been autographed. She almost felt guilty putting them into Baggies and displaying them by the cash register for over a hundred dollars each. But that's what they were going for on eBay, and Louis had lived in Arizona for part of his life.

Today's find was nothing like that, however. Instead of neat stacks, today's haul had been piled into two white boxes that used to hold computer paper. Going down to her knees, Yolanda started going through the books. What made these stand out was their age. All were more than fifty years old. There were original Hardy Boys, even some Boy Scout adventure fiction books. She'd seen one of these at her uncle Juan's house. There was also a couple of Ernest Hemingways and John Steinbecks, unfortunately not signed. The rest were obscure titles that Yolanda hadn't heard of.

Yolanda went back to one of the Hardy Boys and checked the inside cover. Two words were printed there in black ink, in perfectly formed letters, all caps, looking almost like one word.

CHESTER VENTIMIGLIA.

A moment later she'd ascertained that all the books had Chester's name on them. One thing for sure, the little old woman who'd been here last week could not have carried the heavy boxes. Which meant someone had done it for her. Or this was a random donation. But Yolanda didn't believe that for a minute.

She looked down the yard and at the street. It was seven in the morning. A few houses had lights on inside, but no one was heading off to church yet.

Taking a deep breath, Yolanda knelt and started returning the books she'd just gone through to their boxes. She should feel spooked, but she didn't. This last week had been one of the most interesting weeks of her life. Not only because of the bookstore's opening but because of Ivy Ventimiglia's visit.

Carrying the first box into the main room, Yolanda set it on the counter next to the cash register. Gulliver immediately came to sniff.

"I agree, something's fishy," Yolanda said.

Her cell phone sounded—it was her grandmother calling to beg off church.

Sometimes Yolanda forgot just how old her grandmother was. Working in Twice Told Tales the last two days had taken its toll. Yolanda had called Mr. Teasdale yesterday. Gramma Rosi hadn't even complained when he showed up to escort her home. She'd just said, "If Thelma Sheldon comes in, tell her she shouldn't stand in the romance section and argue with herself about what to buy. People are starting to think she's losing it."

Going to church alone never bothered Yolanda. She'd been raised in Scorpion Ridge, and there wasn't a pew that didn't offer a friend. Yolanda hoped Janie would be there, though it was unlikely. She and Rafael had purchased a house in Adobe Hills, where Janie taught, and only drove to services in Scorpion Ridge once a month. Yolanda usually knew when she was coming because they'd organize to meet for lunch at BAA, and they'd set up a lunch date for next week.

It took only one glance at the clock to get Yolanda moving. She had twenty minutes to get ready and out the door. The church she attended was on the outskirts of town. To get there she had to drive by Ruth Dunbar's mini-manse, where she'd worked for most of her teen-age years.

Ruth was in her late sixties, a newlywed, and one of the richest women in town. Her husband had been the richest man in town, and the only reason Ruth wasn't the richest now was because she helped support BAA. In some ways she reminded Yolanda of Gramma Rosi. She was a little overweight, straightforward, liked all people and was bossy.

Funny, Yolanda had worked for Ruth Moore as a maid, and Gramma Rosi had been a maid to the Ventimiglias, in the very house they lived in, at age seven.

At seven, Yolanda had been dreaming of being a Spice Girl and trying to learn how to ride a bike.

The mini-manse looked the same as it always had, except for the toys in the front yard and the many cars in the rounded driveway. This morning two collies ran back and forth across the grass. It had been a different scene when Yolanda started. Back then, Ruth had owned a lion she'd named Terrance the Terrible. Because of him, Ruth was a friend to all animals.

He'd died last month. He'd been thirty years old by Ruth's count. Lions in captivity shouldn't live that long. But Terrance the Terrible had two things going for him that most lions did not. One, he was truly loved. Two, he got his teeth brushed every day.

"The crowds love to watch him get his teeth cleaned," Ruth claimed.

The mini-manse disappeared from the rearview mirror, and Yolanda turned in to the tiny church. She found a parking spot, but didn't exit the car. In the handicap spot right in front of the church's side door, the whole Snapp family stepped from Adam's mother's car. It was the first time Adam had attended since he'd been back.

He'd texted her couple of times yesterday. They were friends, she kept telling herself.

He looked around, scanning the parking lot, and Yolanda had to scold herself because she really wanted him to be looking for her.

And that made no sense at all.

"You'll enjoy every minute," his mother predicted as they exited the car parked in front of their church. His mom taught a Sunday school class for three disabled kids. She'd started it when Andy was four, and one of the teachers at church hadn't understood how to handle him. Soon other families started attending their church just for his mother's class.

"I'm sure I will enjoy it," Adam agreed.

Adam's dad looked a little better this morning as he started to escort his wife to her class. "The pathway to Heaven is more crowded because of women like you."

Amazing, his dad was a bit of an artist himself, Adam thought. Only he painted with words.

Closing the car door behind him, Adam looked around. The church hadn't changed except for a circle of picnic benches in the back. "Your father's idea," his mom said. "He thinks members should stick around and visit more. He managed to find the money for the picnic tables, and now in good weather, we often have the potlucks outside."

It was no surprise that his dad had found the money. The man was a deacon and had handled the church's accounts for almost twenty years.

Adam felt a little funny following his mom and brother through the door of the church. Quite honestly, he was afraid. If his dad's portion of the pew was empty, the church should tilt.

They were a good ten minutes early because Andy didn't respond well to being late.

At church he had certain jobs he called his. He made sure the minister's podium was perfectly straight. He also went through and organized the song books and Bibles left in the pockets and made sure no book was left on a pew.

Walking through the front door and taking in the Scorpion Ridge Church—the faded red carpeting, the desk where the church women took turns handing out the bulletin and greeting people, the bulletin board where a Bible Bowl was featured—Adam felt something tug at his heart. He'd attended this church his entire life up until he'd left to paint murals. He hadn't been back since he'd come home.

It had been easy not to go to church when he'd first returned to Scorpion Ridge and had been living at BAA. He'd been busy, so he claimed. But he hadn't fooled his parents. They both knew he was mad at God. He'd been telling himself it was because he'd not made it in the big city and had allowed himself to be taken advantage of. But he'd been denying his true fear—that he was going to lose his father. His parents reassured him that his father's illness was the cycle of life.

Life wasn't always fair.

The fact that Adam's dad was with them now, though, and not in bed, showed that when life wasn't fair, one needed to fight back.

His father had gone through a battery of tests yesterday in Phoenix. They'd gotten home well after Adam and Andy had returned from the competition. All Mom would tell him was "the doctors say attitude is half the battle, and your dad has attitude to spare."

Adam believed it. Snapp's Studio had been born out of his dad's attitude.

For the first time in a long time, Adam wanted to be more like his dad. He wanted his dad to be proud of him.

Standing in the front foyer, watching the congregation gather, felt different—both wrong and right. Wrong because he'd been gone so long and too many changes had occurred, and right because he felt as if he'd never been gone.

It took only a few minutes before he'd had his hand shaken a dozen times, two suggestions that he get a haircut and one elderly man asked if he was a visitor.

"Adam Snapp," Adam said, even though the man asking had been the first minister before Tom Sheldon took over. "Robert's son. You baptized me fifteen years ago."

"Of course," the older man said, looking as if he didn't believe it.

Adam had always been polite to the older members of the church. He opened doors for them, gave them hugs and called them all by name. But today he felt as though he really knew them because he knew their history, and that made everything more real.

He noted how the hair stuck over Otis Wilson's ears, even though the man was bald everywhere else. Otis's father had looked the same. Then there was Thelma Sheldon. She wore white gloves to church: the only woman to do so. Many of the drawings in Yolanda's book showed women wearing gloves. Even Yolanda, when she walked through the doors, had a hint of the past. Something about the curve of her cheek. But he wasn't noticing that because of the book. Yolanda's family wasn't pictured there. He noticed it because of how many times he'd drawn her likeness lately.

Because he'd been thinking about her.

Way too much.

And if her Gramma Rosi had been beside her, Adam would have noted how the two women didn't resemble each other much.

Because Yolanda looked a lot like her biological grandfather, and also took after him in height.

If Adam was correct.

Right now she was standing next to Thelma Sheldon and nodding at something the woman was saying.

"Good to see you, Adam." William Huckabee

held out his hand for a shake. "I'm glad you're coming on Tuesday. I enjoy everything you did at BAA so much. Sometimes I go there and walk around and pretend I'm ten again. I think I like the farting bench the most."

"Thanks." Yup, a farting bench was just what Adam wanted to be famous for. Maybe eight years ago, when he'd designed it, that had been true. Not today.

"I've been looking at murals online," Huckabee said, "and I had an idea that you could really do something unique with ostrich feathers."

The difference, Adam had figured out two murals ago, between being an amateur artist and a professional one was that an amateur basically did what he wanted, while a professional had to follow the job's parameters. All those years ago at BAA, Adam had designed his work based on his creative whims. Luke Rittenhouse had smiled, shook his head—sometimes in awe and sometimes in disbelief—and let Adam go on his merry way.

Adam wanted that back.

"Do ostriches fart?" Adam asked.

"Ew, I've joined this conversation at the wrong moment." Yolanda came up and gave William Huckabee a quick hug.

"Adam and I were talking about ideas for my

mural," Huckabee said. "I'd like him to do for my place what he did for BAA."

"And what he's done restoring my Victorian. It's amazing."

Huckabee turned and studied Adam. "It's wise to spread your talents. It seemed when I drove by Yolanda's place a few months ago that you were replacing the balusters."

"Yes, I did that first," Adam admitted. "The porch was leaning so much I kept expecting it to fall into the ground."

"What are you working on now?"

"I'm finishing up the kitchen. When the appliance guy put in the new stove, he dinged up part of the wall. I'm also inventorying the upstairs' doors. Many of them have lead paint still. I want to see what we can salvage."

"I admire a man with talent," Huckabee said.

A year ago Adam had been a mural artist. Now he was a home renovator, Tae Kwon Do instructor and general go-to man for his parents. Come the next weekend, he'd add caricaturist to his list of jobs.

Now, too, he might be able to add muralist back to his job description. "I'm teaching a class on Tuesday from ten to eleven, so I could be there about noon."

In two days Adam would offer his hand again to Huckabee, agreeing to do a mural. He knew he could do it, with Yolanda at his side. But would she still stand beside him when he told her the secrets he was keeping, both about her parentage and about possibly owning the Victorian.

"I'm helping." Andy walked up and joined the conversation, more so he could be near Adam, his presence reminding Adam that they were on a schedule, and Adam should be in the auditorium sitting in their pew.

"Why not tomorrow?" Huckabee asked. "Bring Andy. He'd like the ostriches."

"I'd rather not risk it. We had goldfish growing up. They were the closest thing to a pet that Andy could handle."

"Ostriches smell." Andy sniffed as if he could already smell them. He wasn't done talking, though, because he added, "Maybe a bit like cigarettes."

Adam could only shrug. How his brother deduced that ostriches and cigarette smoke were the same surely made sense in Andy's own mind.

Turning to Yolanda, he said, "I'm suggesting Tuesday because you mentioned wanting to go into Phoenix to buy some books. I thought Monday, since you're closed, we could do that. Maybe after I'm done teaching?"

Her reaction was exactly what he'd hoped for. Her eyes lit up, and her smile was just for him.

He hated to think that he'd be responsible for that smile fading. There had to be something he could do to make things right.

For everyone.

CHAPTER THIRTEEN

THEY WERE SPEEDING toward Phoenix in his van, which smelled a little like paint.

Yolanda was amazed. "You haven't even started the mural and already your van smells like art," she said.

"I'm just glad it overwhelms the scent of the Tae Kwon Do students from Saturday's meet. One of the younger kids took off his shoes in the back. I thought I was going to have to stop."

"How did the meet go?"

"Good. I was surprised. They had me acting as a judge, first time ever. It gave me something to do. Andy earned a silver in sparring."

"Sparring?"

"It's a bit like fighting. My job was to give points to the competitors as they hit their specific target."

"The target being?"

"Another competitor."

She winced. "How would you know if they hit their specific target?"

"Because in Tae Kwon Do, there are certain

hit areas. I could show you if you want. I'll stop the car."

She laughed. He looked as if he really wanted to show her his moves, but she knew he wasn't thinking martial arts moves at all.

A good thirty miles flew by the window as she imagined that. "This feels weird," Yolanda finally said.

"What does?"

"You and me, acting as if, well, acting as if we're more than friends."

"Is that what we're doing?" he said, his tone so serious that Yolanda wasn't quite sure how to interpret it.

"I don't see you squiring any other woman around," Yolanda pointed out.

"You asked me to take you scrounging for books," he reminded her.

"Oh, you're right."

The van was silent for seconds that felt like minutes. Then Adam cleared his throat and said, "I'm not sure what we're doing, exactly, either. When I first started working for you, you barely said anything to me except to argue that I was staying too true to the original intent when you wanted to modernize a bit."

"And," she agreed, "most of your suggestions were spot on."

"Your house has character. I didn't want you to lose that."

"I didn't plan on losing it. But really, Adam, tastes change. And your suggestions have made the renovation a bit more expensive. Such as the pine floors."

"They look great."

"Carpeting would keep the place quieter. I agree, the salmon-colored carpet had to go, but—"

"Only because it didn't go with the Kool-Aid orange door you wanted for your office."

"You keep bringing up that door," she protested. "I gave you free rein in the kitchen."

"You did," he agreed. "And I went home and told my mom that I didn't think you cooked. You have no food in that kitchen. Plus, I never see remnants of a meal."

"I cook."

"My mom reminded me that you made Ruth's meals when you worked for her."

"As a maid."

"Does it bother you that you were a maid?" Adam asked, his voice gentling.

"If you asked me that question a year ago, or while I was working for Ruth, I'd have said no. It didn't bother me a bit. Now, since finding out Gramma Rosi was a maid, I've really been thinking about the choices we make in life and how people make choices for us."

He stared straight ahead, but his hands became taut, fingers tightening on the steering wheel.

"Three generations of my family have been domestic help," she said. "Is that to be our lot in life?"

"No, look at you now," Adam pointed out.

"Only because my mother skimped and saved." Yolanda turned so she was gazing right at Adam. He, wisely, kept his eyes on the road. "How many times did you go to Disneyland?"

"Six or seven."

"I've never been. We couldn't afford it. My mother was too busy working and saving money."

"You can break the chain," Adam advised. "Your children don't have to work as domestic help. But remember, there's nothing wrong with being a maid. Lots of people are maids."

"I know that, but something else bothers me."

"What?"

"When we went out with the Salazars, do you remember what Rafe pointed out?"

"No."

"Well, the Salazars have been around a long time, too. He noted that neither his family nor mine, the Acuras, were mentioned in the book."

"There are lots of families who are not mentioned."

Yolanda agreed. "The unimportant people."

"So," Adam said, carefully, "you're saying maids are not important."

"Not in the history of Scorpion Ridge."

"I think they're very important."

His voice changed. Yolanda looked at him, at the expression on his face, so serious.

"What's going on, Adam? You keep talking about history and maids and what is and is not important. Why do you keep bringing it up?"

For a moment she wasn't sure he'd tell her. But she stayed quiet and waited patiently.

"Do you remember when we toured the museum and Thelma said there was a rumor that Woodhull had gotten a local girl pregnant?"

"I remember. But she also said none of the town girls had a baby nine months later."

"No, what she said was that none of the girls she hung around with had a baby nine months later."

"What are you trying to say?"

"Just hear me out. I've been mulling this over for days."

Yolanda felt a slight chill go down her spine. This wasn't the usual banter they had, the typical sharing of ideas. He'd had this idea for days without telling her. Why?

"Your Gramma Rosi worked for the Ventimiglias. She stopped just before her father purchased the house. How old was Rosi when your mother was born?"

"Sixteen, or maybe seventeen."

"How old was she when she moved into the house."

"Sixteen," Yolanda said slowly, remembering her Gramma Rosi's words. *Nineteen hundred and forty-six or four, maybe earlier or later. I had just turned sixteen.*

"What if Woodhull got your grandmother pregnant?"

"No," Yolanda sputtered. "No, she'd have…"

She had to give Adam credit. He didn't push. He just let her mind work for five or ten minutes until she finally said, "Oh, wow. But I could never ask her to confirm that."

"It would," Adam said, "explain how it came to be that your family got the Victorian."

"And the Ventimiglias moved away in shame because Rosi got pregnant. Nah, that doesn't make sense. They'd just pay to push the scandal under the carpet."

"Not if they were having other problems, as well. Particularly money problems. Do you know how much Rosi's father paid for the Victorian?"

"No."

"Did you see the Ventimiglias' name on the paperwork when your grandmother signed it over to you?"

"She hasn't yet. Oh, wow. Why didn't you tell me what you were thinking sooner? This isn't something—"

"I was going to the night we went to dinner, but then you found the books on your bed and the Salazars ended up eating with us. There just didn't seem to be a right time."

Yolanda nodded in agreement. There could never be a right time to share something like this.

She could be related to the Ventimiglias.

Gramma Rosi, what happened all those years ago? Do you also know more about how Wood-hull died?

Yolanda looked at Adam, but didn't voice what was in her head. She wasn't ready to discuss whether or not Woodhull had fallen into the well or had been pushed. One thing Gramma Rosi had shared about her family was that her father had always taken care of his own.

He'd gotten them the best house in town.

What else had he done all those years ago?

Yolanda started tapping her fingers on the door frame, somewhat relieved when Adam changed the subject by asking, "So, where are we going?"

When she answered, her words sounded a bit distant. "I've three favorite secondhand stores. Plus, I did an internet search and found one bookstore that's closing. Much as it makes me feel as if I'm taking advantage of someone else's misfortune, it's good business."

Two hours later the back of his van was loaded with books. "Good thing I cleaned out the van. Are we done?"

"No, we still have the bookstore that's closing."

The Bent Cover was in a strip mall and took up three stores. No lights were on inside.

Yolanda jumped out of the van after Adam parked and checked the front door: locked. She checked her watch before getting back in the van. "I'm meeting the owner's daughter. She should be here in a few minutes. She just wants to get rid of everything."

"Why?"

"Her mother passed away last month. I guess the store's contents were left to the three kids, but they hadn't a clue what to do with them. The daughter we're meeting finally put the whole lot up for sale online. That's how I found it."

"She's liquidating," Adam said.

"That's it," Yolanda agreed. "It's what Agatha did in Gesippi when the library closed. Only I think she took half the books home with her."

"I couldn't bear to sell my paint supplies even though I'm not using them." His serious tone touched her heart, reminding her that the man beside her had left Scorpion Ridge a boy but came back a man. Quite a man.

"What happened, Adam? You said you came back to help family, but there's more to it. Remember, I've known you all your life."

"You've watched me all my life," he responded. "That's not really knowing."

"Oh, I know you," she said, wagging her eyebrows.

He barely cracked a smile. "Okay, how did I break my arm in eighth grade?"

"Skateboarding. You were coming up out of the bowl and tried to do a three-sixty and instead landed full on your left arm."

"Too easy a question. Everyone heard about that."

"Sure, because you milked it."

"Okay, let's try something harder. What's the first thing I ever painted?"

"A flower in preschool."

Adam laughed. "As a serious painter."

"You painted Terrance on the wall at the back of BAA. The wall where the shrubs grow through the cracks in the wall. You arranged it perfectly so that the shrubs formed Terrance's hair. For years, you sneaked back there and watered the shrubs so that Terrance wouldn't go bald."

Adam was still laughing when an old green truck pulled up beside them, and a harried-looking woman got out. "Sorry I'm late. My husband was dealing with an outside customer and didn't come home…"

Yolanda interrupted with, "No problem. We aren't in a hurry." She remembered from being on the phone with her that this woman was a talker.

And she was finding it hard enough to focus on the task at hand as it was. Right now even a first-edition *To Kill a Mockingbird* would have a tough time trumping Yolanda's inner turmoil.

Am I a Ventimiglia?

It took some doing, but Yolanda pushed her musings aside and focused on business. An hour later Yolanda had filled the rest of Adam's van, all the while agreeing with the woman that the bane of a used bookstore owner's existence was lack of storage.

"Thanks, Adam," Yolanda said, getting into the van and putting on her seat belt. "If I had to lift all those boxes by myself, I'd be crying."

Adam wasn't even out of breath. "The past three months of filling in for my dad have really gotten me back in shape."

"You were in shape when you got home."

"Painting murals is a lot harder than most people assume. I'm hauling supplies and climbing onto ladders and scaffolds constantly."

"I went on the internet and searched out the murals you painted over the last five years. They were very good. The one in Telluride is the best, in my opinion."

"That was my third job. I'd hit my stride. It was hard being away from home and all alone. The first two, I was always looking over my shoulder. At BAA, people were always interrupting me, asking questions. But I knew I could joke with them. When I first started painting for patrons, the only interruptions came from the people paying, and they always wanted to make changes to the original."

"Did that bother you?"

He let out a long breath. "No, not really."

"But you didn't have an audience of admirers like you did at BAA."

"I had admirers, but they didn't really talk to me. They asked a few questions, but mostly watched. At BAA, the staff and a lot of the visitors had known me from the time I was born. When I left Scorpion Ridge and went other places, I felt a bit like I was on a pedestal. People looked at me, admired me, but didn't really see me. It was lonely."

"I hadn't considered that you might be lonely."

They'd both been lonely. Funny, even before Ivy showed up that morning, Yolanda had been aware that Adam was nearby, working. She'd ignored him. But, in his presence, she never felt lonely. "The mural you painted at Wildrose is different than all the rest. Why?"

Adam looked at her, surprised. "No one," he said, "not my family, not the people who paid for my murals, and not the critics, have mentioned the differences. I expected some backlash. When it didn't come, I figured maybe I was wrong."

"Wrong about it being different?"

"Wrong about how different it was," Adam admitted.

"So what made it different?"

"I painted it with someone else. She was acting as my assistant, learning the trade."

"Like you worked with Janie all those years ago?"

"Janie did what I asked her to do. She didn't always like it because she's more of a realist artist, but she always followed my direction. Stacey didn't."

"Stacey?"

"Stacey Baer."

Finally Yolanda knew what had stymied his paintbrush, filled his eyes with sadness and erased the smile from his face.

Another woman.

THEY STOPPED FOR an early dinner at a truck stop where the owners sold Native American jewelry in a back room and the chicken-fried steak was almost as good as prime rib.

At least in Adam's opinion. Yolanda merely nodded in agreement but ate only half of hers. She still, obviously, was chewing on the idea of being related to the Ventimiglias. She offered the rest to him, and, as if he'd been doing it his whole life, he took it.

Today had beeen a surprise. He'd offered to drive her to Phoenix, to get to know her better. And he had.

He'd realized that he'd mistaken her shell of protection as haughtiness. She was vulnerable, but strong. She wasn't someone who would use others to gain advantage.

Not like Stacey. When the waitress brought their dessert—two hot fudge sundaes—Adam waited until she'd taken a bite or two. Chocolate always made a girl more willing to listen.

Understand.

"I probably should thank Stacey," Adam began.

"Who?" Yolanda said, but Adam could tell she was being facetious.

"I met her about a week after I moved to Wildrose, Illinois. I didn't figure out until later that she'd planned the meeting. At the time, I just thought she was a young artist looking for a mentor. She was beautiful, and I stumbled all over myself wanting to help her."

Yolanda took another bite and nodded, saying nothing.

"I took her through the whole routine. She watched as I drew thumbnail after thumbnail. Sometimes she sat beside me doing the same thing, mimicking exactly what I was doing. I even took her to a few meetings so she could see how negotiations went. I only painted two canvas models of the mural. The businessmen paying for the endeavor liked the second one so much that they wanted to go with it."

"The final product was the one I saw in the *Wildrose Gazette*."

"Yes."

"I saw it in color, too. It's on the town's website."

"Under both Stacey's and my name." Adam finished his hot fudge sundae, unsure if he felt stuffed because of all he'd eaten or because of the heartburn that always came when he thought about Stacey.

"I was negotiating three more deals, assuming I'd take Stacey along. I mean, how cool, someone who loved painting as much as I did and was also a bit of a vagabond."

"You still feel like a vagabond?"

"No, but I also no longer want to be."

"You still have your muse," Yolanda predicted. "Everyone has setbacks."

"Not you."

"I majored in accounting. But in my second semester of junior year, I was sitting in a laundromat when I realized that I hated numbers, hated sitting still at a chair in front of a computer all day. I also knew there was nothing I could do about it. By that time, I was twenty thousand dollars in debt and had a mother who'd have a heart attack if I told her I wanted to change majors."

"What would you have changed it to?"

"Probably library science. When Mom left me her money, I almost went back to school."

"I wish I'd taken a few accounting classes or at least spent time with Dave Ramsey and Financial Success. Maybe I'd have been wiser with my money."

"What went wrong? Why aren't you still with Stacey?"

"Everyone was impressed with the completed mural. I made the front page of not only their tiny *Gazette*, but also the Chicago papers featured it in their Sunday edition. A news station from Springfield came out and did an interview with me. Stacey was right there for everything."

"That's amazing."

"After the mural was completed, I had planned to come home for a visit, to show my parents how well I was doing. And I was going to introduce Stacey to them. I'd not even mentioned her name. Not sure why, except we'd only been dating for four months. My final night in Wildrose, there was a cocktail party in my honor. Stacey didn't want to go. She said she wasn't feeling well. When I got home she was gone."

He'd felt the strangeness right when he opened the door. It was a certain kind of quiet. Oh, Adam appreciated quiet. Growing up with Andy had instilled in Adam a need for peace. But the quiet when Stacey left was the quiet of emptiness.

Luckily, he acknowledged, it had been an external emptiness. Which told him now that he'd not loved Stacey, not really. He'd enjoyed her company, liked having her help, but she hadn't touched his heart or his soul.

Not in the simple but pure way Yolanda did.

Stacey, however, had definitely touched his sponges, paint and matte gel. She'd even walked off with his brush soap. Nothing he was willing to call the police about.

"She pretty much took everything. Of course, we rented the apartment furnished, so she left the furniture and my clothes. But she took all my art supplies, my iPod and even what few groceries we had."

"And you had no clue this was going to happen?"

"None." Adam tried to picture Stacey. He remembered short blond hair, curly. He remembered a lithe body always in motion. She'd run up the ladder when they were working on the mural. He felt like an old man sometimes, but then he was always carrying something. She'd wanted to go out every night, and oh, could she spend money.

Looking across at Yolanda, he thought about how she sat down every day and balanced her budget. Her lips would purse and she'd tap, tap, tap a pencil as she made notations on the paper. She was careful. He could learn from her.

"It gets worse," he continued. "I came home, headed for BAA and moved into the caretaker's cabin. That night, I took Andy out for a hamburger. I thought it would be like old times. My debit card didn't work. Thank goodness we were at Rafe's mom's place. She said I could pay her later. The next day, I called the bank. Stacey had cleaned out my account. I'd given her my check book and Visa card more than once, as we were both buying paint and such for the mural. She took more than twenty thousand dollars. To her credit, she left me with fifty."

"Did you call the police?"

"Right. And tell them that the girl I lived with for four months took money out of my bank account. Oh, yeah, plus I'd given her blank checks. And she was sort of my work partner, so for the last two months of our relationship she had my permission to take money."

Too many afternoons sitting with Loretta and watching *Judge Judy* reruns gave Adam an idea of exactly where his pursuit of the injustice might end.

"Do you have any idea where Stacey is now?" Yolanda asked.

"She took a job painting a mural for a suburb in Boston."

"So you taught her well."

"Too well. It was one of the jobs offered to me. She called them, apparently a couple of days before she left me, and offered to take the job. Her name is on the Wildrose mural. There was a photo in the newspaper of both of us working on it. She got her foot in the door and threw it wide open."

"And left you standing outside in the cold."

Adam nodded. "I never felt more betrayed. I've heard people talk about being shell-shocked, but I never understood the concept. Standing in the doorway of our empty apartment, I understood the importance of trust and the importance of knowing *who* to trust. Unfortunately, the lesson was costly, both in money and…" He glanced at his hands, the ones that no longer painted.

"Why didn't you tell me this when you first got back?" Yolanda reached across the table and took his right hand. Her thumb gently caressed his palm.

"I didn't tell anybody. And if you remember, we weren't cozy those first few months."

"You had a chip on your shoulder," Yolanda said. "Now I understand why."

"And you had a deadline," Adam reminded her. "You'd decided August 28 was going to be your grand opening, and nothing was going to stop you."

"Not even a mystery," Yolanda agreed. "I think you should tell your parents. Your dad spent most of his life doing accounting. He might have some advice."

Adam shook his head. "Dad's just now seeing that I can be successful with art. I don't want to give him cause to doubt again. It's my own fault I let myself be taken advantage of. If I'd paid attention, I'd have money to help my parents. I wouldn't be a glorified handyman, having to paint caricatures on the weekend."

"You enjoy painting caricatures," Yolanda pointed out. "You always had a line and—"

"And made enough to survive, not get ahead."

"You sound like my mother."

Adam blinked. He wasn't sure Yolanda had meant it as a compliment.

"Tell me, were you paying Stacey for her help?" Yolanda asked.

"She didn't ask for pay. She volunteered. Once we became a couple, though, I paid for everything."

"You mean rent and groceries and going out."

Adam nodded, thinking that Stacey had gone out a lot more than he did. "You know," he said slowly. "The last essay I wrote in high school had the topic: An Event that Changed My Life. Kids wrote about divorce, death, car accidents. I couldn't come up with a topic. The only thing that caused me any stress was Andy. I wrote about having to deal with a special needs brother."

"I remember that essay," Yolanda said. "It was about the time he got lost."

"We found him in three hours. That was the most traumatic event in my life up to that point."

"You were very blessed."

"What did you write about?"

Yolanda looked at her hands for a moment. "I haven't thought about that essay in years."

"So you don't remember?"

"No, I remember. I wrote about going to the

thrift store with my mother and buying school clothes for sixth grade. Then on the first day of school, Mona Pagat announced to the whole playground that I was wearing her clothes from last year. I was so embarrassed."

"But so many others were writing about divorce, death and car accidents. We were both blessed and didn't realize it."

"I guess we'd have things to write about now," Yolanda mused. "You'd write about Stacey and I'd write about the Ventimiglias and my possible connection."

"It would be a book instead of an essay if I wrote about Stacey. All I've ever witnessed were healthy relationships. My parents have been married almost thirty years. GG still talks to her husband, and he's been gone thirty years. My aunt and uncle have been together so long they're starting to resemble each other."

"What would have happened to your and Stacey's relationship if the shared interest in art went away?"

Yolanda's question wasn't one that Adam had considered. He hadn't been into the nightlife scene nearly as much as she had been. He was more a get-comfortable-in-the-neighborhood kind of guy. He preferred books; she had the television on all the time. He didn't mind quiet, but she avoided it at all cost. If they were driving, she filled the space with the radio, singing along, or endless conversation.

"If we didn't have art in common, there'd be empty space," Adam realized. "She'd have filled it with noise, and I'd have filled it with contemplation. But we wouldn't be together."

He should have realized that the moment she moved in. She'd not tried to make the apartment her own. Now Adam recognized that she'd only been killing time.

"I guess this proves your mother's opinion of me was correct," Adam said.

"What do you mean?"

"She didn't think I'd amount to anything. She told me so more than once when she was still working at the mini-manse. She even warned me not to sniff around you."

Yolanda looked appalled. "She actually told you to leave me alone?"

"More than once."

"She was wrong," Yolanda said. "Those who are willing to risk are willing to grow, and Adam Snapp, that's you. You've really impressed me lately, especially with the drawings you've done from the book. The one of your ancestor, Jedidiah, is downright scary. It's as if he's really looking at me. I never thought about the art I'd have at my bookstore. Now I keep imagining what you could do with each room. I was even imagining putting up Halloween masks the other day. All your fault. I don't want blank walls any longer. I want color, imagination and…"

She didn't finish, but Adam could almost hear the whispered word: *you*.

Staring at Yolanda, he felt the memory of Stacey dimming, the scars vanishing.

Stacey had introduced him to the idea of sharing his life with a girl. But it had only been a trial run. What he wanted to do next was share his life with a woman twenty-four-seven for the next fifty years.

It was the worst time for such a realization. He had nothing to offer. Worse, she had everything to lose.

Like her house.

CHAPTER FOURTEEN

TUESDAY MORNING, ADAM rolled out of bed early. Again. This was becoming habit. Good thing since he had a lot to do today. Quietly, he made his way to the kitchen.

In his younger years, he'd only drawn in his bedroom, afraid of other people's opinions and interference.

After five years working outside in front of God and spectators, he no longer minded an audience. And at the Snapps' house, the kitchen was the heartbeat. What better place to draw the people who'd made history in Scorpion Ridge?

Today he was enlarging Jedidiah, still in pencil.

Tomorrow, if everything went well, Willy would commission him to paint a mural. Good. He wanted to feel a brush in his fingers again, rub his hand on an oilskin rag, blur the colors that brought a vision to life. Yolanda had been right; his muse had been with him all along.

Too bad he couldn't make some changes in Yolanda's house. She'd let him now, he knew.

At least until he revealed that the house might not be hers. Adam needed to get to the courthouse and look at the papers that were there. Then he wanted to talk to the lawyer Ruth had hired when she'd realized things weren't right with her deeds.

He returned to his drawing. This morning he noted that Jedidiah's nose might be a bit bigger than the ones boasted by the current generation of Snapps. As a creator, Adam could fix the flaw, but that would be messing with the truth.

After an hour of reworking a few of the details, Adam decided that maybe Jedidiah's ears really weren't parallel.

"I want you to paint the family." His dad's voice came from the doorway. "I've picked just the photos I want you to use, and I want you to merge them into one big canvas. We'll hang it in the living room."

"I can do that."

"Don't make my nose that big," Dad cautioned. "I've always been grateful to Loretta. I think her small nose offset my own father's big nose, skipping a generation. You and Andy got lucky, too."

Then Adam's stomach started making noises. Quickly, he put away his project. More than anything else, he wanted to see Yolanda this morning. Yesterday, when he'd bared his soul, had changed their friendship, but how much?

"If I make pancakes, will you eat them, Dad?"

His dad wrinkled his nose. "This morning I think I'll just have some crackers."

Adam started mixing the batter anyway. Even if his father didn't eat the pancakes, his mother would appreciate the gesture.

"You heading over to Yolanda's today?" his dad asked.

"Yes, I'm going to work in her kitchen for a few hours."

"You two have been spending quite a bit of time together," Dad noted.

Adam had had this conversation before. "She's my boss." But that wasn't true. Lately, she was more than his boss. Yesterday had been both enlightening and exhausting. He'd actually enjoyed squiring Yolanda around from book drop to book drop. He'd even purchased a few new horror and sci-fi books.

As for their hours—two, at least—at the truck stop, he'd come away with a different perspective, on quite a few areas of his life.

He'd realized that Stacey had worked for him and she'd deserved payment. Maybe she should have discussed it with him, especially when her name garnered some recognition. Taking the money, the way she did, was petty. He'd not deserved that. But it had taught him a valuable lesson about trust and about appreciating what he had, namely talent and the people he could trust.

"We've a couple of mutual goals," Adam admitted as he turned on the stove.

"Besides work," his dad teased. For a moment Adam saw a glimmer of his dad before he'd gotten sick, lost so much weight and started staying home instead of going to work.

"This surgery you're going to have?" Adam stood, headed for the pantry and came back with pancake mix. "What will happen? Both during and after."

"Because I have pancreatic cancer, there's not much hope."

"There's always hope."

"You sound like your mother."

When Adam didn't respond, his father continued, "It's a pretty drastic surgery. I'll be losing my gallbladder as well as parts of my pancreas and stomach. There's a lot more, but that shows you how serious the surgery is. The good news is that my cancer hasn't spread to my liver or any major blood vessels."

"And after the surgery?"

"It will improve my quality of life for my remaining years."

Adam felt the breath fan out of him. Making sure his father couldn't see, he leaned against the countertop and closed his eyes. Then he opened them and slowly made a circle with the pancake mix onto the griddle. "You didn't mention this when we were having our talk with GG the other morning."

"She's aware that it's serious. That's all she needs to know."

"Mom and I are the only ones who understand how serious?" Adam asked.

"Yes."

"I told Yolanda," Adam said, first to the countertop and then turning around to look into his dad's eyes.

"I'm fine with that."

"I'm staying in Scorpion Ridge, making it my home base. Dad, I've really thought about this. Last night Yolanda and I had a late dinner, and I realized that I'm happiest here. It's where the best of me resides. Scorpion Ridge is where my muse began, thanks to you."

"Don't give me credit. It was your great-grandmother and mother who pestered me into giving you those art lessons."

Adam had forgotten those lessons. The summer he'd been thirteen, his dad had driven him into Phoenix every morning and dropped him off at a summer program one of the art charter schools had offered. For the most part, it had been fluff. But Adam had learned about mixing color and about always locking away his stuff in a secure place. Valuable lessons, both.

"Dad, do you remember GG saying that she dated Woodhull Ventimiglia?"

"Yes."

"I think I know why they broke up."

His dad raised an eyebrow.

Quickly, Adam shared his suspicions, adding, "I told Yolanda my theory last night."

"Is she going to ask Rosi?"

"I'm not sure."

"Are you going to ask your great-grandmother?"

"I don't want to cause her to have another panic attack."

"Is it worth the risk? Does learning the truth change anything?"

This was the moment when Adam should share his suspicions about the Victorian's ownership. Instead, Adam finished setting the rest of the table and thought about how he could fit a trip to the courthouse into his day. And, for some reason, it was important to Adam to speak with Yolanda about his concern before he spoke with his father.

"Dad, why did you come back to Scorpion Ridge?" Adam headed to the stove again and flipped the pancakes.

He was familiar with his parents' story, how

they'd met in college, fell in love and then married their senior year. Once they'd graduated—Dad with a degree in accounting and Mom with a degree in English—they'd settled down in the house Dad had grown up in.

"I wanted to live in this house. I wanted to fill it with kids and play basketball with them."

Adam knew about his father's dream of having his own basketball team. Andy loved basketball but if you decided to play with him, you needed to be ready to play for hours. Adam had been more a soccer and baseball kind of kid, but his height had certainly been enough to encourage coaches to toss him the ball.

"Do you regret not having more children?"

His dad surprised him by answering, "Yes. We decided not to, because Andy's needs were so daunting. But once you boys turned six, we realized we could do it. We thought a little girl would be a nice addition."

"Then why didn't you have more?"

"Just didn't happen. We decided to wait for grandchildren."

"That would be my responsibility, right?" Adam set a plate of pancakes in front of his father.

His dad grinned. "Maybe."

All Adam's life, they'd carefully moved around what Andy's autism diagnosis meant.

He was a genius in math, able to add series of numbers from the time he hit first grade, but he'd never raise his hand to provide an answer in class. In school he'd sit in the back row, left corner. Nowhere else. It was unlikely that he would marry or have his own children.

"He's doing better," Adam said. "Since I've been home, the only time he got antsy was the end of the day on Saturday while we were waiting for one of the moms to arrive at the studio to pick up her son."

"He's always on the outside looking in," Dad said.

"No, you made sure that didn't happen," Adam said, "when you opened the studio and gave him a life. He's more social, he rarely has outbursts and he's happy."

Adam's mother came into the room, took one look at her husband and sat down, carefully leaning against him with a "Good morning, dear" kind of gesture. They'd always been a team, finishing each other's sentences, building a business, making time for family, friends and God.

Adam needed to tell Yolanda the truth today.

They'd been a true team until he'd stumbled across her heritage and the possibility that his family owned her house. Teams didn't grow stronger by hiding truths. He'd learned that much from Stacey. They grew stronger by tackling obstacles together. He wanted that chance with Yolanda.

He hoped he hadn't already blown it by waiting.

YOLANDA PULLED A stack of books from a box on the table by the cash register and glanced out the door. Gulliver promptly jumped into the box. Yolanda took him out again and set him on the floor. He scampered after a gum wrapper that hadn't quite made it to the trash can. It quickly became his favorite possession. Across the street, the Wilsons were walking to the sidewalk and greeting someone getting out of a car.

"They're selling the house," Gramma Rosi said.

"Really? Otis has lived there for how many years?"

"About forty. His family used to live up on Munro Street. His favorite aunt lived in this one. Otis spent a lot of time with her. He inherited the house when she died."

"What did Otis do for a living?"

"He took over his father's business. They owned the five and dime in the center of town. It was a pretty thriving business even into the seventies." Gramma Rosi came to stand beside

Yolanda. Across the street Otis was leaning on his cane and shaking his head.

No one paid attention to him.

"He still looks as if he can take care of himself. Maybe they should—"

"That's what I thought, too. But now that I'm in Red Roses Retirement Home, I'm enjoying the freedom. Believe me, Otis will enjoy the rest and security."

Otis had walked over to the Victorian every day since Yolanda had moved in. Sometimes he just stared at her front porch. Other times he came in, helped himself to food, or lately, sat in a chair on the porch with Gulliver in his lap.

Adam's van—slightly worse for wear after its breakdown last week— pulled up, and he parked in front of the bed-and-breakfast next door. The owners wouldn't complain, Yolanda knew, because they'd been asking whether Adam would come do some work for them.

Yolanda checked her watch. Adam had already taught a class, and here she stood on the front step not even restocking.

"We're talking about Otis across the street," Yolanda explained, when he finally joined them on the porch. "They're putting the house up for sale."

"He was in the painting," Adam said.

"The one in the museum," Yolanda explained when Gramma Rosi looked confused.

"Oh, lots of the young folk from my day are in that one."

"I don't remember seeing you," Yolanda said.

"I was inside helping with the food they were going to serve afterward. The Ventimiglias' whole staff was there. The night was guaranteed to be special. It had to be so. Ivy had painted all the backdrops. Woodhull was the main character. The most prominent family in town did shine."

"They served lemonade and cookies," Yolanda remembered.

"Otis wanted to be in the play. I heard he punched a hole in the wall of the boys' lavatory when he found out he wasn't chosen. He aspired to be an actor, but his parents told him absolutely not. I've always wondered what might have happened had they let him have the freedom to try."

"Why didn't he just leave?" Adam asked.

"Times were different then. Kids paid a bit more attention to their parents and their wishes. I know I did," she said wistfully.

Yolanda wondered just how much. She opened her mouth to ask, but didn't have the courage. Instead, she queried, "What would you have changed if you'd had the chance?"

"That's the kicker," Gramma Rosi said. "I'd never have moved into this house. But then, it wouldn't be your house, and I'm so glad it is."

"You don't like the house?"

"No, not really."

"Why, Gramma? You can tell me."

Rosi Acura looked at her granddaughter for a moment, a pained expression flitting across her aged face. Adam knew what Yolanda needed to hear, but obviously Rosi wasn't willing to say it.

If there was something to say. He could be wrong.

"I'd love to see the deed," Adam said, changing tactics. "Do you have it?"

"I'd have to find it," Gramma Rosi said. "I'm sure it's with my father's papers."

"Adam," Yolanda scolded, "what a thing to ask."

"He's right." Gramma Rosi looked a bit stressed. "If I'm going to sign the place over to you, I should get the paperwork in order."

Two customers came up the steps, and Rosi hurried to greet them before leading them inside, talking all the while about a romance she'd just read.

"She's a natural salesperson," Yolanda said. "I was worried she'd be giving books away. This morning she sold a World War Two book to a man, and he paid more than double what I was asking."

"Why?"

"She told him I forgot to add a two to the price."

"You might want to advise her not to do that too often." Adam followed Yolanda into the house and then the kitchen. He had work to do.

It only took him fifteen minutes to drill holes in the cabinet doors and screw in the handles. She leaned against the wall, watching him.

"Not as busy in the store as Friday and Saturday?"

"No, and Gramma Rosi's doing a fine job. I've been restocking and such."

"I'm heading to Huckabee's Harem next to finalize the commission," Adam told her. "It's a start toward helping my family."

"How's your dad doing?"

"This morning he ate a whole pancake. He'll have surgery next week. Then we'll see." Quickly, Adam laid out his plans—all that he was doing today and how much he thought he'd be able to make in a six-month period.

Yolanda took a moment to respond. "And after that?"

"I've the names of five contacts that wanted to hire me to do a mural. I was thinking I could make Scorpion Ridge my home base and travel three days of the week. Plus, there are plenty of homeowners in Scorpion Ridge who've approached me to help restore their houses. Then, too, I'll be working at BAA on weekends."

"You've thought this out."

"I have. Things are finally falling into place."

"How much do you make drawing funny likenesses of people who come to BAA?"

Adam finished the last door handle and then opened all the doors to see if any hit against the wall. Two did, and he attached two tiny clear bumper pads to their corners. "Five years ago, on a good weekend, I was averaging about eighty-five dollars an hour."

Yolanda's mouth dropped open. "What?"

"I'd expect to make about the same now. BAA's gotten busier, but I don't want to raise my prices. The economy has tanked, and most people coming to the zoo have little kids, so I'm competing with cotton candy and the carousel."

"Eighty-five dollars an hour? Luke paid me fifteen an hour, and I thought he was being gracious."

Adam stopped her. "I set my own prices and brought my own supplies. If it rained and no one came to BAA, I made nothing. You still made your fifteen dollars an hour if you made just one sale all night."

Yolanda's grandmother chose that moment to

enter the kitchen. "Looks good," she remarked. To Yolanda, she said, "Mr. Teasdale's here. He's going to sit and read in the history section. He doesn't plan to buy anything. I told him that would be just fine."

"Do you need me out front?" Yolanda asked.

"No, and Mr. Teasdale just sorted the rest of the books from the last box you were unloading. You should see the display he made for the *Readers Digest* collection."

Sometimes Yolanda felt as if the town of Scorpion Ridge owned the bookstore. Mr. Teasdale arranged books; Otis Henry went through her refrigerator; Gramma ran the cash register.

"Come with me to Huckabee's Harem," Adam suggested.

"I can't. We could get busy and Gramma might—"

Rosi interrupted her granddaughter. "Gramma might what? Fall down of old age while charging a friend two dollars for a used book? I don't think so. Besides, Mr. Teasdale is here to help." She leaned close and whispered, "He appreciates having something to do with his time." Louder, she added, "You go. Have some fun. Ride an ostrich."

Yolanda raised an eyebrow. "You don't ride them, do you?"

"I researched his place this morning online.

Huckabee has a lot going on, but I didn't see one photo of someone on the back of an ostrich. I get the idea they're not easily trained."

"Like some men I know," said Gramma Rosi as she sailed out the door, leaving Adam and Yolanda alone.

"Come with me," Adam said again. "After we leave the Harem, I'm heading to the court-house. I want to look at the deeds that were in the trunk we saw at the museum. Something just isn't adding up."

"Is that why you asked Gramma about her deed?"

"Yes."

He was relieved when she didn't question any further. If the deed to her house was in his great-grandmother's name, he wanted the proof in front of him when it came time to face the truth.

He really hoped he was wrong and that the deed had the Acura name on it.

But if he was right, he wanted her to know that he'd do anything he could to help her keep the Victorian. That they were in this together.

They took his van, although Yolanda mut-tered about breaking down in the middle of no-where and gas prices.

"She's fixed as good as new, and I'm the one footing the gas, so relax."

He watched her as her fingers strummed the

side of the car door. To his surprise, he knew what she was worried about.

"Rosi will be fine. When we left, she was sitting behind the cash register with a book in her hand, a glass of tea on the counter and a cat in her lap."

"I know, but someone broke in just a week ago."

"Broke in to take books and then waltzed in to return them. I doubt there's much danger."

"But this—"

Adam raised a hand to stop her. "I agree. Something is going on, but it's more likely that Ivy, or whoever it is, is searching for what she's lost. And I have an idea of what it is."

"The name Ventimiglia gets Gramma Rosi's hackles up every time it's mentioned. It's about more than that we live in the house that was once hers. It's also that she's not in the painting, the one in the museum, because she was in the kitchen working." Yolanda paused then said, "What do you mean you have an idea what it is? It's the book? Isn't it?"

He shook his head, aware that this was an opportunity to lay the groundwork for what was coming.

It was the last thing he wanted to tell her; it was the one thing he had to do.

"You know how the courthouse fire keeps coming up?"

"Yes."

"It happened in 1946."

"The year my mother was born."

"The year the Ventimiglias left town."

"Because their son died or was murdered."

"Yolanda, it's possible that the fire was set, probably by Richard Ventimiglia, on purpose to destroy deeds so they could later be replaced by false deeds."

"What do you mean?"

"Remember my mentioning that Luke saw the name Ventimiglia on a piece of paper when Ruth was transferring ownership of BAA to him?"

"Yes."

"Well, I went to see her day before last. The deed she has may not be valid. She's hired a lawyer to verify that the Moores owned the land the mini-manse and BAA are on."

"What?"

"Seems that Richard put a lien on the property because of back taxes, which Ruth says were never owed. Plus, there's the property between BAA and Huckabee's Harem. It belongs to Ruth, but the deed reads Richard Ventimiglia.

"Wow."

"The deed's a re-creation. It's dated after

the fire. So it could have been forged. There's more," Adam continued. "Ruth says the lawyer she's hired has turned up a few more discrepancies."

"Such as?"

Before he could answer Yolanda's question, they turned into Huckabee's Harem. The dirt parking lot was about one-fifth the size of BAA's. Right now only two cars and one large van were in it. Adam stopped and hurried around the car to open Yolanda's door.

In front of them, Huckabee's gift shop was no more than an outdoor tent sale. One side displayed overpriced giant egg shells—some with pictures painted on them, not very good pictures—and ostrich feather dusters. On the other side, Huckabee was selling ostrich magnets, T-shirts and stuffed animals. A girl, with at least two kittens prowling around her feet, sat at a picnic table. She couldn't have been more than fifteen and was painting an ostrich egg as casually as most females painted their fingernails: one glob of color, slick, and then on to the next. She wasted little time blending and hadn't diluted the acrylic paint.

But she had talent.

"Is William Huckabee here?"

"Dad's giving a bus ride. They left about five

minutes ago. He won't take another group out
until there's at least ten of you."

"I'm Adam Snapp. I'm here to talk to him
about a mural."

Now he had her attention. "You did the ones
at BAA."

"I did."

"Oh, they're awesome! I paint on the wall in
my bedroom. Elephants. They're the saddest
creatures. I'm glad BAA doesn't have one. They
don't belong in captivity. I like how you used fur
in your bear mural. What did you do with the
elephant at BAA? I can't remember. I thought
maybe tusks that stick out, but that could get
dangerous."

"I designed a moveable trunk with a hose inside that water could shoot out of."

"Oh, I can't believe I didn't remember that."
Then, as if just remembering her manners, she
stuck out her hand. "I'm Heather Huckabee.
Willy's my dad. I'm the one who told him about
all you did over at BAA. I made him go see it.
He was convinced."

"Thank you," Adam said gravely. Maybe he
was meeting his number-one fan.

Heather turned to Yolanda. "Are you his girlfriend?"

"No, just a friend."

Heather didn't look impressed as she stood

up, leaving the egg half-finished and her brushes exposed. "Come meet my mother. She's given Dad a budget when it comes to the mural, and she's researched how much you've been paid. Did you really paint all those murals for free over at BAA? I painted all these ostrich eggs for free. Dad says he's teaching me the business. I think he's looking for cheap labor."

"Painting the murals at BAA was short-term free labor that turned into long-term profit. By the time I left BAA," Adam said, "I had a portfolio and had been featured in a few magazine and newspaper articles."

"You're all over the web," Heather agreed, leading them around the sales tent and across a road. Yolanda walked beside her, about the same height, her head swiveling right and left, taking in the sights.

Adam noticed a nice home, ranch style, next to what looked like a giant barn.

"But really," Heather repeated, "who's ever gotten famous for painting ostrich eggs?"

"I'm famous because of a farting bench," Adam said.

That gave Heather pause. She walked up the driveway to the porch, opening a door and gesturing them inside. "Maybe the ostrich eggs are a good place to start."

Before Adam could comment, Heather shouted,

"Mom, Mom, Adam Snapp and some girl are here." A muffled response came from the back of the house.

"She's with my great-aunt. We take care of her. She's kinda losing it."

"Seems to be happening to a lot of people," Yolanda said. "I caught my Gramma Rosi eating a ketchup sandwich for breakfast this morning."

"I told you to stock up on groceries," Adam put in.

"I did," Yolanda protested.

"You two sound like married people." Heather disappeared down a hall, leaving Adam and Yolanda to gape at each other.

"We're spending way too much time together," Yolanda said.

"Or maybe, "Adam said, "it's just that we get along."

Yolanda didn't acknowledge his contribution. Instead she sat on the couch. A kitten climbed up the side of the couch and headed for her lap. Idly, Yolanda—getting used to the quirks and needs of kittens—stroked its neck and back while she gazed around the house. "Very much a mixture of old and new."

"Lots of great antiques," Adam agreed.

But Yolanda wasn't listening, instead she was leaning toward the coffee table and picking up a yellow cup with an orange daisy painted on the front of it.

Her voice cracked a bit as she whispered, "This is the one that was taken from my bookstore."

Before Adam could answer, or even look at the coffee cup, the front door opened and Willy Huckabee walked in, all breathless and smiles.

"I'm so glad you're here." He shook Adam's hand. Then he gave Yolanda a hug. "It's usually slow on Tuesdays, but I had a group of Senior Saints drive all the way up from Gesippi just to see my place. I had to take them for a spin."

Yolanda nodded, only half listening to his words, instead intent on asking, "Where did you get this coffee cup?"

"I'm not exactly sure," Willy said easily. "Guests leave things all the time. Yesterday I found somebody's false teeth sitting on the picnic table under the sales tent. I must have stared at faces all day, thinking I'd find someone gumming it."

"I'm sure this cup is mine," Yolanda said.

"She has a set exactly like that," Adam added.

"Then keep it. Wife keeps complaining about not having enough shelf space in the kitchen anyway. You'll be doing me a favor."

"Somebody stole it from my bookstore." Yolanda went on to describe Ivy and all that happened that day that felt so long ago now. While she spoke, Willy's eyes dimmed.

"That sounds like my great-aunt. She came to live with us a month ago. Her landlord called us because she started leaving her dishes on a table outside her apartment door. When he questioned her, she said the maid would pick them up."

"So she's wealthy?"

"No, but she used to be. Her family lost everything and had to start over. But that happened many years ago. Maybe you've heard us praying for her at church. Bitsy's getting real forgetful. We—" Willy looked around "—brought her here so she'd be comfortable, with family. But she isn't really happy with us. She says Scorpion Ridge is a horrible place."

"Does Bitsy smoke?" Adam asked.

"If I'd let her," Willy said. "No, I take that back. If Heather'd let her. Heather scolds our paying guests if they so much as take out a cigarette. That doesn't mean I haven't caught Bitsy outside talking to the guests and bumming a cigarette. Don't tell Heather. I think her third-grade teacher did too good a job with the health unit. She glares at me when I drink coffee. Something about caffeine at my age."

"What's Bitsy's real name?" Yolanda asked.

"Ivy. Ivy Ventimiglia."

CHAPTER FIFTEEN

"MY GREAT-GRANDMOTHER SAID she was dead." The minute Adam said it, and based on the dirty look Yolanda shot him, Adam wanted the words back. He gave her a *What? I'm just saying what we're both thinking* return stare.

She smiled one of her famous Mona Lisa smiles, one that was more of a reprimand, and then switched her attention to the Huckabees. "How much of the Ventimiglia history do you know?"

"Not much of it," Willy admitted. "Only what Ivy and Grandpa Chester have told me."

Yolanda almost slid off the couch. "You know Chester!"

"He was my grandfather. Greatest guy ever. He owned a construction company in Flagstaff, where I grew up. Acme Construction. Maybe you've heard of it. It's located just over two hundred miles south of Phoenix and—"

"Yes, I've heard of it," Yolanda and Adam said at the same time.

"How is it," Willy asked, "that you're so interested in my family's history?"

In response, Adam explained about Ivy's visit to Yolanda's bookstore.

"This makes no sense," Yolanda added. "I searched the internet for his name. If he owned a huge company, why didn't I find his name?"

"Oh, the business was incorporated under his wife's maiden name. She managed the place, really, and made it a success. He got some type of tax break because it was a female-run business."

Willy seemed to sense that they wanted him to continue, so he went right on. "When I was in high school, he donated time and materials to a local charity, and the shop students from our school built a house for a needy family. That's the kind of guy he was. When the wife and I decided to move to Scorpion Ridge, we designed and helped build this house. I could do that because he taught me exactly what I needed to do." Willy looked around proudly.

"Did you come to Scorpion Ridge because of your heritage?"

"No. Mostly I came here because Chester left me this land. I'd been paying taxes on it for thirty years. Wife and I drove out one day to see it, liked what we saw and decided to retire here."

"You didn't retire, though," Adam observed. "You started this."

Willy chuckled. "I watched a documentary on ostriches on television. I got it in my head to raise them much like you would cattle. Best part is they don't require all that much room. But once I had my first herd of twenty, they became personalities, and I couldn't bear to slaughter them."

"So you opened this place to the public," Yolanda said. "Is it profitable?"

"Not yet, but we break even, and someday we hope to make a profit. Right now we're living our dream. It's kinda cool. The wife makes all the feather dusters, and we get orders from as far away as Florida. People enjoy getting a picture of the ostrich that donated the feathers. Plus, Heather is saving the money she makes off the ostrich eggs for college. She's a real artist. Bitsy taught her. I was ready to retire, but not ready to be bored. The ostriches give me something to do."

"He means driving that crazy bus gives him something to do," came a voice from the hallway.

Adam stood. He'd not met Willy's wife, and she wasn't quite what he expected. Willy looked like a good ole boy rancher, who had the money and heart to try anything. Connie definitely personified the hippie era. Her long hair had probably once been blond, but now it was silver-streaked white. She was a good two inches taller than her husband.

Heather had returned, too, smiling and helping her mother. On her arm was an old woman with startling blue eyes. Surprisingly, the elderly woman walked upright, and although it was just a regular Tuesday afternoon, she was dressed in a red polyester dress that had a matching jacket with white trim.

"Very Jackie Kennedy," Yolanda murmured.

Adam had been questing for a connection; Yolanda supplied it. If Adam included Ivy in the exhibit he planned, this was how he would paint her.

No, not true, because Ivy took one look at him and stopped her slow steps. She hung back, glancing over at Willy as if he'd done something wrong.

"Why is George here?" she asked. "We don't associate with their family. George Snapp, you need to leave."

"My name is Adam. George was my great-grandfather."

Ivy looked at Willy, still accusingly. "That boy's father shot…" her words tapered off, and her face scrunched in consternation. "Oh, I can't remember which cousin it was. He was down from Flagstaff."

"Really, Aunt Bitsy, I don't remember this story," Willy said. "Are you sure?"

"Of course I'm sure. He was out walking, just to get some fresh air. I don't know how he got all the way over to where the farms were. That man's father, Jedidiah, said our cousin was trying to steal a cow. Now, why would he want a cow? Makes no sense."

"I'm sorry," Adam said, all serious. "But it was before my time, and I had no control over the situation. I'm sure if Jedidiah were here, he'd apologize."

"Hurrumph, not that man. He didn't apologize for anything. He thought he was something."

"Bitsy," Connie said gently, "you're getting all upset. These young people are here to paint a mural for Willy. Something that will help us advertise the ostriches. They didn't mean to upset you."

"But he is a Snapp, right?" Ivy asked.

"Yes."

Then Ivy turned her attention to Yolanda. This time she didn't stop or hang back. Instead, she took a step forward, staring, her voice hard. "I remember you. You worked for us."

"Aunt Bitsy, sit down." Willy guided his aunt to a rocking chair. After she settled in, he adjusted the pillow behind her. She was sitting ramrod straight and had clenched her hands together. Yolanda glanced at Adam. "Is the book in your backpack?"

"Out in the van," he answered.

To Ivy, Yolanda said, "You left a book when you visited my bookstore."

"Why would you have a bookstore?" Ivy asked, clearly confused. "Do maids know how to read?"

Turning to her nephew, Ivy said, "She used to do the silver. She'd sit in the kitchen at the table all day, buffing, buffing, buffing. We were about the same age. Did you know that? I'd walk by holding my china head doll, and she'd stare at me with those big brown eyes. She must have sat at that table every day for seven years. Then she started helping in the kitchen, and another little girl took over the silver. I never got her name. She didn't last long."

"You have quite a memory, Aunt Bitsy."

"I do. That doll came from Germany. I was the only one in town who had one. Everyone was jealous. Except for you." She glared at Yolanda.

"I never played with dolls, ma'am."

"And you're still in my house, sitting at the table, only now you think the house is yours."

"It is mine. I've turned it into a bookstore. You came in searching for a book last week."

"Yes. When Connie drove through town, I saw the sign. She dropped me off for a short visit. I was sure surprised that my house would be a bookstore. But then, I've been trying to find my book for a very long time."

"Your book? So you didn't leave one behind at my store?"

"No, why would I ask for it and then leave it behind? I wrote that book a long time ago. Then I misplaced it. I really want it back."

"I'll go get it," Adam said.

Her eyes went wide, and her hands went to the armrests. She clutched them so hard her fingers were white. "You have it." Her voice gasped a bit, coming out in a half cough, as if she needed air.

Connie got Aunt Bitsy a glass of water, and Yolanda tried not to squirm as the elderly woman caught her breath. "You'll give me the book back," Ivy said.

"If it's yours, you can have it. I'm honest."

"Your father wasn't." Ivy's tone was monotone but her blue eyes weren't. They were alert and unwavering, unsympathetic.

"Aunt Bitsy!" Willy scolded. Turning to Yolanda, he said, "This visit really isn't what I imagined. Aunt Bitsy usually keeps her opinions to herself."

"I was raised to do that. Be seen but not heard.

Well, that's why I wrote everything down. I knew someday the words would be read. I'm just surprised it took this long."

"She doesn't keep her opinions to herself," Heather protested. "She's all the time telling me what I should do."

"Maybe," Willy continued, "we should plan our business for another day. I don't want Bitsy worn out or upset. This isn't good for her."

Adam knocked on the door, opened it and slipped back into the living room. He held *Stories of Scorpion Ridge, Arizona,* in his hand.

"Oh." Ivy clapped her hands a few times. "It's been sixty years, maybe more, since I've seen the book. Please, give it to me."

Yolanda nodded and Adam handed it over.

Ivy's gnarled hands stroked the cover, the spine and then opened to the first page before she pointedly stared at Heather.

The girl jumped up from the couch. "I'll get your glasses."

A moment later Ivy read the name on the inside cover. "Chester Ventimiglia. He was my uncle. I gave it to him, watched while he wrote his name in it and then he put it in the bookcase. He started reading it, but he got upset. The truth does that to people. My father cheated him out of a lot of money, his whole inheritance, and then left town in the middle of the night.

He showed up more than twenty years later at Chester's door with no money left."

"Did Chester take your family in?"

"Yes, for all of a week. It was all very embarrassing. Living with him was quite a change after the Victorian, let me tell you. Chester's house only had three bedrooms, and he allowed us the tiny one in the back. They didn't have servants, either. And my mother cried every night for her house and for my brother. My father disappeared a week later. Packed his meager belongings one night and took off." Her voice shook. Yolanda wasn't sure if it was from the memories or from her age.

"Later," Ivy continued, "we found out that he'd gone to a small town in Kansas, pretended to be a widower and became a judge. It only lasted four years. He cheated somebody else, the wrong somebody, and wasn't heard of again. Mother and I think he was murdered. Just like Woodhull."

"Family secrets." Willy sighed. "Neither of you plan on putting this in the town paper, eh?"

"Soon we didn't care about what had happened to my father." Ivy paid no attention to Willy's comment. "It was nice living with Chester. I learned how to cook and took art lessons. The house was full of laughter. It was a nice change. When he died, I mailed the book to—

Oh, look here. I'd forgotten." She fell silent, going through the book, every once in a while smiling then frowning. She got two-thirds of the way through and gave a little gasp. When Connie made to go to her, she held up her hand. "No, just the truth knocking. It gave me a start."

Yolanda had to give the Huckabees credit. They were learning their history the hard way. They looked half intrigued and half shell-shocked.

Connie put her hand on Bitsy's and said, "You don't have to share all this. It's the past. Nobody will judge you."

"Everybody gets judged," Ivy said. "Some when they're supposed to, and others a bit later." To Heather, she said, "Go to my bedroom and get me the scrapbook in the bottom dresser drawer."

Heather, looking somewhat mesmerized by everything she was hearing, hurried from the room.

"I'm amazed that we're getting the answers today," Yolanda told the Huckabees. "Ever since this book showed up in my bookstore, we've been trying to find out who left it."

"Why didn't you tell me you had it the day I came?" Agitated, Ivy started rocking. "I've worried about it so."

"Why did you worry about it so?" Adam

asked. "The pictures are stunning. Did you draw them?"

"One of the few things a girl of my station was allowed to do. I loved to draw. Mother made sure I got supplies even when Father said no. After Chester's wife died, he and my mother married. She told me that all those years ago, he'd sent her money for art lessons because he knew my father wouldn't give me any."

Turning her attention to Yolanda, she said, "So, I take it you've read the whole book. Then why would you return it to me? You know the information in here can change lives, hurt some, heal others."

"I've read part of it. Adam's read it all. Please believe me, this book wasn't at the store when you came," Yolanda explained. "And we weren't exactly sure who you were."

The Huckabees' heads ping-ponged as they tried to keep up with the conversation. Ivy had no such problem.

"What do you mean it wasn't at the bookstore? You said you found it."

"I found it," Yolanda explained, "on the floor in the children's room when I went to clean up. Almost an hour after you left."

"We assumed you had left it," Adam explained. "But if you didn't, who did?"

"The old rascal had it the whole time," she

murmured. "Well, he did what I asked him to do. He told everyone I was dead, and they believed it."

"Here, Aunt Bitsy, your scrapbook."

"What old rascal?" Yolanda asked.

She was ignored. Ivy took the oversize scrapbook. The cover was red vinyl, and the thick, black pages inside were so full of mementos that it accordioned out. It crackled with age when she opened it. After a moment she came to the page she wanted. She pulled out a manila envelope that held photos. She put them upside down on the lamp stand. Then she drew out two pages and handed them to Adam.

The missing pages from the book. So much had gone on since finding it that he'd almost forgotten the missing pages.

"Do you mind if I look at these?" he said to Willy.

"You don't need my permission. They belong to Bitsy."

"I told Otis that when it was time, the book should be read by those who needed the truth."

"Otis?" Yolanda said. "My Otis from across the street?"

"He told me you were a good girl. He insisted on returning the books he took from the attic trunk even though I said they belonged to my family."

"And," Adam said slowly, not letting Ivy get sidetracked. "you think we need the truth."

She nodded.

"What if I already know the truth?" He glanced from Ivy to Yolanda, both the same size.

"Wood didn't deserve to die." She looked from Adam to Yolanda, her gaze going soft. "He loved her. She was the first thing he wanted that he couldn't have. So he went after her. It didn't work out quite like he planned, though."

"Did my gramma know he loved her?"

"Oh, yes. Wood tried to make sure she would be taken care of. But my father was a bit trickier than that. We were losing everything, everything, because of my father, but still he blamed the losses on Wood and your grandmother. But he was the one who set the fire at the courthouse."

Adam stared down at the pages Ivy had just given him.

There was no doubt what he was seeing. Ivy was a much more detailed artist than he was. The image showed Ivy's brother at the bottom of a well; his own father stood at the top.

IVY HELD OUT the pages to Adam, and Yolanda wanted to snatch them from him. This was *her* story. Ivy had threatened *her*. Otis had left the book in *her* children's section. Her grandmother had worked for the Ventimiglias and had their son's child.

The only connection Adam had was that his great-grandmother had once gone steady with Woodhull.

"Aunt Bitsy, you don't have to do this." Willy was starting to look alarmed, not at the pages exchanging hands, but at Ivy's pallor, the way her hands shook, the sadness in her eyes.

"I do. I've wanted the truth known for a long time. It was my uncle who rebuilt the courthouse. He found out my father had set fire to it. But if he revealed that fact, more men would be ruined, so Chester had the courthouse rebuilt. I never got to see it until a few months ago."

"'Erected in nineteen hundred and fifty because of Richard Ventimiglia and by Chester Ventimiglia, by his hard work and money,'" Adam recited.

Ivy clapped her hands. "Chester always said that someday someone would make the connection. I never thought it would be a Snapp. They were about the only ones my father couldn't swindle. Old Jedidiah didn't trust him. He did his business at other places. And when my father put pressure on him, Jedidiah got out a gun. You could do that back then, you know."

Slowly, Adam opened the pages and laid them on the coffee table so that everyone could lean over and see them. Only Ivy didn't lean; instead, she rocked. Her eyes were staring straight ahead, and her lips were pursed.

"Is that Otis?" Adam asked, pointing to a drawing of two young men standing by a well. One was clearly Woodhull.

"Yes, he was at the well with my brother. I think they were planning how to get out of town without being caught. Wood wanted to take Rosi along. Otis just wanted freedom. They probably would have gotten away with it, too, but my brother was starting to have a conscience." Ivy looked at Yolanda. "Thanks to your grandmother."

"Rosi's pretty special."

"Wood had watched my father that day, watched him filling out deeds. Because of my father's job, he had all the certificates and forms."

"Because he planned to set fire to the courthouse," Adam said.

"You are a bright boy." Ivy reached out and patted him on the cheek. "Definitely a Snapp."

"I'm a little lost here." Yolanda spoke up. "The changing of the deeds, is that why Ruth now has to prove she owns the land her house is on?"

"Wait!" Willy leaned forward. "Aunt Bitsy, are you saying that your father changed legal documents in this town so that he owned more than he was actually entitled to?"

"We were broke. It was only a matter of time before everyone found out. My father came up with this scheme so we'd keep everything. He didn't care who he hurt."

"Do I own *this* land?" Willy asked.

"You do, thanks to Chester."

"And Ruth owns the land that BAA is on. You can testify to that?"

"Yes, Otis would be able to, as well, as Wood showed him some of the forgeries."

"All these years," Yolanda wondered. "Why didn't Otis speak up?"

"Because he knew my father killed Wood, and that my father wouldn't hesitate to kill him, too. I also imagine that by the time he felt safe from my father, he was terrified to face the townspeople who would be affected by the changes." She looked right at Yolanda.

"When my father was changing the name on the deeds, he put Loretta Munro down as owner of the Victorian. My father figured everyone knew that Woodhull would marry her and then the Victorian would be restored to our family. Didn't work out that way."

Yolanda stared across at Adam. He didn't blink, just gazed at her with compassion and something else. His dark brown eyes offered something that just yesterday she'd been prepared to take.

He wasn't surprised.

He'd already known the Victorian was in his great-grandmother's name.

And to think she'd believed in him, believed that the kiss had been the first of many. That she could trust him.

He took too many risks, and this time the risk had been to her heart.

"I want to get all this said." Ivy spoke up before her family could offer any advice.

Willy nodded. "All right, Aunt Bitsy."

Adam moved, coming to sit beside Yolanda on the couch. She wanted to move away from him, but the couch was old, and the cushions formed a sunken V. She turned a little, nestling closer, leaning into him. In some ways he was like a shelter. In other ways he made her feel trapped.

But it wasn't just him. It was also the history being poured at her feet.

"This is why Gramma Rosi was so upset when we mentioned Ivy's name. All these years the Ventimiglias had been gone. Her secret, about her oldest daughter, had been safe."

"Does this mean we're cousins?" Heather asked Yolanda, looking intrigued at the possibility.

"Distant," Willy responded.

"Very distant," Ivy agreed, glancing at Adam. "And not supposed to be."

"Loretta said she was Wood's fiancée." Adam stayed next to her, his hand on hers.

"Father didn't want Rosi or her family to have our home."

"Why was that even an option?" Willy finally had a question.

"Her father showed up at the door, demanding that Woodhull do what was right by his daughter. At that point, I think my father knew we would be leaving Scorpion Ridge. The Snapps had never done business with us. The Moores were severing ties. Our credit at Otis's store was embarrassingly overdue. Quite frankly, the only thing we had left was pretense. Father knew that Rosi's family could restore the Victorian. So he drew up the paperwork and signed it over to the Acuras. But it was paperwork that would never be seen because he was planning the fire."

"Just," Adam said, "one more manipulated deed so that someday he could return to Scorpion Ridge and claim land that didn't belong to him."

"And that's why Loretta might own my house?" Yolanda whispered.

"He wanted the deed to be in her name. The Acuras would live there for a while, but he'd take it back once he regained his fortune else-where, claiming he'd signed it over to Loretta on Wood's behalf as a wedding gift."

"This is really convoluted," Willy said.

"Better than *Twilight*," Heather agreed.

"My father made a career on being convoluted and manipulative. This was a small town, and he controlled it for many years."

Looking at Ivy, Yolanda said, "Are you sure your father pushed Woodhull in the well?"

Ivy nodded at the picture. "Look at the trees. I drew us in there, me and Otis. I saw the whole thing, and I never told anybody."

"Until today," Yolanda said.

Ivy stopped rocking. She folded her hands in her lap again and straightened her spine. "Woodhull was stronger, but he didn't know how to fight. He'd never worked a day in his life. My father had bullied people from the day he was born."

"Thank you for telling me all of this," Yolanda said, standing, feeling out of breath, betrayed and somehow empty. "It answers a lot of questions."

Adam stood, too. She cherished his presence, but in the same breath wanted to push him away.

Truthfully, she didn't like to think of the consequences from some of these answers. She'd barely had time to digest the fact that she might be related to the Ventimiglias—pretty much a certainty after what Ivy had revealed—but now she had to deal with the fact that his family "might" own her bookstore.

"Are you going to tell Rosi what you know?" Ivy asked. The look in her eyes seemed to dare Yolanda.

"Yes. We're a family that supports each other. We don't keep secrets like that."

She eyed Adam, telling him without words just what she thought about *his* keeping secrets, breaking her trust.

CHAPTER SIXTEEN

IVY PUSHED HERSELF up from the rocking chair and beckoned for Adam to follow. Looking back at Yolanda, he shrugged. They'd spent a week trying to find this woman. Part of him wished they hadn't.

The Huckabees were busy trying to figure out exactly how they were all related. Adam could hear Willy's wife say, "If Woodhull Ventimiglia was Yolanda's grandfather, and Chester Ventimiglia was Willy's grandfather, then Yolanda is our cousin."

Yolanda, the cousin, apparently didn't have much to say. Well, she was worried about her house, about what his family would do.

Heather, on the other hand, was very excited. "Finally, a relative close to my age!" was her welcome.

Adam knew Yolanda wanted to go home. She had to be shell-shocked. He'd be polite to Ivy and then he'd take Yolanda away from all this, convince her that everything would be all right. He'd win her back. He'd paint a million murals, work day and night and buy the Victorian if he had to. Buy it from his grandmother. Even if it took the rest of his life.

Because he wanted to spend the rest of his life with her. Now he understood why his dad had returned to Scorpion Ridge.

Adam imagined a basketball net attached to the Victorian's carriage house… He couldn't think of anything more exciting than shooting hoops with his children, inviting Andy over to play, too.

"You coming?" Ivy asked.

"Right behind you." Adam was half-afraid of what Ivy wanted to show him. After all, she'd just turned Yolanda's history into a Lifetime movie. He didn't want to know any Snapp secrets.

"You think my pictures are stunning," Ivy said, walking through a doorway into a bedroom that contained a bed, a dresser and more than a hundred canvasses stacked against the wall. "That's what you said earlier."

Adam stopped, staring around the cramped room. There was no need for him to re-create the drawings from the blue book. Ivy had already done it. They were all here.

"I was impressed by your work when I saw it over at BAA. When I heard what your last name was, though, I never wanted to meet you." Ivy picked up first one canvas and then another, studying them, studying Adam and looking somewhat sad. "I was wrong." She turned a canvas around. "This was Otis when he was just eighteen. He wanted to be an actor, you know."

Adam nodded. A part of him wanted to go through the canvasses with her, discuss technique, ask if there were any drawings in the book that she hadn't enlarged. Another part wondered how she could be so calm.

The only story he had was Stacey leaving him. Compared to the tragedies in Ivy's life, his didn't seem so bad. He'd recover, be a better person, make sure it didn't happen again.

Plus, the only person really hurt by Stacey's betrayal had been him. Nobody else. And maybe in the scheme of things, that was the biggest blessing of all.

Looking at Ivy's face as she stared at the canvas bearing Otis's likeness, he thought about all she'd suffered. Maybe now that she'd told the story, her final days would be happier.

"What do you think?" Ivy asked.

She'd been talking the whole time.

"I'm sorry. What did you say?"

She frowned but repeated, "Willy wants me to put on a show. He's said it for years. I never put much stock in the suggestion, but now I like the idea. Only, instead of my drawings alone, the show should include your work."

Adam was having trouble keeping up. Sometimes Ivy seemed to be living in the past, and now she seemed to be firmly in the present.

His eyes swept the more than one hundred canvasses in the room. Here was Scorpion Ridge's past, drawn by someone who had lived it. He couldn't compete. Didn't want to.

"What we need," Ivy said, "is today's perspective." She held up the canvas. "If I have the Otis of yesterday, you could create the Otis of today. Scorpion Ridge is alive, and our past should complement that, not overshadow it."

Ivy surprised him by saying, "Think about it, Adam Snapp, but in the meantime, go to her. I can't say I approve of what my brother and her grandmother did, or that I'll ever consider her a Ventimiglia, but it's clear the two of you belong together."

Looking around the room, she frowned.

"Are you tired?" Adam asked. "I'll send Heather in, she can—"

"No, don't send Heather."

"You want Connie?"

Ivy gave him a glare that clearly said *No*.

"I'll fetch Yolanda," Adam said. "She needs to get back to work."

"At the bookstore," Ivy agreed. "You'll definitely want to draw that. My father must be turning over in his grave."

"I've got things to do, too," Adam continued.

Call Rafael, tell him about a murder. Call Loretta, tell her that her name might be on a forged deed granting her ownership of an eight hundred thousand dollar Victorian.

And suddenly, Adam was no longer worried. Based on Ivy's story, and with Otis to corroborate it, it was unlikely Yolanda would lose the home her grandmother had given her, as the deed with Loretta's name on it was a forgery. And the Snapps would make no claim on it.

Maybe they could include the deeds that Richard had re-created as part of the display they'd put on in the courthouse.

Oh, it wouldn't happen for years, but by then, there'd be closure, the best kind of closure.

When he walked back into the living room, Connie was hugging Yolanda and talking about having both her and Rosi over for Thanksgiving.

Yolanda didn't say no, but Adam could tell by the way she held her shoulders so straight that she wanted to.

When they got into the van, he turned to her and said, "Look, I'll do—"

She held up a hand, stopping him.

"Just take me home."

He started the engine and backed out of the parking lot. "But I want—"

"I don't care what you want. If I had the strength to walk, I wouldn't be in this van with you. I don't want your help, not with my house, not with my life. Just take me home," she repeated.

"If you'll just…" he began as he pulled out onto the road, but then he noticed the silent tears streaming down her face.

Maybe he hadn't put them there, but he'd definitely put himself in a position where he was part of her problem and not part of her solution.

Regaining her trust might be the hardest task he'd had in life yet.

"PHONE'S FOR YOU," Gramma Rosi called.

A full week had gone by. Each day, when Yolanda walked into Twice Told Tales, she worried that it would be her last.

"Who is it?"

"The arbitrator that Ruth Dunbar recommended," Gramma Rosi said. "But if you'd just given Adam a chance, that boy—" Yolanda held up her hand, palm out. Even though Ivy could testify that the deed with Loretta's name on it was a forgery, the deed with the Acuras' name on it—if they could find it—could only be a recreation of what was lost in the fire. Ivy could also testify that her father had never intended to truly sell his house to the Acuras. So what would a judge decide? Yolanda was not at all confident the law was on her side.

She took the phone, listened a minute to the arbitrator before pulling her calendar out of the desk drawer. They agreed to meet the next day.

"I should have told you the truth," Gramma Rosi said. "I knew something was wrong years ago. I wanted to take out a second mortgage, and when I went to the courthouse and asked for a copy of the deed, I realized I couldn't prove I owned the place. If my father ever had a bill of sale, I couldn't find it. I decided I didn't want a second mortgage."

"Don't worry, Gramma Rosi. We'll figure something out. And it's just a house. I still have Mama's. If this belongs to Loretta, I'll move."

"But…your dream. Your bookstore."

"Depending on what the arbitrator does, maybe I'll buy Otis's place across the street. It doesn't have quite the same personality, and I won't be able to live upstairs, but it would make a nice bookstore."

The door opened, a customer came in and Gramma Rosi disappeared out the back door. Lately, the townspeople had come more to talk to Rosi than to buy used books. And each time

Rosi told the story, she seemed to find a peace that Yolanda couldn't.

More than one customer also mentioned how truly sorry Adam Snapp was.

"The boy certainly is moping around." This came from Mr. Teasdale.

"Customers at BAA are complaining," Thelma Sheldon said. "Adam's caricatures aren't as funny as they used to be."

In the week since Ivy's confession, Yolanda had seen Adam twice. Once at the sheriff's office when she had gone to give her statement. And second time at church.

Andy had waved.

Tomorrow she'd drive to Adobe Hills and sit across from an arbitrator who would help sort out who deserved what.

Adam should have told her everything. She'd have understood. His father's life was worth more than a house. Love was worth more than secrets.

After making a sale, *Frankenstein* by Mary Shelley, Yolanda peeked out the front door. When she didn't see any customers, she hurried out to the yard to find her Gramma Rosi sitting in the swing.

The backyard had always been Gramma Rosi's favorite place. Now Yolanda suspected why. There were too many memories inside. Maybe the outside was Gramma Rosi's alone. Growing up, Yolanda had planted gardens, dug holes and even driven the riding lawn mower years before she was old enough.

The tangy smell of oranges wafted across a slight breeze. Yolanda made her way down the path and sat cross-legged at her grandmother's feet.

"I'm glad there are no more secrets. I just wish my mother were still alive. She always wanted to know who her father was."

"And I didn't want to tell her. She'd have been appalled. Your mother was a Ventimiglia through and through. She was prim and proper from day one. Oh, and stubborn and haughty." Gramma Rosi laughed. "She had dreams that I couldn't afford to make come true, and nothing I offered came close. She went away for a while to try to make it on her own. When she came back, it was as if all her dreams had died. Then she married and had you. I think that made her happy."

"And she didn't want my dreams to die."

"That's what love is," Gramma Rosi said. "Worrying more about the dreams of the one you love than about your own."

"But if you love and support each other, can't everyone's dreams come true?"

Mr. Teasdale came to the back door and called out, "You ladies want some hot tea?"

"Old fussbudget," Gramma Rosi said fondly, getting up and taking one step toward the back porch. "Dreams do come true. I mean, just look at me and Mr. Teasdale. I'm just barely eighty and being squired by a man who insists on being called Mr. Teasdale. It's all great fun."

Yolanda raised an eyebrow. Barely eighty, right. Gramma changed her age at least twice a month.

Gramma Rosi made it halfway to him before turning around. "Not all dreams fall in your lap, though. Some you actually have to pursue. Your mother never figured that out."

Yolanda didn't respond, just considered her mother's favorite saying: *Men leave.*

As if reading her mind, Gramma Rosi said, "Those two rockers on the front porch, your father made them."

"He did?"

"Man made the most wonderful furniture. He wanted to build a shop in the backyard of your house. And start his own business. Your mom wouldn't let him. I always thought she killed his dreams. I think she knew it, too."

The next day Yolanda left Gramma Rosi and Mr. Teasdale in charge of the bookstore. Driving to Adobe Hills, where the arbitrator had an office, she mentally listed all the paperwork she'd gathered in the last week. She had tax records, insurance records, general upkeep receipts, as well as utility bills going back decades. She'd searched everywhere for a bill of sale, but if it had ever existed, it was gone.

Using her GPS, she found Doss Ricardson's office. She expected to face both Adam and Loretta today.

The office complex was made of red brick and cooked cement. Yolanda hurried between two arches and found the right number. Inside was a small waiting room. No one was there. She followed the sound of voices, jovial voices. Guess everyone involved was in a good mood.

Except her.

"Ah, Miss Sanchez." A tall, somewhat chubby man with thinning hair combed to the side stood and held out a hand. "I'm so glad we're meeting in person. I'm Doss Ricardson."

"Good to meet you." Yolanda took a breath, offered him a smile and then nodded at Adam and Loretta.

Another man stood up. "I'm Bill Whitman."

Adam had brought his lawyer, the one helping Ruth Moore with her ownership issues.

"Please, sit down."

Yolanda sat, putting her briefcase on the table and opening it.

"Let's hold off on that," the lawyer said. "If we need it, you'll know."

The only thing on the table in front of Adam was a blue book, shiny and new, with a pencil next to it.

"Usually," Ricardson said, "during conflict resolution, a lawyer is not welcome. However, Whitman here has waded through the documents, the ones falsified by Richard Ventimiglia as well as the ones that are legitimate. He has knowledge to bring to the table that will help both sides. The Snapp party says they want everything aboveboard."

"I appreciate it," Yolanda said, trying to keep her voice strong.

She was facing this alone, and today, sitting across from Adam, she remembered how much she'd liked having him by her side. She could pretend otherwise while she worked among her beloved books and while she went about town on her days off, but in the same room with him...not possible.

The lawyer began, "According to Ms. Ventimiglia, we have reason to doubt the legitimacy of both deeds. However, since the original deed in Mr. Acura's name was destroyed and no other documentation exists supporting the Acuras' ownership, the deed in Mrs. Snapp's name seems to be the most legitimate."

Yolanda wanted to scream. And she couldn't claim squatters rights because no one in her family had filed intention.

She choked up but said, "That's fine. I know they need the money."

Adam had been fairly quiet while the lawyer presented the case. He tried to speak now, but the arbitrator motioned for his silence.

The lawyer gave a tight grin and picked up another piece of paper. "This document has to do with the property, two hundred and fifty acres, situated between Bridget's Animal Adventure, and Huckabee's Harem. It belongs to a descendant of Richard Ventimiglia's. That would be you. His only heir. Ivy Ventimiglia says she has no desire to make a claim now."

"What?"

This time Adam spoke quickly and didn't look at the arbitrator. "It's the document that Luke noticed the Ventimiglia name on back when Ruth was signing the habitat's land over to him."

"The Ventimiglias own the land?" Yolanda asked.

"And you're the Ventimiglia," Adam answered.

"There will be some negotiations with Ruth Dunbar," the lawyer said, "concerning taxes paid in good faith. Apparently, a trust was set up by Moore's father-in-law years ago, and she's been paying the taxes for you."

Yolanda nodded.

"Usually," Ricardson said, "we start by identifying the conflict, with a goal of avoiding legal intricacies. Before you arrived, the Snapp party offered a solution that I strongly recommend you consider. Truth is, this might be my easiest resolution ever."

"Stop preening," Loretta said. "It was Adam's idea."

Yolanda took a closer look at Adam. There were dark circles under his eyes, but other than that, he was as handsome as ever.

"We'd propose a trade," Adam said.

Yolanda frowned.

"Straight across the board," Adam said. "We'll take the property near BAA to sell, as we need the funds. In exchange, you'll take the Victorian located at 2014 Main, to do with what you will."

"The Victorian's worth more," Yolanda said. "So the exchange is *not* across the board."

Loretta tapped the table and said, "I said the very same thing to Adam, but he countered with his intent to marry you and live in the Victorian and that the monetary difference could be considered a wedding gift."

Yolanda blinked. Then she checked her watch. They'd been negotiating for only six minutes.

"Really," Loretta said. "You have to take pity on him. You're affecting his work."

"Can't draw?" Yolanda asked. She wasn't sure she liked having the same effect on him as Stacey.

"The opposite," Adam said. "I can't stop drawing." He pushed over the blue book.

Yolanda opened it to the first page. Adam's handwriting wasn't book perfect like Ivy's had been, but he'd started with the perfect picture.

It was Yolanda's Victorian, the day before the renovation began. She was standing on the front porch talking to one of the builders. Adam was in the background. Flipping through the pages, she saw that he'd depicted the last few weeks. Her Gramma Rosi was there, sitting on the bottom step of the staircase with her arms circling her knees and a smile on her face. Gulliver the cat was also shown, curled up in his box beside the cash register. Even Otis was in a picture, his head stuck in her refrigerator.

He'd drawn Yolanda in many ways. Her favorite was in the museum, in front of the high school painting, one finger pointing at something or someone on the canvas. But she also liked the one of her and Adam in his van, driving.

"Flip to the last page," Adam said. "I think Mr. Ricardson has another appointment soon."

Ricardson didn't look as if he cared at the moment.

Yolanda flipped to the last page. It was the front porch of the Victorian. Yolanda sat in the rocking chair with Gulliver on her lap. The front door was open and just inside, Gramma Rosi was handing a customer a book. On the other side of the door was a rocking chair. But no one sat in it.

"You're not finished," Yolanda accused.

"No, I'm not," Adam agreed. "I need to know if I can add myself to the drawing, plus maybe a golden retriever…a stroller or two."

"See," Loretta said. "He wants to marry you. I might be a bit prejudiced, but I say go for it."

"There's too many people here." Adam stood. "Let's go outside for a minute."

Before Yolanda could decide whether she wanted to go or not, Adam had her by the hand, and she was under the arch in front of the office.

"I know you're worried about my job, that I'll have to leave. But I've got enough work to keep me busy for the next decade," Adam said. "And it's all here, in Scorpion Ridge. There's no place I'd rather be."

"Men leave," Yolanda whispered, unable to forget the words of her mother.

"Not the Snapp men. My parents have been married for almost thirty years. My dad's parents, I've seen pictures of them, and the way they looked into each other's eyes. Loretta and George were married almost half a century. Even Jedidiah stayed true to Amelia. I went to the cemetery and found their graves. You know what the epitaph read on Jedidiah's? It read 'Beloved Husband.'"

"You keep secrets," she accused, but her voice was soft, her eyes warm.

"Not anymore. After we left the ostrich farm, I went home and I told my dad, my whole family really, just how much I loved them. I'd not appreciated them enough.

"I asked my dad why he returned to Scorpion Ridge. He had the education and opportunities to go just about anywhere. He told me that this is where he wanted to raise his children."

"Children?" Yolanda was still whispering.

"Yes, and I know just where I want to put the basketball hoop."

Yolanda hadn't realized he'd managed to bring the blue book with him. He opened it and showed her the last page again. "There's no place I'd rather be."

She pointed to the rocker. "You see how empty

that rocker is? Well, that's how empty the bookstore's felt without you there, complaining about my color choices or tripping over toolboxes."

"So, what do you think?" Adam asked. "One Victorian house in exchange for a giant vacant lot. The deal includes a man willing to love you for the rest of your life."

"*Our* lives."

"Is that a yes?"

"No, this is."

And she kissed him, both hands going around his neck and pulling him to her. For the first time in her life, she felt sheltered and loved and whole and—

"Ahem."

Yolanda gave Loretta a disgruntled look.

"Sorry to interrupt but Rosi called my phone when you didn't answer your phone, Yolanda. She wants to know if you have anything to tell her."

"Marry me," Adam whispered in her ear, his breath hot, tickly—something she wanted to feel again and again. "Tell me you want to marry me," he ordered.

"I do."

It was enough for Loretta, who ran back into the arbitrator's office with the news. Just what news, Yolanda wasn't sure. Could be that the trade had been approved. Could be that Adam and Yolanda were getting married.

Yolanda didn't care as long as Adam kissed her again.

* * * * *

LARGER-PRINT BOOKS!

GET 2 FREE LARGER-PRINT NOVELS PLUS 2 FREE MYSTERY GIFTS

Love Inspired®

Larger-print novels are now available...

LARGER-PRINT BOOKS!

**GET 2 FREE
LARGER-PRINT NOVELS
PLUS 2 FREE
MYSTERY GIFTS**

Love Inspired®

SUSPENSE
RIVETING INSPIRATIONAL ROMANCE

Larger-print novels are now available...

LISLP15